THE CASHIER

GABRIELLE ROY

THE CASHIER

ALEXANDRE CHENEVERT, CAISSIER

TRANSLATED BY HARRY BINSSE

INTRODUCTION : W. C. LOUGHEED

GENERAL EDITOR : MALCOLM ROSS

NEW CANADIAN LIBRARY NO. 40

MCCLELLAND AND STEWART LIMITED

The Canadian Publishers
McClelland and Stewart Limited
25 Hollinger Road, Toronto

0-7710-9140-0

PRINTED AND BOUND IN CANADA

THE CASHIER

INTRODUCTION

In *The Hidden Mountain* (1961), a study of the instinctive artist, Gabrielle Roy has Gédéon, the trapper, remark to himself: "Every man is precious and unique by virtue of what life has made of him, or he of it. . . ." Here, in her earlier novel, *The Cashier* (1955), in the character of Alexandre Chenevert she considers one man to show what is precious and unique in him. Admittedly, at first impression, the cashier seems an unlikely and unrewarding subject for such a study. This little, beak-nosed, misanthropic, overly self-reliant paying teller in Branch J of the Savings Bank of the City and Island of Montreal, this heir of all the ills of spirit and flesh, is immediately repelling in body and mind; yet he merits sympathy and wins it. This novel at its close has become a classic of empathy. Here, if ever, is illustrated that view of fiction held by George Eliot: "If art does not enlarge men's sympathies, it does nothing morally. . . ."

The time-span of *The Cashier* extends from the early spring of 1947 to the early winter of 1949—in effect, the last two years of the life of Alexandre Chenevert. The period historically witnessed such internationally important events as the Nuremberg trials, the death of Gandhi, the Berlin airlift, and the war between Israel and the Arab League; fictionally such events as these are woven into the novel as sources of the anxiety which spiritually oppresses the cancer-ridden body of Alexandre.

Alexandre is city-born and bred, a denizen of the modern metropolis, of the billboard jungle, laced by the cables of electrical, communication, and transportation systems, reeking with exhaust fumes, raucous with the noise of traffic, offering quiet and rest for many of its inhabitants only in hospitals, providing no privacy, but supporting loneliness. On a few occasions Alexandre has escaped this man-made environment; in his youth he has taken trips into the country; once in the dawn he climbed Mount Royal; but his sole escape within *The Cashier* is a week's vacation spent in a kind of Canadian Arcady at Lac Vert in the Laurentians. In that "land of heart's desire" he encounters the Gardeurs, who, independent of other men, live on the extra-sufficient bounty of God apparent in field, forest, and lake. Such is the integration of this novel that neither of these settings is a mere backdrop; both are highly relevant to the narrative; for, while the city exacerbates Alexandre's nerves and oppresses him by its "terrible lack of concern for him," the cultural primitivism of Lac Vert bores him by its very sufficiency; his reaction to each environment is a condition of his final knowledge that peace in this life is to be found in the tenderness of the human heart.

In narrating the quest of Alexandre—*The Cashier* is the story of a quest—Gabrielle Roy acts as the omniscient novelist, as the reporter who knows all and tells all that is relevant to the significance of her narrative. Often, and particularly often in the case of Alexandre, she enters the minds of her characters to report the interior monologue; witness the opening pages of the novel. Sometimes she summarizes, as when she passes quickly over the months between Alexandre's return from Lac Vert and the resumption of his visits to the doctor's office: "And Dr Hudon said to him: 'You can't continue like this; it can't last.' And yet it did last. For months and months. His stomach powders, and especially the pills aimed at his sympathetic nervous system helped him a little. These tiny tablets did to some extent withdraw Alexandre from his day, from himself . . . from others." Sometimes, as in Alexandre's early visits to Dr Hudon, she renders the narrative in setting and dialogue; in this particular instance she drops the mask of authorial objectivity to comment directly: "More and more nowadays doctors' offices are getting to look like travel agencies, with all the mass of advertising that daily floods their mail. Most of the pharmaceutical products represented therein are backed up with a barrage of anatomical drawings, in three or four colours, vermilion for blood, green for the bile, mauve for the nervous system; to suggest the menopause, a reproduction of an autumn landscape . . . complete with falling leaves." The comment here is implicitly adverse; it is sometimes ironic as in her statement that the French-speaking tram conductor was "instinctively more polite when he spoke in English."

Yet withal the narrative line is chronologically straightforward; the infrequent brief flashbacks do not interrupt the progression; they support and amplify Alexandre's present experience and actions—as when he is moved by the sudden memory of the hospitable bustling of his mother to lose himself, happy for the moment, in re-ordering the furniture of the tiny apartment to accommodate his daughter and grandson, or as when the memory of his having scolded his mother for her apologetic explanations to strangers leads him to acknowledge "that you never had enough love for the living." Within the progression of the story time slows and quickens its pace at the need of the narrative; the first six chapters, in which the character of the protagonist is established, deal only with a part of one day in his life; the six chapters of the second section, in which external action is of less importance than internal development, recount Alexandre's spiritual struggles at Lac Vert and come to the ironic climax of his being unable, in his terrible inarticulateness, to proclaim the knowledge he has won to; the final four chapters, given over to the three weeks of Alexandre's final illness, explore the irony that it is only in the very approaches of death that he realizes what life could have meant if lived in sympathy and communication. Durationally the novel expands and contracts to register the required emphasis upon significant incident and period of time.

The Cashier in Harry Binsse's translation is marked by an economical precision of style. Even in the descriptive passages in which one might expect a certain lushness of rhetoric one finds a spareness of word and a tautness of syntax. Consider the description of the Gardeur homestead:

> It was the Canadian dwelling as in the land's yester-years. A big lean-to on its side served as kitchen during the mild season. The main body of the building was topped with a steep-pitched roof, which flattened out a little before coming to rest on the balustraded porch. Small attic windows looked on the cleared area, and on those same purple-spired flowers Alexandre had seen on the land freshly claimed from the forest. The house had never had a coat of paint, but the wood because of its fine quality had decayed but little and had acquired a grey-blue tone, very ancient and cosy.

Perhaps the best word for such a style is austereness, a severe simplicity, admirably suited to the "drama which is the life between men and God."

Because Alexandre Chenevert is the protagonist of the drama, Gabrielle Roy has lightly sketched the subordinate characters who are important only in relation to Alexandre and his struggle. Eugénie, Alexandre's wife, a woman at her climacteric, now only occasionally sympathetic to her husband, whose continued welfare remains a burden to Alexandre even in the final weeks of his life; Irène, his daughter, the wife of an irresponsible husband, the mother of an ill-trained child, the inheritor of her father's independence of spirit, a reflector of his misery; Godias, like Alexandre a paying teller in Branch J, healthy of body, slovenly of dress, sluggish of emotion, whose insensitivity and unconcern for all not immediately his responsibility preclude complete communication with Alexandre; Monsieur Fontane, the manager of Branch J, in appearance the man in the Swift-Arrow shirt advertisements, materially successful, immured in habit and custom (his home is decorated according to the standards of *Ideal Home* and *Perfect Housekeeping*), whose superficial kindness is the grease of the business machine, and whose prudential guarding of his limited happiness contrasts with Alexandre's openness to pain; the Gardeurs, Edmondine and Etienne, simple, hospitable people of good will, "the salt of the earth," whose life at Lac Vert is for Alexandre a cherished myth of a kind of happiness no longer possible for him; Father Marchand, the hospital chaplain, grossly healthy among the sick, a fighter on the side of God, not of men, who is humbled by the suffering of Alexandre to admit that he does not know the meaning of suffering; and Dr Hudon, the competent, kindly, harassed physician, disappointed in his own aims, aware of all the suffering in the world, and at times overwhelmed by it, who fights to the end by the side of Alexandre: these, and other more minor characters, all sometimes hinder, sometimes help, and finally sympathize with the suffering of Alexandre as he moves towards death and towards understanding.

F. H. Bullock in reviewing *The Cashier* (*New York Herald Tribune Book Review*, October 16, 1955, p. 12) said that the protagonist, "Alexandre, is, in a sense, a frustrated Everyman"; Elizabeth Janeway (*New York Times*, October 16, 1955, p. 5) believed that in creating Alexandre, Gabrielle Roy "began with a type who slowly but inevitably became an individual." Both reviewers were perceptive; yet there is another dimension to the character, for Alexandre is the non-hero who becomes hero. His quest is the quest of the rationale of suffering, the understanding of pain and evil; the boons he grants through his dark journey include the valorous endurance of pain and the creation in those about him of affection, love, and sympathy; nor in this novel is the last of these the least, for through sympathy in suffering all men are united, one with another.

As Dr Hudon recognizes, in "this epoch of appalling tedium" the Alexandre Cheneverts are legion. They are the minor white-collar workers, the clerks, the stenographers, the cashiers, submerged in the accounts and records, the paper work of our civilization, ungenerously paid, ill-nourished mentally and often physically. For the sensitive and thinking among them the sources of anxiety are many; and Alexandre Chenevert, this ugly, puny little fellow of fifty-two (he is proud of his physical resemblance to Gandhi), irascible, independent, bearing a loveless faith in God and a loveless impatience with and suspicion of man, who has been eighteen years a paying teller, is both sensitive and thinking. When Dr Hudon suggests that he take up bowling as a preventive of thought, his mental reply is "what? take all that trouble to prevent yourself pursuing the only activity that matters, the only rational activity?" So, in his insomniac nights this minuscule Atlas takes all the cares of the world upon his shoulders; his brain seethes with problems, petty and important, personal, national, and international: the loose button on his overcoat; the new silk umbrella which he mislaid; the unrest in Greece; the Palestinian question; peace as the ultimate human desire; the ironic incongruity between man's spiritual potential and his body's functions; "the Bolshevik peril," the economy of war; the accumulation of human knowledge, the predictable routine of noises from the neighbouring apartment; the slanting of the news, and so on and so on. Nothing is too small or too great for the mill of his mind whose anxious and indiscriminate turnings are as debilitating and enervating as the routine of his life in bank and home. Yet, he continues to struggle, for "he felt there was something humiliating in being a man and in not wrestling with misfortune." Once he gives way to his longing to escape; an error of one hundred dollars in his accounts is an excuse for his resignation; but the cheerful manager arranges that the amount should be repaid in monthly instalments, thereby adding to the weight of Alexandre's treadmill. To lift that debt and others he takes a job straightening out the accounts of a Jewish merchant. The extra work strains his already weakened eyes and debilitates him more: "Once the debts were gone, he could afford to be sick, and once he had been sick, he'd attend to the glasses." Before he can be sick, his wife must be hospitalized; and a visit from his daughter and grandson depresses him more, for he realizes that "his slight power over the accidents of life" cannot shelter his daughter from a misery akin to his own.

Unable to afford a serious illness with its promise of rest, Alexandre seeks from Dr Hudon a few pills to allow him to carry on. The doctor recognizes Alexandre as a man "made to suffer"; he offers palliative medication and advice: "Go, Monsieur Chenevert. . . . Go away. Shed your excess baggage. At least once in your life do what you have always wanted to." And Alexandre, who, with the perverted economy of the poor, has squandered a part of his vacation in taking the doctor's tests, spends a part of what remains in sanctuary at Lac Vert.

At Lac Vert Alexandre achieves a kind of temporary reconciliation with life. He recognizes himself like the reeds by the lake as a part of the cycle of nature; in the contentment and material sufficiency of the homestead he finds a certainty of God and of God's beneficence towards man; in the happiness of the Gardeurs he discovers reason for forgiving "God for the suffering so freely scattered over the four corners of the world"; and through his dependence upon the knowledge and skills of past generations he realizes that the generations are linked. But these thoughts are consoling only temporarily; his inarticulateness precludes communication of his consolation; he perceives that the happiness of the Gardeurs rests upon mere sufficiency: " 'Because I lack not vines nor a hearth, because I am not sick, I look upon God as my benefactor.' Basically, for what did the happy man give thanks if not for inequality on earth." And he is overcome with homesickness for the city, "for the crowded lives there, for the intermeshed lives." So he returns to Montreal, only to experience more sharply than before the apparently callous indifference of the city towards him, only to feel more deeply the prevalent misery and suffering.

Within eighteen months—months of insomnia, months of irascibility, months lacking in joy and happiness—he is hospitalized for a cystotomy, an operation which proves pointless, for the cancer has spread even into the bone-marrow. Yet Alexandre in his suffering still questions and seeks the significance of suffering. In the seesaw battle waged for the prolonging of his life, in the very narrows of death, he finds happiness; he has "time to glimpse a little of Heaven on this earth." Locked in his anxiety, personal misery, and immediate responsibilities, Alexandre in the past has failed to enter into community of feeling with others; he was moved to take flowers to his wife in the hospital by the example of other men; he gave his mite to charity and benevolence not through sympathy but through obligation; he found no liberation of sympathy in suffering. Now in the hospital, with his affairs in order, his misanthropy turns to an outgoing love which finds its community in common suffering; in acts so simple as clasping the hand of a fellow-patient and ordering to be gone the two young clerks from the bank who come to visit him, he shows himself entering into the feelings of others. The kindness of those about him, a kindness which ironically has always been present, even in himself, but which he has never fully recognized, leads him to discover a divinity in man; as he says to Father Marchand, "If God has as much heart as a man, that would already be a fine thing . . . a very fine thing. . . ." And in his final meeting with his daughter, who "for the rest of her days . . . would be forgiving her father for the anguish he had transmitted to her . . . he seemed to glimpse what might be God's intention; how beings would never be truly severed, one from the other . . . ," for they are united in love, in pity, in sympathy, "in that tenderness for human beings which goes furthest beyond the bounds of reason," as well as in suffering.

Queen's University   W. C. LOUGHEED

ONE

CHAPTER I

IT WAS still dark. The bed was warm, and the room quiet. Alexandre Chenevert had been awakened by what he thought was a noise, but was really a nagging recollection. One of his overcoat buttons was dangling loose by a single black thread. And then too, it was spring. Spring reminded him of the income tax. "If I should forget to have that button sewn on . . ." he reflected, and then the notion occurred to him that perhaps there wouldn't be any war, simply because the weapons of today have such terrific killing power.

He did hope, however, that he would remain master of the thoughts about to wander through his mind. In days gone by, when he could still enjoy a good night's sleep, he had occasionally gotten up at an unusually early hour, but it had been to take a trip into the country, to catch a train, and then once— what seemed a whole lifetime ago—it had been for an expedition to climb Mount Royal in the dawn. His present cruel sleeplessness, despite everything, was linked to former joys. He felt as though he was off on a jaunt, as though he might come back a new man; he even had some feeling of self-importance. His brain tricked him into the belief that he was refreshed after so brief a rest. "Seeing I can't get back to sleep," Alexandre Chenevert cheerfully told himself, "I might as well turn it to good use. . . ." And he began thinking of Marshal Stalin, with his seminary education, of Tito, Yugoslav dictator, and of the brand-new silk umbrella he had mislaid yesterday, most likely on the streetcar. For a very long time he had bought himself only cotton umbrellas, the cheapest ones, the cloth of which wore out in no time. He had believed that in the long run it would be more economical to buy an umbrella which would be serviceable for years. And that was the one he had had to lose. During his life he had lost a great number of things, and almost always the best things—first his youth, and then his health, and now his sleep. But of the two of them —the Russians and the Americans—which possessed the bigger supply of atom bombs? A very important thing, superiority in atomic bombs. Because after a fashion it promised security. Gandhi had just started a new hunger strike. Alexandre Chenevert had a liking for him ever since the day when, glancing at a photograph of him, he had discovered what he considered a certain resemblance to himself; like the Indian Mahatma, he was thin, almost skeletal, and, Alexandre thought in his heart of hearts, perhaps good into the bargain. The stevedores were on strike too; food intended for starving peoples was rotting on the wharves. Then again, Alexandre told himself, if people weren't hungry, and if food were not perishable, would the dock workers have any means to assert their rights? Justice, it seemed to him, was won only at the cost of fearful pressures. What was more, air travel was far from a safe business. Again yesterday a plane had crashed somewhere in Newfoundland. THIRTY-EIGHT DEAD. The poor old world hadn't stopped spinning for a trifle like that. Alexandre envisioned the globe as you see it at the movies, at the beginning of a newsreel. A lion roars; a dancer swings her hips; a tank bursts into flame; then Mussolini, hanging by the feet, his features horribly swollen; beside him swayed the stripped body of Clara Petacci; a background of skyscrapers; a faceless man talking into a microphone. He announced: The world has become one and indivisible. "Indivisible, indivisible . . ." Alexandre began repeating. He chanted the word, broke it into its parts, counted its syllables. Five syllables.

Now how would you spell Hyderabad? Two r's or one? Today's newspaper headlines certainly mentioned some weird places. And the crossword puzzles called for some stranger still. Alexandre had tried everything to make himself sleepy, even racking his head for hours to find a three-letter word which was the name of a Swiss canton. But the Pope didn't get much sleep either. His Holiness, Pius XII, was looking at Alexandre with those huge eyes—gentle and overburdened—so prominent in his pictures. Christ's vicar on earth, and hence favouring neither the one nor the other among the enemy peoples. How could he avoid worrying nights, his head also tossing on his pillow, twisting from right to left, from left to right? Switzerland had eleven cantons. Or were there more than that?

The war had vastly broadened Alexandre's knowledge of geography. Just as certain travel stories leave us with a lifelong fondness for such odd regions as the Cordillera of the Andes or Tierra del Fuego, so the correspondents' dispatches and the radio news had engraved on Alexandre's mind names that powerfully attracted him—Murmansk . . . Ankara . . . Teheran. He knew just where Dunkirk lay, and most of the Normandy beaches; Arromanches, for instance—what a pretty name, which despite everything called to mind the tireless motion of the sea. Stalingrad still clung in his memory, and it retained an echo of some such syllables as "Sarroya Roussa." Even into the desert had the armies pursued each other. And in the desert dwelt graceful gazelles. Truly, without the war, what would Alexandre have known of the great, groaning world, resplendent and more thinly populated than most people said?

Nor were they getting along with each other in Greece. The papers had said the war was over. But fighting had not stopped. What's more, Alexandre had foreseen it; we shouldn't have started rejoicing. Nowadays he envisioned a huge portion of the map of the world coloured red. You know very well that some fifteen years ago nobody said much about the Russians. There were those who wrote about the Red Peril and the Bolshevik Menace. Alexandre had barely had time to grasp it when the Bolsheviks became the "allies of democracy." The press did not frankly say "our friends." There were differences of opinion, but in all the editorial tone had been favourable. Headlines told of the heroic defence of Stalingrad, the brave Russian offensive, the vast efforts of the Russian people. Alexandre had been slow to overcome his distrust. The attack on Finland still weighed on his heart. And yet the existence in his mind of two hundred forty million Russians hinged upon certain insignificant if human details. The Russians wore loose-fitting shirts gathered at the waist by a belt and high leather boots. They were musicians; they sang in choral groups; their novelists were the greatest of all time. Moreover, it was not their fault if they remained backward and barbarous; their masters had long held them in serfdom. One day Alexandre read that they had reopened the churches over there in Russia. Thereafter he became a lukewarm apostle of the alliance, asserting, "There's a chance we may come to an understanding with the Russians."

But now we were back to terms of abuse. One fine evening Alexandre had turned on his little radio and had once again heard talk about the Reds. Thenceforth no more human touches. Just the Bear, the Soviets. And yet this radio voice through all the years seemed the same to Alexandre, always urbane, always persuasive, so deeply convincing: "We must be on our guard against the Soviets. . . ." "Our allies, the Russians. . . ." When had it spoken truly? It was even to be expected that America would some day join forces with its former German enemies to stand off the Russians, yesterday its allies. "In that case, it wasn't worth fighting them." Alexandre protested. Allies, enemies, allies. . . . He lit his small bedside lamp, glanced at the alarm clock. He had only been awake for twenty minutes.

Beside him Madame Chenevert lay asleep. How could she

rest quiet when war threatened to break out at any moment? In three years. Perhaps five. As soon as they were ready.

When she went to bed, Eugénie Chenevert wrapped her hair done up in curlers in a net that had become greasy with use. Thus exposed, her face was red and puffy; her lips half open, her cheeks sagging; she had a doltish look which disgusted Alexandre with sleep. Must not a person who slept so soundly lack any capacity for thought and real feeling?

Besides, supposing there were no longer any reason for going to war, it would be impossible to destroy the munitions of war: that would be waste; they would have to be used.

He got up.

In the bathroom he began to meditate even more intensely. He kept studying his toes, misshapen by corns; he had ugly feet, thin and rawboned. Once again he was struck by that emancipation of the mind which takes place at some of the most inopportune, least worthy moments in life. To reflect on the immortality of the soul while staring at his toes seemed to him almost shocking. Yet, when you came down to it, why was it indecorous? What was unseemly: such thoughts, the heights they reached, their remoteness from human bondage? Or else the too-frequent needs of a nervous man? It was shot through with irony; either a man should not think or else he should not have to eliminate the wastes of the body.

Alexandre began to pray. He was prone to prayer whenever he became aware of his sickliness. It was as instinctive with him as the cry of distress he sometimes cast into the void, a cry to his mother dead years ago. "Mama!" he would beseech, himself already old, adrift amid his wandering thoughts, alone in the night.

Suddenly he was off headlong on the Palestinian question. He had read that boatloads of immigrants, near the port of Jaffa and in sight of the promised land, found themselves refused permission to leave the ship. In desperation a handful of these refugees had tried to swim to shore. One of the bathtub faucets would not close tight; a little water had collected on the enamel bottom of the tub. Alexandre saw a Jew from Poland, his hat pulled down over his ears, thrashing about in the Red Sea. Somewhere else in an office a top bureaucrat was settling the affairs of mankind on a slip of paper. He it was who determined how many immigrants might be allowed to land. In the distance riders appeared mounted on the nimble little horses of the desert, and Alexandre envisaged burnooses, black bears, ferocious eyes . . . Arabs! How he hated them. He hated the English bureaucrat in his office. All his pity went out to the

Polish Jew he had espied drowning in the trickle of water in the bathtub. People shouldn't be treated that way, Alexandre told himself.

Barefoot, shivering in his rumpled pajamas, he wandered around the room. With all his heart he wished the Jews had a country of their own. He went into the kitchen and turned on the light. The Palestinian problem seemed to him beyond his competence and responsiblity. Indeed war, treaties, the atomic bomb—none of it was within the range of Alexandre's powers. "What of it?" he said out loud. "There's not a thing I can do." Nevertheless he felt there was something humiliating in being a man and in not wrestling with misfortune. He took a dry biscuit from a big, round, cream-coloured box marked "Biscuits." In China, how many Chinese were there by now? But wasn't it India that was the most overpopulated country? Alexandre asked himself. He had a notion to look it up right away in the encyclopaedia, but began searching instead for the bicarbonate of soda. Wendell Willkie had proclaimed on the radio: The world has become one and indivisible. Eating sometimes helped insomnia. Alexandre had read that it drew the blood from the brain to the stomach. Bicarbonate of soda . . . bicarbonate of soda. . . . Eating always suggested to Alexandre some sort of medicine. It was not true hunger, indeed, which tormented him—rather a nervous gnawing sensation. "I'll end by dying of cancer of the stomach," Alexandre told himself with a certain archness, as though he would thus at least attain a fate wholly his own.

He stood in the cold blank light falling from a white ceiling on the enamelled cabinets, on the sparkling sink and shining linoleum of a little kitchen as clean, white, and dismal as a room in a hospital.

He was a small man, almost puny, with a huge worried forehead. Two deep wrinkles framed his thin-lipped mouth, drawn tight by stomach cramps—or perhaps merely by life's frightful complexity, which on occasion he imagined he alone in all the world fully appreciated. The top of his head shone. Along the sides, two skimpy tufts of hair protruded, disarrayed by the movements of his sleeplessness. His rather long and slightly beaked nose lent him a certain likeness to those unsociable birds of prey reputed to be vicious, yet perhaps merely ill-starred. Alexandre was absorbed in thought. Sometimes, while he probed the night in the white silence of the kitchen, he suffered a feeling of such strangeness that it constricted his very heart. What business had he to live in such an age? Like many imaginative men, Alexandre felt that he was not made for the century in which he lived, this epoch of appalling tedium all too little relieved by gadgets, by nickel, aluminum, plastic, celluloid, Bakelite, nylon, zylon. . . . For some time, now, the refrigerator had been silent; its motor clicked back into action with a dull explosive rumble. The machine purred gently. It put you in mind of an experimental laboratory. Alexandre sensed his utter inferiority as a man, with all his little stomach troubles, his endless colds, his confused problems. The machine's smooth functioning threw into bold relief his hopeless yearning. What more did Alexandre ask of life than his refrigerator—the last payment finally met—what more than a sure meal ticket and a new suit every two years? Then, just as he asked himself the question, he realized that he was far from being alone in the world. Almost everyone on earth, had Alexandre been able to question them that night, would have replied: Peace, it's peace we long for. Even the men of Lapland would have agreed with him. Mankind's common hunger lay everywhere about him. Whereupon a piercing joy possessed Alexandre. It could not be very wicked to win our case in the end, since we're all agreed, he told himself with a smile. He rubbed his small hands together. Surely the insomnia that brought such a discovery in its wake had something good about it! Alexandre felt a deep content. All mankind offered itself to him at that moment, so varied, so astonishing, responsive to the most exacting affection. And his impatient heart set forth somehow to span the globe.

And almost at once he again ran headlong into the Bolshevik peril. He perceived neither men nor children nor women nor towns nor countrysides: only a vast area all tinted one disturbing colour over which was spread in black letters U.S.S.R. Germany also became clouded over when he thought of Dachau. Who could forget Dachau? Who could be friendly toward the Nazis? Alexandre had seen a few spy films and he knew what the Nazis were: blond, squareheaded young men with crew cuts who spoke in harsh, abrupt, metallic voices. And all the ss, dressed in black, hidden behind dark glasses, driving their motorcycles at breakneck speed ahead of the tanks.

What had Alexandre set out to find when he had started round the world? He most certainly would not find it among the English. You had only to watch their actions here in Canada to discover their taste for dominion. Of course for Alexandre the English were the hereditary enemy, nominated by history, the schools, his whole environment—the enemy he could scarcely do without, for were he to lose him, what would become of his grievances?

The French Alexandre reproached for having done injury to religion by bad books and the great number of freethinkers they had spawned. Nor could he forgive the Jews their control —he had only lately read that it was beyond denial—of the fur industry, hatmaking, the press, and the motion picture. He caught a fresh glimpse of that Polish Jew, but he wondered whether he had not been invented out of whole cloth by the Jewish imagination, as skilled in winning the world's pity as in every other form of propaganda. As for the Americans, they were guilty of having set up material progress as the basic goal of life. Alexandre fell back upon his own people, his compatriots. Their faults at once sprang to view: envy, the habit of feeling sorry for rather than asserting themselves, hate rather than love; yet very arrogant when they proved to be the stronger—in short, the faults of men in general, but in this manifestation they hurt Alexandre. From them he turned to his intimates, to his small circle of acquaintances. This chap, whom he had once helped out, avoided him; another had not paid him a small loan made long ago; yet another, in whom he thought he could confide, kept telling people behind Alexandre's back that "poor Chenevert was turning sour." A very real bitterness stirred within him. He was uncovering most precise reasons for being pained at mankind. Certainly, his stomach bothered him. Alexandre's fine trip had merely led him into the desert. How could anyone return home from a journey so poor in spirit? The kitchen clock kept ticking away. And there was still the noise of the motor, pumping coldness. An extraordinary invention. Would the Japanese go back to making inexpensive toys? "Made in Japan." One day in a cheap novelty shop Alexandre had seen a toy, a small porcelain object, a kind of figurine representing a human being, quite a bit of work, and it was marked "five cents." Alexandre had picked it up and looked at it closely. It was not at all badly made: features, dress, a certain attitude—all that, and for only five cents! He had been on the verge of understanding the Japanese. But then came the attack on Pearl Harbor, and since that everyone knew the Japanese for what they were—crafty and underhanded sons of Nippon! No one in the world could you trust, not even that poor little Nipponese who had moulded a human expression into his five-cent figurine. Alexandre's heart remained heavy with disappointment. Then the face of a man whom he had seen occasionally, almost the face of a stranger, came back to him; he reflected on this human being whom he scarcely knew: Constantin Simoneau at least was an excellent man. And there remained, as a resting place for his eager heart, one man who was dead and whose whole life was to him very nearly a closed book.

Without the dead, the absent, the folk you had never even seen, whatever would become of man's faculty for love!

Alexandre went back to bed.

"Eugénie, are you asleep?" he asked quietly.

At the grey hour which comes before the dawn, there was always a moment for Alexandre when he saw himself a new man. He made resolutions. He would wholly change his life. First of all, he was going to sleep. Then his health would be better and it would be easy for him to love and be loved. And eagerness to begin at once his fresh life tortured him with impatience. He felt as though he must physically grasp his good intentions that very instant, otherwise they would slip out of his reach.

"Eugénie," he implored.

Had she awakened at that moment, Alexandre might perhaps have succeeded in expressing to her feelings sensitive beyond anything she had ever suspected in him, feelings of which he himself was aware only when overtaken by insomnia. At such moments he was less ashamed than usual of his heart's deepest and truest impulses. He would have liked, for instance, to have explained to Eugénie that the Japanese were not as crafty as people said. They found themselves, as it were, forced to sell tiny figures for less than five cents. For, after all, how much profit do you think that could bring them? he asked. But she was sound asleep. And her state of well-being was enough to rid Alexandre of his good intentions. He thought of her in terms of abuse he never would have dared utter aloud. He wondered whether he did not hate Madame Chenevert. What could this heavy woman, this dull, unfeeling woman, understand about the fate of the Japanese? He sat on his pillow, his back against the bars of the bed, and he beheld his soul, grown tender for an instant, fill with bitterness and suspicion.

This time he had waked up Madame Chenevert.

"Aren't you asleep?" she asked drowsily. "How often have I told you you read too much, Alexandre . . . all those murders and catastrophes. . . ."

But before she could finish scolding him, she was slumbering once more.

You had to read. Modern man was the heir of such a mountain of knowledge. Even had he limited his curiosity to that which was published in his own day, he could never have succeeded in absorbing it all. And where did truth lie in all this mass of writing? Aexandre lived in the age of propaganda.

Take an aspirin tablet. Aspirin is spelled A-S-P-I-R-I-N. I repeat, A-S-P-I-R-I-N. Buy a cake of Lux soap. Germany must be destroyed. Germany must be put back on her feet. What sudsy suds.

Still everyone knew very well that Lux soap made no more suds than any other. From life's beginning to its end, a man listened to interminable discourse, and must keep asking, Is it true? Is it false? Alexandre had to acknowledge himself wholly alone in this limitless thicket of men's convictions. He became angry. He cast aside everything written, explained, reiterated; and then like a slave he came back to it, seeking its support. He took to heart a violent editorial he had read a few days before. He became deeply indignant with the English. They had let the Jews down in this Palestine business. Promises, secret treaties, and then shift for yourselves. We're washing our hands of it. Well, since that was the way things went, Alexandre also would wash his hands . . . of Palestine and the rest. The man at the microphone kept repeating: indivisible, indivisible.

If I were President Truman, Alexandre wondered, what should I do? And he pitied President Truman.

He imagined a deep forest. He moved along, clearing himself a path, in perfect silence. He found an abandoned cabin. He let himself fall upon a bed of sacking. Here were no newspapers, no radio, no alarm clock. Alexandre was becoming less tense; his hands began to unclench; his mouth lost some of its grimness. The trees of the forest stirred in the wind. As Alexandre imagined them, these trees were full of kindly welcome, tender, green, and his unconscious nostalgia imparted to them a gentle motion which charmed him. It was like a soft patter of raindrops all around Alexandre. A feeling of restfulness overwhelmed his soul as it found ease in the absence of all but vegetable life. But he had no umbrella. He had lost his umbrella. What would he do without an umbrella? His hope seized on a halfhearted foresight—perhaps it wouldn't rain much this spring. But such optimism seemed to him terribly imprudent, likely to invite long spells of wet weather that would soak him to the bones.

He was jerked away from the cabin in the woods. Now he was journeying through the city. The rain beat on the pavement. The street lights glowed, each in its aureole of dampness. It was one of those rainy nights in spring such as Alexandre had loved, but his pleasure was spoiled by silly trifles. His shoes would be ruined. He could not help stepping in large puddles of water. His overcoat was soaked. He would catch cold. He would have to buy medicines. Perhaps, taking everything into account, he would do better to buy another umbrella. On the very edge of sleep, Alexandre was overtaken by paltry considerations of prudence. If he had so greatly loved rainy nights, it was because they seemed to set up a sort of justice on earth. At night, beneath the rain, all men walk with their backs arched, their heads sunk between their shoulders, barely noticeable save when they passed before bright shop windows. Alexandre was filled with love for his neighbour when he beheld him thus from afar, faceless, and moving rapidly out of his own orbit.

A dog began to bark in the street. Irritated beyond measure, Alexandre got up. When he opened the slats of the Venetian blinds, he was surprised to see a portion of the sidewalk flooded with cool light. The sun had risen while he was imagining a night of justice wherein everyone moved with his back hunched against the gusts, elbows tight against his sides. The black dog was scurrying about, its nose in the wind, quite beside itself with eagerness to pick up some scent. At a distance he could hear a milkman whistling, and his horse's hoofs echoed briskly as they came closer. To Alexandre life seemed all the more bitter if only because he saw others find in it a joy beyond his comprehension.

He went back into the bathroom and opened the small medicine cabinet. He examined—always freshly surprised at their number—the phials, the pillboxes, the bottles, the salves which crowded each other on the narrow shelves. There was something there for every ailment, and at a glance you might realize the unbelievable variety of affliction to which a human being is subject.

"Are you irritable these days, down in the mouth, and in a bad humour? . . . It's because your liver is not secreting enough bile. . . ." For long years Alexandre had listened to such instructive utterances, and that was why his little medicine cabinet was well stocked. But he always got up just as ill-tempered and out of sorts. Never did he recover the "pep" they promised him and which, to be sure, he had never had. Alexandre was not the "peppy" type.

Salts, effervescent powders—the small cabinet did not contain merely correctives for that affection general in our age, almost as common as good health, to judge by the advertising devoted to it in streetcars and newspapers; there were likewise little brown pills for the kidneys; vitamins; and finally a whole section devoted to remedies for the common cold: drops to clear up congestion, some to be sprayed deep into the throat, others to be inhaled through the nostrils. On the top shelf at the back he at last discovered the object of his search.

Dormine. To be taken a half-hour before retiring with a hot beverage.

He reached for the little bottle.

Here was indeed the only thing that tempted him.

For years he had slept badly, and less and less as time went on.

It was beyond his endurance to continue thus fettered to himself.

But were he at last to savour sleep, how could he do without it afterward? The drug that conferred this boon he would long for, no matter what the price, and he would lack the strength of will to give it up.

Slavery for slavery, were there any grounds for preferring one to the other?

Till then he had only very rarely taken sleeping-pills—five or six times perhaps in the space of several years, just enough to have known the most comforting of certainties: this time I'm going to sleep—to delight in it a few minutes—then, immediately afterward, to drift off without the least recollection. But the next day he had continued for a long time in a state of torpor, his mind muddled, as though a stranger to himself, heavy and dull. Appropriately enough he had read in a popular article on medicine that nothing weakened the will and the faculties so much as the use of soporifics.

Now Alexandre Chenevert prized his faculties. He was a small man without any special gifts who had nothing extraordinary to offer the world but who, for precisely that reason, would have found it heart-rending that the entire harvest of his thoughts should be lost forever. Yet he no longer did anything about them, having even ceased jotting them down in his black-covered notebook, which he still kept handy, but which he would have been ashamed to see surrendered to another's curiosity. Why indeed had he ever begun? Perhaps through respect for the wanderings of his captive soul. Without any real ability for self-expression, his soul had genuinely aroused his pity—so completely was it a prisoner. For a long time he had envied the men who were able by their speech or by a written phrase to set free their inner lives, for it seemed to him that he had much to say. As he saw it, what he lacked were not things to say, but the manner, the skilful words, the talent, which have nothing to do with the secret depth of the soul. And then it was that he had bought the bottle of Dormine.

But before that, even before the notebook, Alexandre had thought it incumbent on him to write open letters to the press. One of them had been published on the second page of *Le Sol*, beneath an advertisement for soap and with the heading "A Citizen Protests." Even today, just as on the evening when he first saw himself in print, Alexandre could shut his eyes and see how the column was placed, could visualize the type of the title, could read his signature and the street address at the end of the letter, for he had not hesitated to reveal its authorship.

Then someone had answered him in the columns of *Le Sol*, and it could have kept on, a fine exchange of views. But the editor had written Alexandre that space was lacking in his paper because of the press of advertising which, alas, as he was careful to explain, produced revenue. At first Alexandre had accepted this explanation as having been offered in good faith. Then he had thought that he detected in it a polite intention to discourage him. And at last, as the years went by, the mere recollection of his letter to the editor had become hateful to Alexandre. It seemed like proof of the sort of proficiency achieved once in his lifetime and never again to be approximated.

In his hand he still held the bottle of sleeping-tablets. Through the glass Alexandre saw the capsules, their very appearance soothing, so tiny were they. This morning he was tempted beyond measure. Perhaps a single dose would not destroy his will. Yet that was the way such things began, Alexandre warned himself. Moreover it was almost six o'clock. Were he to take a sedative now, he would never wake up at seven. And half-doped he could not do his work properly. Granted that, as he scarcely slept at all, one fine day he would most likely commit some dreadful blunder in any case.

He returned the little bottle to its accustomed place.

Basically he was abstaining from it as he would from sin, sin against the reason, against the soul. As long as his soul should live, could he ever offer it, as he might offer his ailing body, the affront of a capsule taken with a bit of water?

Meanwhile, thanks to his having resisted temptation, he hoped he had deserved sleep. He went back to bed, wearily drawing the covers over him. Just as though it had been awaiting this moment, the wandering dog began to bark again, immediately under the bedroom window. A frightful rage stirred in Alexandre. Suddenly human existence seemed to him truly unbearable. At one moment consumed by a desire to change the world and to change himself, within an instant man found himself powerless to make even a dog stop barking. Whatever had Alexandre come into this heartless world to accomplish! The barking became more distant, then ceased altogether. Alexandre thought he should hasten to take advantage of the silence to fall asleep. Soon other noises would make it impossible. He arranged himself on his right side, in the most restful position; he tried to count sheep, following the advice so freely given the whole world over by people who can't sleep. It was just like getting your hair to grow back. Alexandre told himself; the recipes always came from the bald. Perhaps what he should try to do above all was to avoid letting sleep know how eager he was to obtain it. Alexandre turned so as to lie on his back, his hands folded behind his neck, concentrating wholly on the idea that he must beware lest he seem to seek sleep. They would try to bluff each other, he and sleep, and we'd see which one carried the day! But sleep was sharp-eyed and crafty; it saw through any attempt at scheming. Probably absolute indifference alone could move sleep. Basically sleep was cruel and not to be bought, like good health, love, and even that talent Alexandre had for so many years timidly desired from afar. Everything was beyond purchase, save perhaps unhappiness. After a sleepless night, vexed to his very depths, Alexandre imagined that he had at least elected to be unhappy, and for that he felt a certain pride. If he didn't sleep, it was because his soul was too sensitive, because his conscience was subtle, because, thank God, he was above the indifference that beset the generality of men. And meantime he anxiously dreaded the sounds which would prevent his enjoying at least an hour's slumber.

The streetcars were now operating on their regular schedules. Alexandre began to wait for the approach of each tram and, when the clangour died down, for the coming of the next. During the interval of silence, if it lasted longer than he had expected, Alexandre got nervous. Whatever had happened to that car? Was it late? Soon the auto horns joined the chorus. The little dog, back from its excursion, barked ceaselessly. A motorcycle passed with a cannonade of explosions. And suddenly Alexandre sat upright in his bed, boiling with resentment, a crazed gleam in his eyes; the whole city was certainly in a conspiracy to prevent his sleeping, all mankind was against Alexandre. Keeping dogs in town ought to be forbidden. And motorcycles—those instruments of the devil—ought to be kept out also: motorcycles . . . expressly invented to shatter delicate nerves. Drivers who needlessly sounded their horns ought to be dragged to the police station. Destroying a person's sleep was at least as serious an offence as robbing your neighbour. A lot of people ought to be thrown into jail so that the rest of us could live in peace and security. Now Alexandre's neighbour was splashing about in his bathroom, and the damn fool was singing. In a moment he would jerk the chain to flush the toilet. The partition was so thin between the two apartments that each tenant could guess at the other's most intimate activities. The thought, however, that the greater part of the human beings in a great city lived in the same hateful promiscuity availed nothing to make that fact acceptable to Alexandre. It revolted him all the more because he could not see with greater clarity for himself than for the other thousands any means of escape. "Beast!" Alexandre flung at his neighbour. He might be a fine fellow. Alexandre knew substantially nothing about him apart from the sounds he made too early every morning, but he loathed him as he would never be induced to loathe the Russians. Heavy footsteps thudded down the stair. Alexandre held his breath; he knew that within a few seconds the street door would slam. And then the old girl next door would turn on her radio.

The weight of his own bitterness, far more than all these noises, kept sleep out of his reach. There he lay stretched out, helpless, his hearing tormented, his eyes hollow with weariness, hating almost everything alive. His limbs were like lead, his throat dry, his body racked with fatigue, and this was the condition in which he must undertake his day's work. That day ahead frightened him, like a barren mountain. How could he ever climb over it if he could not succeed in sleeping at least for one hour?

"I'm going to sleep. I have to sleep," he said to himself. "I must have sleep."

He recalled having read that people went crazy for lack of sleep. He took himself in hand. He reasoned with himself. He harked back to the years when he could sleep, and like many another man, Alexandre fed his self-confidence on the good things he had lost. Since I once used to sleep, Alexandre said to himself, I'll sleep again.

He patted the folds out of his pillow and thrust his head into it. He turned his back on the Jews who had no country of their own. And there began to pursue him a pulsing tick-tock which gnawed away at time with appalling speed. Alexandre could sleep almost another hour, whispered the clicking seconds, eager now to rob him of any time left for slumber. But he had better hurry, for he has already lost ten minutes. He still has fifty minutes, though. The hands were leaping around the dial of his alarm clock. Forty more minutes of sleep for Alexandre. Now only thirty-five. That's always better than nothing, whispered the seconds. Quick, quick, Alexandre. Hurry up. Quick, quick.

By his frenzied desire for it, he succeeded only in pushing sleep further away.

It was almost seven. Alexandre opened the dried-out palms of his hands. I won't sleep, he admitted to himself. And it was almost a relief. With something like satisfaction he was at last reaching that dreary calm afforded by the absence of all hope.

"I won't sleep."

Then Alexandre began to go under. The old terrestrial globe started revolving once more, but at such a rate that Greece and his heavy-footed neighbour, the Jews in Palestine, and the U.S.S.R. were fused into a single hazy image. *Would the kingdom of God one day be established on earth? Or would it be only in another world that men would no longer do evil to one another?* The questions fell apart in Alexandre's mind. His identity had faded to a button lacking on his fall overcoat. The thread must have come completely loose and then broken. Alexandre was sinking straight down. He passed through the rind of the earth and came to regions remote and dark beyond compare, situate perhaps before the flood, even perhaps before the separation of the waters from the land. Under slime and waves of black water, he seemed to remember that he should have gone to get his umbrella. Then his mouth yawned wide; it opened, then tightened in the slow, pathetic movement of fishes' gills.

The alarm went off. Strange was this tiny voice of the earth, irritating and futile, plumbing into the obscure depths where Alexandre, like a minute detached particle of chaos, began to stir.

Madame Chenevert was saying, "Wake up! Wake up, Alexandre. And to think the man complains because he can't sleep! Turn that thing off, will you? For heaven's sake turn it off!"

Alexandre started up in a cold sweat, looking utterly bewildered. Her words, distorted by sleep, seemed to say, turn that fellow in! For heaven's sake turn in Alexandre Chenevert! Look! He's going to run for it; he'll get away from us; he's going to fall asleep!

And his first concern then, even before turning off the alarm clock, was to stretch his arm from his bed and fish his denture from its glass of water; still bleary, scarcely knowing what he was doing, his eyelids heavy, he fitted it into his mouth.

CHAPTER II

AT TWENTY minutes of nine on the dot you could see entering Branch J of the Savings Bank of the City and Island of Montreal a short man of ashen complexion wearing a round hat. As he crossed the threshold he took off his coat, which was still neat but of an outmoded cut—blue with a narrow black velvet collar. He put it away, taking care that the hanger properly supported the shoulders, with the neck opening in the centre, and faced it to the wall, for the worn spots were in front, near the pockets, where his arms rubbed. He slipped by the accountants' offices, one or the other of whom, at this hour, was usually at work. A few absent-minded good-mornings greeted him. Before acknowledging these by an abrupt nod of the head, he seemed with a sensitive glance to gauge the precise degree of cordiality each face entitled him to bestow. When, on the infrequent occasions of that gentleman's having arrived, he bowed to the manager, he suffered an embarrassment which made his Adam's apple bob up and down in his throat. Ten seconds later he walked into his own cage.

It was not one of those iron-barred cages such as you used to find in every bank but which today are not often seen; it was a transparent cabin, harbouring indeed as few secrets as a shop window. Surrounded on three sides with panels of glass and open to the high vault of the ceiling, it was the second from the entrance of five identical cages. Near the wicket a tiny inscription proclaimed:

> Whether your account is large or small,
> You are entitled to our courtesy.

Presumably this was to reassure bashful clients whom some trifling transaction, or a mere whim of fate, occasionally brought into the awesome premises of the Savings Bank of the City and Island of Montreal, the most solemn financial institution in that metropolis.

The vast banking room with its three massive columns, as spacious as a railway station, seemed empty, despite the table desks lined up beneath the high window and, parallel to them, the severe counter of polished wood which acted as base for the glass partitions. A portrait of the bank's founder was hung high on the wall: a disdainful face with a short white beard, made more rigid by a starched collar; his hand grasped the arm of his chair, and his features were the embodiment of a sound Presbyterian conscience. Calendars bearing the name of the bank and the grand total of its deposits carried a legend:

Let us give our work the full power of our arms.
Let us bend our wills to follow the path religion points out to us.
Let us spend our strength in the spirit of Sacrifice and Thrift.
Prosperity and Happiness will reward our efforts.

Such was the outstanding glory of the Savings Bank of the City and Island of Montreal, certainly one of the few banks in the world to extol and, if you will, place on the same honourable footing Religion and Prosperity. Everything here bore witness to this formula's effectiveness, everything demonstrated that indeed hard work summons success, except perhaps for the few pale faces glimpsed through the glass partitions, except especially for the little man in cage number two.

He had already laid out his books, lighted his gooseneck lamp, and wiped off with the end of his sleeve a glass-covered name plate, which he placed on the counter within the lamp's rays and where now you could see glowing in sober letters: A. Chenevert. Thereupon A. Chenevert spilled on the counter in front of him the contents of his cash drawer. In a twinkling he had sorted it out: the quarter-dollars on one side, the dimes on the other, and, a small mound all my themselves, the five-cent pieces. Alexandre then began making up his rolls of coins. He stacked the necessary quantity of each denomination, rolled them in slips of paper, and pinched the ends to hold the coins in place. For almost eighteen years now, Alexandre had made rolls every workday morning. He could prepare them very quickly, without having to pay any real attention to the movements of his fingers, which had long seemed aware by themselves of the exact bulk required for the various quantities of coin. Thus he remained reasonably free to cogitate. And from this very vantage point, just as he was starting his thirtieth roll, Alexandre beheld eternity. He found himself facing incommensurable time, stretching into the invisible. The impression of this vastness suddenly overwhelmed the teller like a lowering threat. After all, he could not at the same instant devote himself to his cents and to his soul. For if he attended to the latter, how could be continue piling up his pieces of change? Abruptly he turned to face the two young stenographers behind him. Their whispering annoyed him. His glance, as he peered between his visor and the tops of his glasses, which had slipped down his nose, became severe. The two girls burst out laughing; they were very young. Not long ago Alexandre had heard one of them—probably Alice, the little redhead—refer to the "old owl." He had immediately realized that they must be talking about him. Even though he at once had recognized himself in her unkindly words, he had all the same been hurt at the injustice they conveyed. Silly idiots, when you came to think of it! Those painted fingernails, those sheer silk blouses! Was such flightiness suitable in a bank? But everything was changing nowadays . . . and probably the time was not far off when there would be stationed at his own wicket one of these young magpies, without the least knowledge of the public or of psychology. . . . He rapped irritably on his wooden counter.

"Keep quiet!" cried Alexandre. "Enough chatter! We're here to get some work done."

Then, amazed at his own outburst, he felt his features shrivel and looked even more crabbed. He picked up his pen once more and made a dollar sign; next to it he noted some figures.

At ten o'clock the blinds were drawn and the doors opened. When this daylight flooded the bank it almost always aroused a kind of surprise: the employees looked out at the street, the cars, the pedestrians, brought back to life for them by this instant in time. Alexandre took up his post, his bills ready beside him, his cash drawer handy, his small, dry face framed in the wicket.

He had little hair left, and what he had was brushed down firmly, almost hair by hair, on either side of his skull. Some flesh still sheathed his hollow cheeks, and under his wrinkled eyelids, in his sunken eyes, life still gleamed. His well-pressed suit—this was the week for the grey Oxford—did not show too much wear. Who could have realized that Alexandre was at the end of his endurance? What attracts less attention than a small man installed in his niche!

His first customer of the day was approaching timidly. An old lady in black. She handed him a government cheque for her old-age pension. Its back already bore a laborious signature made with an old-fashioned stub pen. This was the age of ball-points, of magic inks. Such a writing instrument dated a person. And even her given name placed the poor old woman.

"Madame Honorine Blanche Mathieu," he inquired, scrutinizing the endorsement.

The old lady indicated that she was the individual named as though she were a little embarrassed at the fact. Her hands flat on the edge of the counter, she seemed to assume some imagined sympathy in the man who was to give her her money. She smiled at him and, perhaps wanting to say something wholly different, began to thank him.

"You shouldn't endorse your cheque before coming here," Alexandre reproved her. "Above all a government cheque."

He felt a tickling in his throat; he must have caught cold earlier that morning, when he had had to wait for precisely eight and one-half minutes for his streetcar. Yet what was the use bothering your head about careless old women? He had already had to warn this very person, and sure as shooting she would do the very same thing the next time. Still, as though to bolster her sense of importance, he inquired, "How would you like it?"

She answered with a thin laugh, not wholly lacking joy and gaiety, that it would be wiser to give her big bills. "They last longer," she explained.

"In tens?" asked Alexandre.

His own mother had had the habit of giving explanations to strangers. And she was forever excusing herself, whether she was giving or receiving. He had often scolded her for doing it; he had kept telling her that nothing puts you in a worse light with people than constantly excusing yourself. Now regret gave him more patience than he had shown his mother for people to whom his mood surely mattered little.

"Yes . . . tens," said the elderly widow. "But a few fives, too . . . to pay my small debts. . . ."

"Let's say two fives and the rest in tens?" Alexandre was already at the end of his forbearance.

He chose brand-new bills for her, though he was perfectly well aware that this additional small courtesy did nothing much to make up for the way he had treated his mother. Not to have loved enough when it was the time for love—that was Alexandre's great sorrow. Indeed his fifty-two years of life had taught him only this—which was no great consolation— that you never had enough love for the living.

"Be careful," he told the old lady, "your pocketbook isn't closed." All he needed was to have the poor soul lose her month's stipend, and lose his own sleep worrying over it.

"Good-bye to you," he added dryly.

It was hard for him to swallow the idea of public support for the country's needy old people. Now there was talk of giving the pension to all aged citizens, whether they needed it or not. Even a chap like Rockefeller might, through the income tax, get a bit of Alexandre's money. And yet perhaps there was good reason for it . . . but would Alexandre himself last long enough to benefit from the advantages of modern life?

A small, sharp-faced errand boy asked for change. His fingers were stained brown and he had just slipped a cigarette butt over his ear. "Smoking? At your age!" scolded Alexandre.

The child made an impudent face at him.

Alexandre drew his hand over his forehead as though to relieve his headache.

He had been young for a short while, not for long, and then it was, with all his ignorance of life and of himself, that he had chosen himself a career. His propensity for accurate work and punctuality together with a gift for figures was what had decided his choice. He had entered the savings bank and there he had stayed, as almost all human beings tend to stay once they have found a safe refuge. Excepting, perhaps, people with a vocation, saints or poets. Who in all the world ever heard of a poor, hungry poet who wants to change places with a bank teller?

"Hello, Mr Chenevert; Do you want my pennies?"

Alexandre pushed back his glasses. He glanced sharply through the wicket. "Oh! Hello, Mademoiselle Leduc."

From the very outset of spring, even in the most unseasonable weather, she wore an old-fashioned straw hat which smelled of fresh varnish. "You have to give spring a bit of encouragement," she claimed. This year Mademoiselle Leduc's hat was yellow; she loved colours fashionable long ago, shades of pearl-grey and violet, a certain mauve in search of which she spent hours in the stores and which did not at all suit her mottled complexion. The very sight of her painlessly, almost pleasurably, brought Alexandre back to the brief moment of his youth and to the girls of those days: careful of their pennies, not a bit independent or bold like today's hussies. What was more, Violette Leduc—her halting gait, her chatter, her spontaneous gaiety—reminded him of his sister Hermance. Now Hermance was one of Alexandre's few dead who left him in peace. He had loved her almost as much alive as he loved her in death. And so he felt no constraint with Violette Leduc.

"Is business good, Mademoiselle Leduc? Everything's going well?"

The business in question was tiny. Just around the corner on the Rue de la Visitation, Violette Leduc kept a one-room store tacked onto the basement of an ugly brick dwelling. Ever since he had known her, Alexandre had occasionally gone a bit out of his way after work to buy a pack of cigarettes there. He took the cotton bag in which she carried her money to the bank and dumped its contents on the counter. First he sorted out the pennies, and there were a great many of them.

"It's the kids, you know," she apologized. "Kids always pay in pennies. . . ."

He indicated his complete understanding. Counting pennies for someone like Mademoiselle Leduc was no bother at all. In fact it made him think of himself as a kid, buying candy at a store on the street where his family lived. . . .

Then he noticed a man come up to take his place behind the old girl; he was heavy-jawed, had a leather brief case under his arm and a dead cigar in the corner of his mouth, and was chewing in an irritated, vulgar fashion; his whole expression said, "Hurry up! Get on with it! I haven't got time to waste listening to your chitchat. . . . Life's too short for that non-sense. . . ."

All the same Alexandre took the time necessary to avoid being abrupt to his old customer. "You have $12.88 in change," said he. "Is that what you make it?" he added "Mademoiselle" with a flourish, and he asked, with a trace of the old-fashioned courtesy he had shown women in his younger days, "Now, if you'll be so good as to sign here. . . ."

Then he bent his body behind the wicket in an abbreviated bow. "Till next time. Take care of yourself, Mademoiselle."

The client with the extinguished cigar was already pushing forward, shoving Mademoiselle Leduc without the least attempt at apology. All kindliness drained from Alexandre's face; once again membership in the human race was an affliction. He became keenly aware of how his head ached. The moment he was through with the man, he began fishing in his pocket. Then, looking guilty, he waited for a moment when nobody seemed to be paying any attention to him to slip a bitter-tasting pill between his lips.

His first job had been as a copy clerk in the Snowdon Branch. Since getting to work had taken over an hour in a tram, he had finally rented a room in the neighbourhood, for he had calculated that otherwise he would spend a seventh of his life in public vehicles. At that time Snowdon didn't please him; it was too far from the centre of the town, scarcely built up at all, and the whole suburb was English. A little later he had been made collection clerk in an East End branch; once again he had moved. But the East End of the city reeked of gasoline, and he began to wish he were back in Snowdon : back there at least there had been open spaces, trees, country air. There must have been a touch of madness in him, because he became fond of the East End too, but only after he had been transferred elsewhere. Then he became aware that in the East End he had been near enough to the river to be able to watch the transatlantic liners glide by and dream of journeying to the Indies, to Martinique, or perhaps the Shetlands, after he had read somewhere that they were the saddest isles in all the world. He was a bookkeeper. He married. He rented an apartment on a terribly noisy street. "But take it in your stride," said Alexandre. "Sure as shooting, the moment I move, I'll be shifted to the other end of town. Let's wait and see. . . ." The Savings Bank at last seemed inclined, however, to leave Alexandre where he was. Of the three children born to him only little Irène had survived. He had become *caissier-payeur* in French, in English *paying teller*. And now he need fear no further advancement, no greater honours . . . unless, one of these days, they should take it into their heads to make him a manager. So keen a fear grasped him at this startling idea that his lips began to move in instant refusal. Every other peril in life he had substantially foreseen, save this—Mr Alexandre Chenevert, Manager, The Savings Bank. . . . A customer who had just rested his elbows on the counter gave Alexandre an embarrassed glance. The man must be crazy, thought the customer. But Alexandre's eyes told him at once what the fellow was thinking.

"Yes?" he said, recovering himself and speaking with his usual stiffness.

There followed a passage at arms with a heavy-set woman, arrogant and unpleasant in manner. "Have you an account here?"

"No," she replied defiantly. But what did that matter? The cheque she was cashing had been signed by a very well-known person.

"That may be," said Alexandre, "but why don't you go to the bank on which it is drawn? It's not far—just the other side of the street."

For a moment the big woman was speechless with rage. Then she raised her voice as though to complain about Alexandre to everyone within earshot: Had anyone ever heard anything to equal it? Here she was presenting a perfectly good cheque, properly made out, and they wanted her to go chasing off, somewhere else. . . .

Alexandre raised his own voice a trifle. "Madame," he said tremulously, "I'm merely following orders. Suppose there were not enough funds to cover your cheque."

She gave him no time to finish his explanation. Very well, very well. But she would remember the way she'd been treated here. . . . And if ever she had any money to deposit, she would certainly never entrust it to a bank where they were so unaccommodating. . . .

"Accommodating," growled Alexandre between his teeth. As was always the case after such episodes, he seemed to seek support from those who had witnessed them. But they were studiously paying no attention, probably embarrassed by the sharp feelings they had seen displayed.

"What can I do for you?" Alexandre asked the next person in line. She was young and timid-looking and must have been terrified at his expression. She had a five-dollar bill she wanted to deposit. Now don't lose your temper with this poor girl, thought Alexandre, and he lost it. "Can't you read the instructions?" said he. "Can't you follow the rules like everyone else?"

The girl's eyes grew round with amazement; she seemed bewildered. Alexandre pointed out to her a notice, very prominently displayed, which requested that depositors, in order to hasten service, write their names and account numbers on slips provided for the purpose in the racks on the writing desks. Very few clients, it was true, would be bothered with even that much trouble. So once or twice a day Alexandre made an effort to enforce the regulations; yet by what strange chance was it that he always selected a timid soul to serve as an example? Was it because such people resembled him? Because he might have been in their shoes? His courtesy was a hollow thing since it was unjust. Was it not employed above all in dealing with aggressive clients, from whom he might otherwise expect an outburst?

The mortified girl was now at quite a distance; two other customers tried to slip in front of the wicket. Alexandre glanced at them irritably. There were six people lined up before his cage; he was still scowling, and unburdened himself to the next in line: "How can I hurry if I have to do everything myself? The public doesn't like to wait, but it won't do its share."

But this customer refused to unbend, seemed anxious not to express an opinion, eager under no circumstances to compromise himself. And indeed, Alexandre reflected, by making excuses he only strengthened the impression that he was in the wrong. Here he was beginning to act like his mother. Was it inevitable that the trait one liked the least in oneself should be the strongest bond one had with others? Now there were seven people in line. Alexandre lost track of what he was doing; he had to begin all over again counting the bundle of bills in his hand. He made each one crackle with a quick snap of his fingers—a trick he must have admired when he was a child. . . . Someone was talking much too loud somewhere toward the middle of the line. . . .

"One hundred and eighty . . . there we are," said Alexandre.

With exasperating care the customer checked the count, and Alexandre began to toy nervously with his papers. He must bend all his efforts to maintain an outward calm; above all he should avoid betraying any signs of agitation on the job —in brief, not let himself act like a human being. Despite his efforts he felt the blood vessels in his temples throbbing. He glanced across the room at the young woman he had casti-gated; pen in hand, earnestly studying the filled-out form in-tended to serve as a guide, she looked puzzled. By now there must have been eight or nine people shuffling their feet in front of Alexandre as though to convey to him their concern, their awareness of time that passed too quickly—or seemed to drag interminably. At the end of the line there was a very tall man who could easily look over the heads of the others, and he stared at the teller, though without the least interest, stared at him as though he were a sort of machine. Alexandre's eyes met the eyes that looked at him as though he were a machine. Another depositor had failed to fill out her slip; this time Alexandre did it for her without protest. Clearly he was be-having without the least feeling for justice. Either he ought to fill out all slips or none. Alexandre looked again at the man taller than the others. Quietly the tall man stared him down.

"Sign," said Alexandre. The old person at the wicket ex-amined him uncertainly. You would have thought that people didn't know how to read. "Here." Alexandre pointed to the line and made a small pencil mark at the end of the dots printed on the slip.

It must be pouring rain. People were now coming in almost at a run and shaking streaming umbrellas. Water dripped from hats and articles of clothing which they shook out violently as though this were a street or a public square. Alexandre sneezed. The girl he had sent off to make out her slip returned. She seemed hurt. The slip had to be made out all over again any-way. Alexandre tore it in two. Perhaps he shouldn't have done that right in her face. Picking up another form, he wrote her account number on it.

"Here, Mademoiselle Huberdeau," he said, perhaps hoping to pacify her if he addressed her by name.

But the young girl seemed to see in this sign of respect

proof that she had been injured. The tall man was drawing nearer. He was still watching Alexandre.

"Sign it, please," said the teller in the second cage.

"Where?"

"On that line," said Alexandre.

There were almost as many persons waiting at his wicket as you would see on the open street waiting at a tram stop. From now on it was he who examined them somewhat as though they were objects rather than human beings. Yet rarely did he fail to retain in his mind some dreadful peculiarity of each one: be it a bloated nose, a wart at the corner of a mouth, a huge calloused paw. . . . Alexandre's head was stuffed with such irrelevant, sometimes annoying, details; at night they would come back, clamouring for his attention, like pieces in a jigsaw puzzle he felt compelled to fit together. The muscles at the nape of his neck were drawn so taut that the least movement of his head produced sharp twinges of pain. Leaning over his papers, suddenly Alexandre heard—almost drowned out in the clatter of the adding machines, barely audible above the shuffling feet—a low voice almost at his ear saying, "Thank you."

He looked up in astonishment. He saw an elderly gentleman with a carefully trimmed, small white beard, very neat in his appearance, with a pleasant manner and agreeable features; his eyes shone with kindness. He carefully examined the name plate on the counter, and repeated, as though it were a real pleasure to say the words, "Thanks, Monsieur Chenevert."

That was all. Quite insignificant. But Alexandre's face contracted; he was as deeply moved as though he had been reviled. His mouth trembled. "Glad I could help you," he said.

A little later, at the very height of the rush, he pulled off his glasses and pressed the tips of his fingers against his eyelids. Then, withdrawing his hand, for perhaps half a minute he stared into the distance. His eyes were stripped naked, iron-grey eyes, weak and blinking in the light, almost sightless and yet lovely for the humanity they contained. In the iris glittered the reflection of the lamp. Through the motionless pupils passed the shadows of wrongs. Meanwhile, in all his remoteness, Alexandre said, "Please sign your name."

"Where?"

Alexandre drew the slip toward him, replaced his glasses, made a cross on the paper at the spot where the word signature was printed in red. Standing upright, or with one hip propped against his stool, he felt a great weariness in his back, as though an agonizing pressure on the spinal column forced him to bend over. Yet all his ills were, you might say, his own fault. Thus, at least, had decided the doctor for the insurance company which had issued a policy on his life—occupational maladies, as the doctor had put it. "Do try to hold yourself erect," he had advised, "so as not to increase the curvature of the spine." Alexandre had a better reason than this advice, he had a vivid personal recollection to induce him to stand straight. When he had been about ten, he had met Uncle Adelard, a civil servant, who was held up in the Chenevert family as a terrible example to warn Alexandre against bad habits—his mother especially kept referring to this case. Although still young, this poor man was so stooped that he almost seemed a hunchback. That dreadful protuberance between the shoulders, that air of looking up at others from under his eyebrows, since of course Uncle Adelard was no longer capable of raising his head straight, were amply sufficient in themselves to determine Alexandre against any imitation of this relative. Even to this day, when he squared his shoulders, he above all felt sorry for Adelard.

"Next, please."

The neighbouring teller closed the wicket of his cage. His few remaining customers had to take their places at the end of Alexandre's line; some of them grumbled; others assumed an expression of resigning themselves to a wait that was in itself offensive. There seemed an endless number of them. Would he ever finish? Would he ever reach the end? Would it ever, at last, be twelve-fifteen?

CHAPTER III

NOW, A tray on his arm and his round hat perched on his head, Alexandre was himself standing in line at the entrance of the cafeteria. Their noses rubbing their neighbours' backs, each laden with his small painted metal tray, men and women were pressing for access to the food counter. It was their hour of relaxation. With them Alexandre gained a little ground, stood still, moved forward a few more paces. To have to stand in line was really no fun; Alexandre had his daily experience of that. But, because of professional fellow-feeling, he perhaps had less sympathy for the fatigue of the people standing than for that of the poor girl at the cash register who had to cast a hasty glance at each tray and, almost instantaneously, push down the keys, make change, and risk—if she erred by a penny—a severe reprimand, perhaps even dismissal. Turning, Alexandre found himself face to face with a man of small stature like himself and a discouraged expression. He noticed other pale, drawn faces; hard-eyed, frowning faces, but less from ill-nature than from weariness, thought Alexandre. Poor people! Would they ever be free of their queues?

He closed his eyes, deeply concerned with the problem of individual identity that would be posed by the Last Judgment. Whereupon Alexandre's wayward imagination summoned up before him the crowding into the Valley of Josaphat: all the earth's queues, the patient waiting lines of all the ages, were stretched out, one after the other, doubling back on themselves like mountain roads, a procession to destroy all respect for human life. Mingled closest together were precisely the races least prone to get along in the flesh—the yellow and the white, the pure Aryans and the lesser breeds. What could be the feeling of the white Southerners and the members of the Ku Klux Klan at their proximity to the Negroes they had not been able to endure? All mankind stood there, and in disorder absolute. The radio, the newspapers, the whole machinery of propaganda had ceased to distinguish ally from enemy. Not a noise, not a word, not a sound throughout the Valley; only the silent movement, step by step, the docile motion of the crowd which of its own accord still obeyed the law of the queue. And opening his eyes, Alexandre was happy to find himself back in a line that was not too tight-packed, the end and goal of which were within his sight. Huge soup pots cast toward him fatty, acid smells; alongside them stew simmered; spaghetti lay in vast buckets. And there were vegetables, other meats, croquettes, minute steaks: dishes in great variety, probably well-enough prepared, and housed in sterilized containers, but so displayed and so intermingling their odours that, suddenly, eating seemed a monstrous boredom.

Once they had put their trays on the chromed bars that ran along the counter, people had to make up their minds quickly. Every sound reverberated as in a station waiting room; human voices, sucked up by the high vault, acquired so solemn an intonation that the patrons were quickly intimidated and lowered their conversations almost to a whisper. With its vastness, its columns, its imitation-marble table tops, its impression of emptiness despite the crowd, this North-Western Lunch was not unlike Alexandre Chenevert's bank. He did not find himself too much out of his element here, at least no more so than in his working environment, with the comfortable feeling it gave him of being a small thing under the distant ceiling, of being unnoticed and perhaps even invisible, among all the others, under the eyes of God, Whom he imagined almost always displeased with Alexandre Chenevert. What attracted him to the North-Western Lunch were the prices, which were quite reasonable and so clearly posted you could not go wrong.

What did they say today, those strips of paper affixed to the wall behind the food counter? Pushing back his glasses, Alexandre began studying them. With the constant rise in the cost of living, you had to expect frequent increases. Then too, certain meals went for a set price, including soup, bread, and a beverage; others were organized in such a way that you might make a mistake. Because he had once been caught and had had to pay separately for each of the items he had on his tray, Alexandre looked very carefully before he chose. And that took time. Time to read through the daily specials, discover on the counter the physical embodiment of what was advertised, calculate the total involved, including tax. Meanwhile the crowd kept pressing him along, and by the time he had about made up his mind, Alexandre found himself pushed far beyond the dish he had chosen. What of it! The goal didn't seem to him worth the trouble of an elbow battle. And besides, he wasn't hungry. Now he was stranded in front of the dessert counter—cakes, slices of pie, cheese, puddings, ice cream, stewed fruit. Alexandre wrinkled his forehead and wondered what he might take out of this choice. That apple pie, perhaps? Of course it would make him sick, but he might just as well be sick for a good reason. Yet it was perhaps somewhat sinful to get yourself sick on purpose. The Christian Scientists held that it was not God Who wanted sicknesses, but man who puts himself in the way of suffering. If this were the case, though, wouldn't we all die in perfect health? This absurd thought made Alexandre scowl. On his tray he had finally placed a bit of cheese, some rolls, and a dish of stewed fruit, which he was already eyeing with disgust. He returned it to the counter, hesitated over a tartlet, and finally took back the fruit. He snatched a pat of butter, picked up forks, spoons, and knives. From a chrome faucet he was served a cup of coffee. He set his tray down on the metal bars. Coffee was still the best bargain at this North-Western Lunch, strong enough to put new life into you. Alexandre fished in his pocket and pulled out his wallet from which he extracted a single bill. A bell jingled; the cash register opened with a rattle! Alexandre's change tumbled down a metal trough. He began counting it—never in these days of Our Lord must you ever slacken your vigilance, even for so much as a moment; why, only last week a cashier had handed him ten cents too much; suppose he hadn't checked, think what the consequences might have been! He picked up the last pennies, one by one, absorbed in the process of adding and substracting. Three people whom he thus kept waiting followed his movement, with irritation. Even the cashier was losing patience. Raising his head, Alexandre became aware of hostile glances that harassed him. Hastily he picked up his tray before closing his billfold and before he could free both hands. . . . He did not like to wait himself; why did these people imagine that he had made them wait deliberately? His eyes were flaming as though he were on the point of starting a fight. . . . Then, at the back of the room he thought he saw an empty seat. Alexandre went off toward it, a fistful of change in his hand, worried about the open billfold he had tucked under one arm. He moved as quickly as he could, taking care not to spill the coffee. His pace was odd, hesitant, constrained, like that of a man carrying some precious burden. And yet every time an elbow nudged him, his cup slopped over. It was maddening; the coffee was far and away the best thing to be had here. He increased his speed. A host of others were crossing in front of each other, behind each other, hurling themselves here and there in search of a table. It was almost like some game in which, rather than balls bouncing from one spot to another, a number of serious adults had been propelled into a complex pattern of movement. Just as Alexandre reached the empty seat he had espied from afar, someone more nimble than he pounced upon it and sat down, beaming. Shaking his head slightly, Alexandre shot him a bitter glance and started out in a new direction. A customer was rising from his chair and wiping his mouth; instantly Alexandre slipped on the still-warm seat. The soiled tablecloth had not been changed; cigarette butts soaked in left-over, stiffened gravy. On one corner of the table Alexandre cleared himself a space. He began his meal with a pill, which he swallowed with a little water. Then he leaned his folded newspaper against a sugar shaker, primarily to afford some privacy from the stranger who was lunching opposite him, a hard-faced individual Alexandre did not find to his taste. And while he munched his bread, he learned that ten policemen had been hanged in Palestine as reprisal for each terrorist condemned to death . . . that there was no hope of coming to an agreement with the Soviets . . . that all the residents of Louiseville had taken a day off to honour the Virgin . . . that Zaco Zopovitch was going home because, having said something scandalous about Pius XII, he had been criticized in the House. You might say that Alexandre never let any part of a printed page go to waste; from amid the serious items, he gleaned the tiny advertisements for hernia belts, harnesses for artificial limbs. Even though he had not yet any need for them, such appliances appealed to Alexandre. For no disease or infirmity could leave him cold.

Turning a page, his eye lit upon something wholly novel :

Honeymoons
$35.00 and up.
Big choice available
No obligation
"Where to Go, Ltd."
Travel Agents

He felt that the first days of marriage must be more distressing than ever under the guidance of travel agencies. He glanced up indignantly and became aware of one of his colleagues at the bank who, laden with a tray, was making his way toward him.

"Hello, Godias!" he called out, pointing to the chair opposite, which was now empty. His small grey face lit up. "Sit down," he said heartily.

Any display of friendship toward Alexandre always surprised him, he was himself so hard to please. He could imagine nothing about himself that might conceivably warrant it, nor could he ever hope to retain a friendship once it was proffered. Which was precisely why he always leaped to grasp at it, tense in his desire for companionship.

Yet once his colleague was installed opposite him—a heavy man negligent about his appearance, his jacket spotted, his shoulders stooping, his thick, blond, still-silky hair full of dandruff—Alexandre almost immediately felt embarrassed at this friendship. Poor Godias! What a sloppy fellow! What a mean figure he cut in the world! How sad that someone with so much goodness of heart and generosity as himself should have no worthier friend than this on whom to bestow them!

"You're putting on weight," he remarked.

"And you're getting skinnier by the minute," retorted Godias, with a hearty laugh that effectually took any sting out of his words.

"At our age it's better to get skinny than fat," said Alexandre.

With honest displeasure he watched Godias greedily swallowing a thick, greasy pea soup the mere smell of which made him feel queasy.

"I fail to understand . . ." he began and stopped short in his resentment.

For where indeed was there any justice? According to all the laws of health, Godias should have been sick long since. He ate voraciously of anything he saw fit without chewing properly and then went straight back to work on his books. Despite this he had pink, healthy skin, a face unmarked by fatigue. He slept eight hours a night, a "dreamless and tranquil sleep," as he put it. And it must be true, for if people often boast of being more unhappy than they are, do they frequently exaggerate the reasons for their well-being?

Yet Alexandre longed to warn this hearty fellow against the ailments from which he himself suffered, however little he deserved them because of any self-indulgence. "There's nothing worse for you," said he, "than to take starches and meat at the same meal. Why, that's elementary. According to the theory of Dr Munroe . . . of the Mayo Clinic, an authority in nutrition . . ." Alexandre was piling it on, raising his voice to force Godias into respectful attention. But he caught his colleague's jeering glance and averted his face in a wounded gesture, deliberately cutting short his sentence.

Today the merest trifle irritated him. Was it really a trifle, though, to see a fellow man scorn all his disinterested advice? "Poor, poor Godias," he commiserated with some irritation. Then as he heard himself speak he realized that he had used the very words of Elise Chenevert when, long ago, she gave up all hope of putting any sense into her son's head. "You poor, poor boy," his mother would say to him, "someday you'll understand that I was speaking to you for your own good." And in fact the bitter experience he himself could now adduce was precisely the same as that he had scorned in his own day. Was this always the way with experience—truth which, after all, you could convey to no one?

Alexandre rather obviously changed the subject. "I read the other day that our planet is warming up. Scientists have studied the arctic icecap, which serves us as a sort of reservoir of cold, and it is melting away. . . ."

"Yet we never had a colder winter," Godias remarked with his mouth full of food.

"That's got nothing to do with the icecap," Alexandre answered in annoyance. You just couldn't talk seriously with the fellow; he made a childish joke out of everything.

"Well, there's one thing that's sure as shooting," said Alexandre. "If the world's population continues to increase at the present rate, there'll be nothing but famine in a couple of centuries."

"You don't expect to be around then, do you?" rejoined Godias with arch surprise.

This levity was about all Alexandre could swallow. As though he were concerned about himself! The gravest possible danger, why, the very extinction of the species, threatened mankind, and this self-satisfied lout didn't care because he wouldn't be here to see it!

"I read an article about it written by a Dutch scientist . . . Van something or other," Alexandre continued solemnly. "Do you know how many million people there are in India alone?"

"Fifteen . . . maybe twenty . . ."

"Fifteen, twenty! Are you crazy, Godias? There are three hundred million people in India, of every religion and every language. The people in one village very often can't understand what the people in the next village are saying."

"That must be a nuisance," Godias remarked out of politeness.

"Three hundred millions," Alexandre reminded him.

"A lot of people," Godias agreed.

"Too many," reflected Alexandre with a sigh.

"But don't worry," suggested Godias by way of consolation. "There'll be less of them after the next war."

Overflowing with bitterness, Alexandre's pinched little face turned toward Godias as though to reproach him. "The Hindus are highly civilized," he said dryly. "They're odd, but perhaps more civilized than we are."

Was it Alexandre's keenness in defending utter strangers? His preference for people Godias was far from considering his equals? In any case, Godias felt annoyed.

He wasn't a bad chap, but a bit easygoing, a fellow who could live surrounded by cosmic tragedy without even being aware of its existence. Generally good-natured and conciliatory to a fault, he saw red when anyone tried to get him excited because some faraway savages were miserable, probably through their own fault. In order to be happy himself, Godias had to deny unhappiness, or at least to imagine it visiting only men very different from himself, backward people perhaps, at least people more hardened to suffering than you might think— or else even deserving what they got. That was what vexed him against Alexandre, who was forever bringing misery so close to him, making it so obvious.

All in all a good husband and father, quite capable of being genuinely distressed when his sluggish imagination could grasp misfortune in visible and commonplace form, by the same token good company, not turning up his nose at a friendly glass or a game of poker with the boys, rather pliable, thoroughly likeable—such was Godias. But when he was with Alexandre —and only then—he was obviously irritable and contrary, and he held Alexandre to blame for it. While Alexandre held it against him that he was happy in a tragic world, Godias reproached Alexandre for doing all he could to make others uncomfortable and wretched; basically he reproached him for trying to make himself different from his fellow men.

And today again with a gesture of impatience he said, "Why on earth don't you try to be like other people! Eat like other people, take a drop of Scotch, let yourself go! Wake up and live! Have some fun!"

Such advice from a big, healthy chap who had never known a day's illness, to a sickly being like himself, who had experienced almost every manner of suffering, was not a thing to anger Alexandre. Certainly not! That would be too silly! Alexandre seemed to say to himself, indicating his superiority by an abrupt movement of his chin. And he continued his sad commentary. "Did you see that in Palestine they're shooting ten hostages for every act of terrorism?"

"A damn good thing!" exclaimed Godias. "The Jews are getting just what they deserve." He had a child's eyes, clear and blue beneath eyelashes so blond that you could scarcely make them out. The directness of his glance framed by the innocent pink of his eyelids freed his expression of any trace of spitefulness. "I certainly haven't any pity to waste on the Jews!" he boasted.

And that set him off on a recital of the generalizations his lazy mind had most easily retained, those most directly based on hatred. The Jews controlled the great trusts, had a monopoly of the fur and hat businesses . . . and don't you tell Godias that it isn't true; he had just read all about it; he could give you the figures if you wanted to spare him the time. And of course the Jews had control of the press. So you couldn't read anything, anywhere, which wasn't coloured and perverted by Jewish propaganda. And so you shouldn't pay too much attention to the alleged sufferings of the Jews in Palestine. It was probably made up out of whole cloth. . . . That was

Godias's summary of the matter as he leaned back in his chair and cleaned his teeth with a toothpick.

"Fairy stories!" replied Alexandre. "It would take a pile of corpses to open your eyes."

He was as cut to the quick as though someone had cast doubts on a thing he had himself witnessed. Or, indeed, on the worth of his friendship. For if there was a man in all the world who could have profited by Alexandre Chenevert's experience, could have enriched his mind by contact with Alexandre's thought and reading; if there was a man whose mind should have worked the same way as Alexandre's, that man was Godias. For twenty years Alexandre had laboured to open his eyes, to make him think things out, to project himself into a larger world. And what was left of all this struggle in the mere lump of flesh now sitting opposite him? Today, more than ever before, his incapacity to influence Godias made the big man insupportable.

"What do you know about all that!" he complained bitterly. "Do you keep yourself posted? Do you even keep up with the news? My friend, all you do is vegetate."

Still and all, what he wanted above everything was to convince. But his deep inner disappointment made him react to any lack of approval as though it were a personal offence, a painful injury. "Basically, what do you know about this business?"

"I know enough anyway," interrupted Godias, annoyed in his turn, "to understand that the Jews are committing plain robbery against the Arabs."

"What do you mean, robbing the Arabs!" Alexandre cried out, pounding the table. "Why, the Jewish colonists have bought and paid for every inch of the land they're farming. Within a few years they've done a better job developing the soil than the Arabs did in centuries. And that's the truth," said Alexandre, defying anyone to contradict him.

Often they had quarrelled about people and events further and further from the reach of their comprehension. One summer evening, amid the rumbling of the streetcars, they had argued, while sitting on Alexandre's tiny balcony, about the Spanish Civil War; Alexandre had expressed doubts as to whether the Reds alone had committed atrocities, and Godias had retorted: ". . . and the bodies of those Carmelites they've lately dug up! You'd have to be a Red yourself to close your eyes to that." The Spanish Civil War had been responsible for their not talking to each other for two weeks. Then they had had a blowup over participation in World War II—not to detail the many others. Yet never had they attained the pitch of animosity with which they now confronted themselves across the small, imitation-marble table. An attendant was noisily piling dirty dishes on her tray. Far off, from near the cash desk, a small radio set was crooning ". . . a woman's heart is like a flighty bird. . . ." It had been discovered lately that music quiets the nerves. Tried to the limit of his endurance, Alexandre for an instant grasped his head in his hands. He felt a knot of pain in his stomach. To be so terribly alone, facing hatred and illwill. Then he was carried away by a feeling of exasperated jealousy against every influence that had outweighed his own with Godias, the influence of people who agreed too readily with a man whose nature loved flattery, the influence of his friends, above all of the newspaper Godias read each day.

He glanced scornfully at the printed matter protruding from Godias's pocket. "Is that where you get your ideas? The most lying, filthy sheet of all of them!"

"The sheet you read is straight Communist!" Godias flared. "A red rag that always sides with every strike."

"Have you ever bothered even to look at it?" Alexandre asked pointedly.

"I know all about it. How about you? Have you ever read the *Pays?*"

Alexandre shook his head; after all, did he need to read the *Pays* to know, as his own paper pointed out, what you should think of the *Pays?* Oh! It required a great deal of good will these days to select one of the more honest papers and, even when you read such a paper, to distinguish true from false. Good will was like a seventh sense which must ever be on the watch. The angel who had extolled it over the stable at Bethlehem had perhaps not foreseen the great weariness involved in the exercise of good will for the men of the twentieth century. The terrible weariness! Obviously poor Godias was incapable of such an effort. He had always been a man of bad will. All the good Alexandre had ever wished him turned into resentment.

"When I think of all I've tried to do for you, Godias Doucet . . . when I slaved to make you study for your accountant's exam . . . when I lent you my finest books which you didn't even bother to glance through . . ."

Several years before, Alexandre, carried away by his perusal of *The Keys of the Kingdom*, had bought a copy to give Godias. Under the pressure of Alexandre's persistent questioning, Godias at last said that he had read the novel and had liked it very much. But a few days later, when Alexandre had stopped by at Godias's apartment, he had happened to notice his gift lying neglectedly under a pile of popular magazines, and quite obviously its pages had not even been cut.

"If you're referring to that old business of *The Keys of the Kingdom*," said Godias, "I did read it. At least I read almost half of it. It was terribly long and damned boring."

This scornful opinion of a work he held in very high esteem added the final drop to the overflowing cup of Alexandre's sorrow. "It's one of the most beautiful books I ever read in all my life," he burst out. "It and *The Rosary*. But you've never made any effort to read fine things." His lip trembled, as though he was about to burst into tears. "You're just like all the rest of them . . . a sheer waste of time."

"You've certainly bored me plenty," said Godias.

Like many another, Godias was perfectly willing to assume that his weaknesses sprang from the influences surrounding him, while his good characteristics had their sole origin in his own being. He was one of that tribe of men who will resist an influence, even when they recognize it as good in their heart of hearts, through need of asserting a spirit of independence they themselves utterly lack. Often the mere realization of Alexandre's rightness had been enough to plug his ears. So that now he was quite honestly convinced that Alexandre's failure with him sprang from Alexandre's own ineptness. Did not his own spinelessness and lack of consequence stem directly from Alexandre's having harped on them so often in the past?

"Yes, come to think of it; I wonder if you haven't been a bad influence on me," he said, upset at the thought of his unhappy fate.

Tears came easily to Godias: as he became aware of his emotion he was very close to believing that his fine qualities would have blossomed in splendour if he had not had to be on the defensive against a constantly tyrannous friendship—at least that his life would have been far happier had Alexandre Chenevert never existed.

Alexandre looked at him fixedly for a moment and began tearing his paper napkin into tiny bits. And he cried in a thin bitter voice, as though appealing to all the strangers in the cafeteria, to the whole city: "I a bad influence on him! Just listen: I've been a bad influence on Godias Doucet!"

"Oh, come on!" Godias was eager to undo the damage he had done. "I didn't really mean it."

But Alexandre continued to beseech some honest witness. Whom could he summon in his defence? "You heard him; so now it appears I've had a bad influence on him. Just think that one over! A bad influence!"

"Alex, good old Alex . . ." Godias interjected, "we've had plenty of disagreements, but never anything serious. Alex!"

That hateful shortening of his name—familiarity, now, piled upon insult! Alexandre could endure no more. He jumped from his seat and marched off without a word, his eyes proud. Godias caught up with him at the door "Come, Alex! I was just shooting my mouth off."

They were out in the drenching wind. Under Godias's big umbrella they trudged lamely and in silence, the smaller man taking three steps to each one of his companion's—two persons who would have seemed ill-suited for intimacy even to a passing eye, acquaintances of the sort a common trade or profession or mere propinquity brings together by the thousand. For what chance has any man to meet, among the globe's millions of inhabitants, that sister soul who may be a Chinese or even an Australian? The rain forced Alexandre to hunch his shoulders. As they went by a shop window, he suddenly became aware of his own small stature, even more dwarfed by Godias's broad bulk. And then it was that he felt the full impact of the outrage he had suffered. He brusquely drew away from Godias and stepped toward the middle of the flooded sidewalk. To share the umbrella of a man who had unjustly judged him suddenly seemed to him impossible. Sharing an umbrella assumed a certain mutual confidence and closeness. Could you conceive of two men aroused against each other to the depths of their souls strolling along under the same umbrella? Looking up at Godias, but carefully avoiding his eyes, Alexandre began to explain, "I've got an errand to do near here. Don't wait for me."

"I'm in no hurry," said the other. "I'll go along with you."

"No, no," answered Alexandre. "You go your way and I'll go mine."

And he added, "Good-bye, Godias."

There was something so absurd about this solemn farewell in the rain, between two men who must continue to work side by side, that Godias almost burst out laughing. But a glance at Alexandre stopped him short.

He became aware of his tininess, his thinness by contrast to his own bulk. He noticed his bad complexion, his puckered mouth, and instead of recognizing the expression of a soul that suffered, Godias believed he saw the hitherto unperceived ravages of illness. "He is sicker than he thinks," Godias said to himself with alarm. "He must be in a bad way . . . worse than he suspects." And an unexpected feeling seized hold of Godias as he raised his umbrella to shelter his companion a few more instants against the downpour. Indeed for those few seconds he felt as though Alexandre had already disappeared from this world.

Yet he felt no lightening of his burden; he was no freer of Alexandre than he had been before. Quite the contrary, he saw his friend as more compelling than ever, faithful, exacting, and too sincere to be thrust aside. The goodness in him shone forth, whereas the defects—unimportant—seemed wiped clean away. A deep sadness invaded Godias. He loved this man who could no longer harass or embitter him. But it was a sad love, heavier than the clouds massed above their heads. Upon Godias's astonished soul love weighed like a burden. Then, alas, he saw Alexandre very much in the flesh: his mouth tight with bad temper—a man you couldn't really make up to as long as the breath of life was in him. His emotion melted away.

"Well, if that's the way you feel about it. Good-bye!"

Alexandre, having taking shelter in a shop entrance, waited until Godias had gone some little distance. Then he continued along the same sidewalk and, careful to avoid catching up with him, followed along behind under the pounding rain.

Godias's broad shoulders ahead of him inflamed his rancour. He was soaked through. The low-hanging sky, the day's sadness, much more like November, the month of the dead, than springtime, were the final blow. Still able to make out Godias's back at the end of the street, he thought: It was over, never again would he have another friend. But had he ever had any? Had he ever found a single being on earth who thought as he did or who at least would grant that he thought as well as his capacities permitted?

And so he would have lived; he would depart from the earth, and "No one," he spat out under his breath at a hurrying pedestrian, would have had the least notion of what it had all been about. Then it chanced that he saw himself in his own heart just as he must appear to the eyes of others: a sharp, contentious man whom he, the very first of all, would have found intolerable.

He stopped in front of a shop window, riveted by this suddenly so hateful view of himself. In the misted glass he sought, as though in corroboration of his judgment, his own pinch-lipped face. A great sorrow suffused his features, so much a stranger to himself and even an enemy, Alexandre wanted to cry.

And yet here and in the rain Alexandre began to feel sleepy.

CHAPTER IV

ALMOST EVERY day that was the way it went. Shortly after his meal, Alexandre would have all the trouble in the world not to fall asleep right where he stood. Even the affront he had received today could not cause him enough hurt to keep him fully awake, and the moment he had re-entered the bank's warmth, it was even more difficult for him to keep his eyes open. He had tried eating little and drinking several cups of coffee, but to no avail: at the hour when sleep reached for Alexandre, his eyelids grew heavy and, independent of his will, sought the rest they longed for.

Which did not mean that when he went to bed he would still be equally disposed to slumber. His desire for sleep would by then have vanished utterly. Alexandre would be in a state of wakeful excitement; his nerves would be jumpy; his brain, a machine gone quite out of kilter, would set to work. Then would he discover the words which would best have served to wound Godias. Now, alas he could easily have slept upright in his cage, his forehead leaning toward the glass partition.

His chin must have slumped a trifle over his chest, his head must have jerked forward a bit. Once again he was battling sleep; but with a very different strategy from that he used at night. Now he was trying to rout it by ridicule. "Imagine," Alexandre was saying to himself, "in Montreal, in full daylight ... found ... fast asleep ... one bank teller ...."

"Sign," said he to a stubby individual called—how many poor chaps seemed to have to him such far from suitable names—Monsieur Auguste Charlemagne. "On this line."

He tried to spread his eyes open, made an unwonted effort over every little detail requiring his attention. He held his jaws clamped tight so as not to yawn.

Happily, even after so many years, it still seemed to him merely a brief interval to be endured. Just like his bad nights, just like the overburdened mornings. Later he could sleep—ten hours, twelve hours. Perhaps around the clock? It was the wasted opportunity to sleep, it was all the wasted opportunities of his life which made life so terrible to bear.

You might describe him as a man who spent his days waiting for the night and his nights waiting for the day.

Yet that was not really the way he spent his life: probably Alexandre had not been niggardly enough with it at the beginning, when life seeemed to stretch far out before him—at twenty-five or thirty. A fine prospect of years, a road bending to the right and to the left. Then it was he may have wasted life's time.

For example, on Mondays in those days he used to wish he were already at the week's end, at Saturday's fine afternoon, which in some fashion belonged to Alexandre for the little tasks he had postponed—painting the closet drawers, repairing a lock, cleaning the spots on his suit; sometimes he even had an hour left to kill, sitting on his tiny balcony; there he would wait for Sunday. Not only had he frittered weeks away, but even whole months. In February he would long to skip six or seven weeks of severe cold to jump right into spring. When July came, hot and sticky, Alexandre would willingly have agreed to forfeit all those summer days, uncomfortably warm in his cage, to shorten the time before the lovely autumn. Then the foliage is resplendent and it's easier to breathe.

A few years later he could admit: "I'm forty-seven. I'm getting older. Can I possibly be forty-seven already?" And in no time, "Here I am, fifty; yet that isn't really old age yet . . ." And then, it seemed to him the next day: Fifty-two! That's not old . . . not quite . . . But I must begin seriously to husband my life."

He looked at the clock and sighed: "If only three o'clock would come!"

But when the bank clock showed that it was three, he was no happier: "If only it could be four!"

He closed his wicket. The last customers were leaving. In their wake the doors were being closed, the blinds drawn. Still it was a lovely moment, when the day's end was in sight. You could breathe. Pedestrians, messengers on bicycles, uniformed telegraph boys, automobiles, trucks, streetcars—they all disappeared, as though behind the final curtain of a play. In the bank they created night at will, at a set hour, summer and winter, even when it was still broad daylight for all the rest of the world. Yet where did life disappear to, life, precious and unique? To each man had been given one life and one alone. Why only one? Were man to have a second life, would he succeed in harvesting from it something worthwhile? One single life . . . it was at once too short and too long to be serviceable. God had not been overgenerous.

With his papers and record book in front of him, Alexandre began to balance columns of figures. There'd be one life for the necessities: clothing oneself, paying for the furniture, the rent, the heat, the electricity. And then another life, this one wholly given to meditation, like Gandhi's in his white loin-cloth. Perhaps given to travel. Still, one fine day Alexandre would decide to chuck the whole thing for good. He bore within him a terrible yearning for happiness which obstacles, if they became too burdensome, could make explosive. "You'll see. I'll make up my mind to go," he had said many times, without being precise as to any destination. Once, however, in tones of utter weariness, he had informed Eugénie that it might be China.

But perhaps all this would not be for the immediate present; for someday in the future, when life really became too intolerably stupid.

Today he would almost prefer to go home and sit down. He began to feel eager to be in his plush armchair, his feet propped on a hassock, listening to the bad news on the radio. So he made up his mind that his working ledger should be up to date no later than four o'clock, and no never-minds, please.

He would still make contracts of this sort with himself, even though he had learned that they distracted his overwrought constitution. His columns didn't balance. And now it was four o'clock, on the dot. Would he ever be at ease in his plush arm-chair if his figures didn't check? He went back to his additions, his pencil point hopping from one amount to the next; with equal agility Alexandre's brain clung to one figure, thrust another aside. Mistrust spurred him on. For it is all very fine to say that a human brain is a wonderful instrument; the fact remains that you never can be sure of this instrument. It isn't foolproof, like an adding machine. If by inadvertence it has made a mistake, it is more than likely to repeat it and repeat it, thenceforth blinded to its error. Alexandre had feared the tricks his brain could play ever since one miserable end-of-the-month, last year, when he had suddenly begun adding wrong. Ten times in succession he must have allowed four plus six to equal eight. Would he now have to slave as he had then had to do through three long evenings in order to set right an error of two cents?

At least he knew exactly, without any possible ambiguity, what had happened to those three evenings of his life.

The bank's lights shone as though it were the middle of the night, the glass partitions reflecting their shaded glow. All around these luminous circles there was a silence so complete that the least crumpling of paper produced a sound like dry leaves torn by the wind. The quiet peace linked to the subdued light would have been easing to the soul if the figures had balanced. But could Alexandre possibly sleep as long as he had not found his mistake?

His bald spot glistened under his shaded desk light. In the dim illumination of the neighbouring cage you could make out Godias's red countenance. Both men had indulged in every sort of subterfuge all afternoon to avoid confronting each other face to face; whenever their glances met momentarily, they had hastily turned away, their features stiff. But now, in tones of deep embarrassment, Godias asked, "Don't you balance? Want me to give you a hand?" Then he added awkwardly, "I'm all O.K."

Clearly fate, against all justice, was still favouring this heavy man who ate everything, slept like a dog, and, to cap it all, practically never had to check over his additions. All the same he was admitting his wrongdoing by being the first to break silence and by offering to help. But Alexandre had no intention of cheapening the insult he had suffered by forgiving too early. An instant pardon would seem to imply, "You didn't say anything too bad; I'll soon forget it" . . . whereas the human dignity within him continued to be troubled: "For if it's true," thought Alexandre, "that I've had a bad influence on Godias, I can't let him off scot-free immediately."

With a kind of longing for the rain, the sidewalks, the crowd, he watched Godias take up his hat and umbrella and go out the door. At least Godias might have been just a little more insistent. . . . A few moments later the two stenographers slipped into raincoats made of some brilliantly coloured plastic which crackled as they put them on. They passed near Alexandre like a burst—here so out of place—of spring. For the bank was old and knew no seasons.

"Night, Monsieur Chenevert."

"Good night."

He grasped his head in his hands.

The correspondence clerk in his turn was leaving. "Good night."

They were all abandoning Alexandre to his error.

Through the door, swung open for an instant, he glimpsed the glistening pavement; between two showers the warm sun was shining and, alongside the buildings, just as in the country, a mist was rising. So it was still daylight: and it must even be spring, if Alexandre's memory did not fail him. To be exact, it must be April. In his mind, snowed under with figures, something else was trying to come back to life, something very distressing, for it was a memory which savoured of joy. Joy was to him even more unseemly than eternity, for it reached him now only through memory, from afar, and therefore with a stubbornness nothing could discourage. What business had that joy from the past coming here, at so ill-chosen a moment?

He must have been about seven or eight; it had been raining and Alexandre, a sickly lad already in love with courage, took off his shoes and stockings; he was running in the water gathered along the sidewalk and was shouting with joy.

Astonished and unbelieving, his glasses at the tip of his nose, the bank teller stared at this laughing youngster. Their encounter provoked shattering surprise in one as much as in the other. "Is it possible?" the runt of a man said to himself. "Oh no! It's not possible; I've not turned into this miserable bank teller." And the child stopped laughing, became quiet, disturbed by this old man without a shred of patience who would certainly get angry and harshly send him packing. Neither one nor the other could believe in their strange relationship. "Get going, you little brat!" was indeed Alexandre's thought, lacking in all kindliness, just as though he had barked at some unknown child whose unruliness had bothered him.

He had just got the same total. Had he had all his wits about him, he would have postponed to the morrow going over his figures, when his head would be rested. But would it be rested? Truly Alexandre had a very sound reason for making it a point to finish each day his daily task; it was the irrefutable truth, he said to himself, "Tomorrow I'll be no better."

"Perhaps I'll be even more tired tomorrow." Again the same total.

His eyeballs twisted quickly and foolishly; his heart thumped several times. It was out of the question that he should have made a hundred-dollar mistake thrice in succession. His additions were correct. Alexandre himself must be short. He must have given a hundred dollars too much to some little-scrupulous client who expected to profit by his oversight.

"One hundred dollars!" Alexandre sighed.

A kind of madness seized him; he put his hand to his head and rumpled his hair. Abruptly he sent his papers flying. Then, as though he might discover the hundred dollars under this pile of foolscap, Alexandre rummaged through it, pushed around in every direction, lifted the leaves in the air to let them fall in disarray.

And suddenly he, who never laughed, began jiggling his shoulders in a movement of extreme hilarity. Abrupt relief relaxed the muscles of his face. Enchanted, Alexandre saw this moment as though it were the moment of his emancipation.

Whoever would have thought that the whole business could come to so simple a conclusion? An unknown person would receive from Alexandre a hundred dollars which were not Alexandre's to give, he would pocket the gift; and Alexandre, enmeshed in the inevitable, would thus be freed of all his burdens. He had certainly imagined all sorts of ways to free himself, but none so radical, so clean-cut, and—in a word—so thoroughgoing. How could he have failed to realize that what he needed to achieve was precisely the pinnacle of misfortune!

"It's all over, finished, done for!" he congratulated himself.

He slammed shut his record book and tossed aside his eyeshade. He seemed to be telling himself something very shrewd and clever, his head nodding sharply up and down in acquiescence to the outcome he saw before him.

He left his cage with a quick, determined step, bursting into the manager's private office.

In the flush of excitement, he cut short his words and had trouble retaining his false teeth, which wobbled on his thin gums. Through their rattling the manager made out a few words: ". . . my resignation . . . tender my resignation . . . all over . . . a hundred dollars . . . over! over! over!"

CHAPTER V

HAD someone forewarned Monsieur Emery Fontaine that because of Alexandre Chenevert he would today be seriously disturbed—even quite upset—he would most certainly have smiled as though at a bit of childish prattle. He would have joined together the tips of his fingers in a gesture habitual to him when he was about to state his views. And he might perhaps have said what he frequently gave as his opinion: that misfortune usually comes from lack of occupation, from failure to follow sound principles. As for him, he had never known a neurotic person who had not become so through his own fault—through idleness, through laziness. Misfortune came to a man through the fact of his not attending to business.

He was not unfeeling, but he was himself tolerably happy,

and he even felt that by keeping happy he put to rout the un-happy, thus doing them a kind of service. Some businessmen like to give the impression that they alone, because of the struggles they have survived, had what it takes to succeed. Such was not Emery Fontaine's attitude. Imbued with a truly democratic spirit, he made it a point to prove in his own person the advantages attainable under a sound social system to a little fellow starting without a thing to his name.

He played golf. He considered physical exercise very impor-tant, of *capital* importance. He injected as much vigour into his recreation after work as he brought with him each morning at nine to attack the problems of the business day. There lay, to his mind, the whole secret of a balanced life. *Play hard . . . work hard* was one of his mottoes, and he had a number of them : Don't lose one minute and time will be yours; Take care of your health, and life will seem worth living. *How to Win Friends and Influence People* was always handy on his bedside table. He would listen to the news summary while buttering his toast, for he owed it to himself to know what was going on in the world, including the hockey results. In all of Monsieur Fontaine's existence there was not one moment which did not serve its purpose. When people congratulated him on having retained so youthful an appearance, not an ounce of excess fat, sound teeth, clear eyes, always a ready—if somewhat conven-tional—answer, Monsieur Fontaine smiled modestly. He attri-buted it all to common sense. Plain common sense !

Thus he had had the good sense to wait until he was well-fixed before marrying. He had seen too many careers at the bank compromised by early marriage, by family responsibilities assumed in youth. According to him, a man should have at least a thousand dollars laid aside before he could let love play a part in his life. And nowadays he might raise the figure to two thousand.

Each evening when he came home from the bank, he kissed his wife on the forehead; he played on the parlour rug with his two handsome children. It at once reminded you of the living-rooms set up as models in the magazines, in *Ideal Home* or *Perfect Housekeeping*. Suzanne Fontaine found in these pub-lications her inspiration for choosing her curtain materials of modern design, for carefully placing an open book on a table, which would remain there untouched for weeks on end. To him there was nothing complex or whimsical about happiness; it followed certain rules; money certainly didn't buy it, but it helped a lot. On this particular evening, in short, as on almost every evening, Monsieur Fontaine was in his usual good spirits when Alexandre burst in so stormily that the cheques and the letters he had signed with his flourishing signature went flying.

The manager gathered them up and bestowed on his second teller a glance somewhat on the hostile side, since lack of self-control had always seemed to him the worst of all breaches.

"Come . . . come," he said at last, all in all a little relieved when Alexandre had finished his story. For Alexandre's excited eyes had made him fear something worse: an unpardonable outburst, the repercussions of which might have disagreeably involved his own responsibility. Nevertheless he must help this poor man regain his self-possession, try to encourage him, make him see the bright side of things. But what a nuisance was this duty imposed on him by kindness—just plain kindness, he thought, nothing else he could do—at the very moment when he was about to go home. The day had been long and especially burdensome. You should never overtax your strength. The moment you were tired, the best thing to do was to quit. Monsieur Fontaine even felt a sort of scorn for the people who never succeeded in relaxing. As for him, after five o'clock he frankly felt the need of that one glass of Scotch he allowed himself before dinner. But now he summoned his reserve energy and forced his features into an assumed alertness; any admission of weariness seemed almost a sin to Emery Fontaine.

"I'd certainly not advise you to get upset," he said decisively. "Certainly not, Monsieur Chenevert. What's the whole business add up to?" he asked rhetorically, spreading out his fingertips as though he could thus encompass the whole problem. "All you have against you is an occupational error. Of course, I'll have to report it."

At these words Alexandre's features became rigid with fear.

Monsieur Fontaine made an admonitory gesture, beseeching him to be calm, and threatened him with a half-smile. "But the bank will take into account your long years of service and the honesty we all admire in you. Frankly no, I should not advise you to be upset. I believe," he added, "that I could arrange matters in such a way that a purely nominal sum would be subtracted from your regular salary cheque—let's say ten dollars per month."

Now stiff with tension, Alexandre nodded his immediate acceptance, but as though in a dream, as though his will played no part in his action. Where had vanished that feeling of emancipation he thought he had grasped at the very height of his troubles? Everything would go on as before, but with a bit more to worry about; not a great deal more, it is true. . . .

"Sit down," Monsieur Fontaine urged him.

Alexandre sat on the edge of a chair. Now he was preoccupied with trying to squeeze out of his salary-less-ten-dollars the same purchasing power as out of the entire sum. For what could he cut out? The price, perhaps, of a few streetcar tickets; this saving, the first that always occurred to him when he was short, was really a silly economy, if you considered the wear of shoe leather it involved. . . . The very pupils of his eyes jumped from one thought to another. How could he really make a big saving? Even yesterday Eugénie was saying that he ought to earn more. And the notion, for someone as much at fault as he, of having dared think himself worthy of a better fate began to appal him; suddenly it seemed to him that here, here was his true failing, more personal, and more serious too, than the loss of a hundred dollars. Now that his job was safe, he felt himself so obligated to feel grateful that truly there remained within him no place for mere relief.

"And that way you'll make up what you're short almost without noticing it," Monsieur Fontaine pointed out to him.

Of a sudden Alexandre had begun to stare at his superior without the least boldness, but with a darting, irresistible interest. For weeks, as a matter of fact, he had been racking his brain to discover Monsieur Fontaine's resemblance to a face he often saw; and now he had found it, probably with the help of his distressed state of mind. That very morning in the tram he had sat just opposite the advertisement for "Swiftarrow" shirts, all broadcloth, choice of three colours, white, blue, pale ivory. The shirt worn by a still-youthful-looking man; yet you were supposed to gather from the few grey hairs—five or six, perhaps—indicated over his temples that he was less young than he seemed; the rest of his hair, smooth and thick, shone with brilliantine. The close-shaven, ruddy-cheeked face, with its brilliant teeth, exuded frankness. And indeed the advertisement supplied the reason for this forceful, straightforward look: "SWIFTARROW shirts," it specified, "dress you for success." It was the man in the shirt whom Monsieur Fontaine resembled; or rather, the man in the shirt looked a little like Monsieur Fontaine. With the manager's eyes upon him, Alexandre lowered his own, as though fearing his thoughts might become visible.

"A cigarette?" Monsieur Fontaine offered.

"I have my own," said Alexandre, hastily fumbling through his pockets.

Then, embarrassed at what might seem a lack of politeness, he quickly took the cigarette offered him. When Monsieur Fontaine extended his lighter, Alexandre darted toward its tiny flame, knocking against the corner of the desk, so as to be sure the manager would not have to take the trouble to get up. Thereupon, one thigh resting on the edge of the chair, he tried to look relaxed, reassured, honoured to spend a minute in his manager's company. Imagine! Monsieur Fontaine did not seem anxious to have him leave; there they were, looking at each other, in a situation entirely without precedent, as though they might now, thanks to Alexandre's mistake, have something in common. But what? Alexandre struggled desperately to discover a suitable subject for conversation. Would it be proper at that moment to make some reference to the weather? It might seem a trifle lacking in seriousness on his part. Yet again, perhaps Monsieur Fontaine did not want to hear talk about weighty things. Alexandre shifted his position. So hugely ill at ease were his drawn features that wholly despite himself Monsieur Fontaine was led to wonder about Monsieur Chenevert's lot in life.

"You've been a teller for quite a number of years?"

"Eighteen years this coming autumn," said Alexandre, trying to present the matter as not absolutely meritorious nor yet absolutely reprehensible.

"A real record," Monsieur Fontaine congratulated him.

He thought to himself: that's his trouble—he's a man in a rut. . . . In the bank you should never get into a rut . . . that was bad business! Monsieur Fontaine, however, was less clear in his mind as to how Alexandre had been so long in a rut. He himself liked to say that he owed his own advancement only to small efforts, within the reach of anyone. He had been sensible, cautious, saving . . . but he realized that Alexandre had been all these things, as much if not more than he. It was certainly hard to see what basic principles Monsieur Chenevert could have neglected: Save and you will prosper, take exercise and you will be healthy. . . . As for hard work, the poor wretch surely did too much of that. The last thing the bank wanted was precisely this—to see an old employee kill himself for its profit. How, indeed, had Mr Jardine, Senior, defined for them the ideal employee at the last executives' conference? "A young man, a very young man, with all his life ahead of him to fulfil his ambitions. More and more the bank should take pains to have young men and even young girls in the jobs which did not involve too heavy responsibility." Whereupon Mr Jardine had undertaken to describe the happy effect on the public of attractive, gay faces. "Have you ever noticed that customers, in a bank as much as in a department store, seem to be drawn toward employees with a cheerful look?"

Monsieur Fontaine sank back in his armchair, a smile on his lips. "Yes, yes . . . but you miss the point, old boy," he said to himself chaffingly. These businessmen's talks after coffee and cigars abruptly seemed to him hypocritical, lacking in logic. "What about the old employees?" wondered Monsieur Fontaine, thinking in English, as he often loved to do—or, to be more accurate, thinking bilingually, as he had every right to. "Those are the people you should have talked about; what are we to do with them, old boy?" Their salaries remained low; a few of them sooner or later would misappropriate funds—but those weren't the really troublesome ones; they were punished and the bank got rid of them. There remained the loyal employees, whom you couldn't reproach for the theft of a postage stamp or even a straight pin, against whom you could only hold their sour looks. Still too young to be eliminated by natural processes, they were all the same too old; in a word, their age simply was unsuitable. Monsieur Fontaine was at last giving thought to Monsieur Chenevert's true offence. "Poor old devil!" he reflected charitably about Alexandre.

He pushed the ash tray a little closer to the overexcited little fellow. Alexandre was smoking as though he wanted as quickly as possible to reach the end of this long Pall Mall. He asked for nothing. He accused no one. Yet he gave witness. In his own way he demonstrated that men—do the best you could, take plenty of exercise—in short, that not all men were endowed for happiness. In any case, wait long enough, and you'll see. Obstinate, self-absorbed, and silent, he testified against the principles of Monsieur Fontaine, and Monsieur Fontaine felt himself under a threat. His well-being seemed to require that Monsieur Chenevert be able to believe in better morrows, at least in better luck.

"Nothing so very out of the way has happened to you!" he exclaimed. "You're short a hundred dollars. Well. In a few months you will have paid it back. Nobody will hold it against you. Do you think it made sense to come offer me your resignation?"

Alexandre indicated that he was indeed well aware of how ill-judged had been his whole outburst; that, moreover, he would be most grateful to Monsieur Fontaine not to remind him of it in future, for now his feelings were utterly different.

"An old employee, honourable and admirable as you are!" continued Monsieur Fontaine. "But I am going to ask you one thing . . ." Alexandre's face betrayed lively anxiety. ". . . to get someone to give you a good check-up," added the manager. "You don't look well."

Yet Alexandre was doing his valiant best to banish the weariness from his features and to seem in fairly good health. *When you are tired, straighten up and throw your shoulders back.*

"If you need your vacation a bit before your turn, I think I could arrange it," the manager suggested. "Perhaps a little rest . . ."

"No, no," protested Alexandre.

Urgently he summoned all the energy he had left to relax the muscles around his eyes and mouth. Truth to tell, Monsieur Fontaine's solicitude sounded in his heart like a knell: a cigarette, good advice, and now rest, a long holiday.

Yet it would be absolutely impossible for him to retire before sixty. If then! With the constant rise in prices, the inflation he had not foreseen, his tiny retirement fund would be wholly inadequate. His worst mistake had been to have faith in the dollar. He would have to stick it out until at least sixty-five; seventy would be even better. Truth to tell, this was the age he had determined he must reach if ever he was to know security. Then he would have the old-age pension over and above his small income; and a bit later Eugénie would also receive her pension. Alexandre became aware that they would then be richer, you might say, than they now were, and that with nothing to do. How sad, all the same, that in a world so well arranged for the aged, men could not live to be a hundred! To have to die as soon as you no longer had any reason to worry seemed harrowing to Alexandre. And he asserted positively, as though by stating the fact he could arrange the years to come to his better advantage: "I'm still hale and hearty. What's more, I come of a long-lived family. My grandfather Chenevert died at ninety-two; my father . . ."

Thus Monsieur Fontaine became aware that the second teller, despite everything, clung to the future; for this he hastened vigorously to congratulate him: "Yes, of course. Yes . . . but see a doctor all the same. I'll give you the address of an excellent man. If there's nothing the matter with you, he'll tell you so, and you'll be at ease."

"It's just a cold . . . I'll be better tomorrow," stubbornly replied Alexandre.

"An ounce of prevention! . . . A stitch in time . . ."

Monsieur Fontaine was reverting to the comfort of tried and true solutions. At the same time he was neatly ordering his papers on his desk. He had done what he could for Monsieur Chenevert; another in his boots might have taken less trouble. Monsieur Fontaine, however, saw no merit in having shown his human side. Certainly he had acquired the right to be happy; yet it was necessary to protect happiness by all sorts of prudential measures: patience toward others, a humane attitude. Frankly Monsieur Fontaine did not too strongly reprehend this kindliness he knew so well how to administer, a kindliness extending perhaps to a certain softness in a man of his position; yet it was better to sin in this direction than by excessive severity.

"Now you're not going to take things so hard, eh? Slow down a bit!" added Monsieur Fontaine, as though to emphasize the tone of good-fellowship.

Alexandre nodded his agreement to everything, but a bit too readily; he seemed to be saying yes in advance to every possible suggestion.

Deep within him two tiny voices had begun their odd duet, two voices at loggerheads: "You must pay the bank back at the earliest possible moment," said one, "get rid of this debt which will prevent your sleeping nights." The other voice, just as compelling, was saying, "But you'll have to get your rest in order to reach your goal . . ." "Free yourself of that debt . . ." insisted the first voice.

"Above all, no more figures, no more work tonight, Monsieur Chenevert. Tomorrow you'll see that the matter isn't so serious. . . . Good night, good night, Monsieur Chenevert."

Until he had gone through the door, Alexandre held his back straight and his chest out. But then his shoulders slumped into their most comfortable position, as bent and hunched as Uncle Adelard's.

Still sitting at his desk, Monsieur Fontaine saw Monsieur Chenevert's back take on its burden of years, and he was much disappointed that his influence should have proved so short-lived. Despite everything his day was spoiled. He had to grant that the world, to a teller's eyes, might well fail to offer any strong incentive to joy; he tried to look at life from a teller's point of view, if that were possible. But at once he was revolted at what he beheld: the whole world to be made over because of one little man. And Monsieur Fontaine became strengthened in his belief that the world had no need for major changes. Never yet had the notion occurred to him that, there being but one life to live, it might seem sad, or at least strange, to spend it merely in a bank. His anguish came from another quarter, at the thought that his world of business, based on "fair play," just and efficient as it was, might not, after all, endure forever. He felt it a grave injustice that God perhaps failed to take sufficiently seriously the businessmen's occupations, even though the businessmen were those who kept His world running smoothly.

He slipped into his pale-grey gabardine coat and picked up his matching lightweight felt hat. That morning, while driving to the bank, he thought he had recognized, even on that sombre, rainy day, a first sign of spring. He had not been mistaken. A soft, fresh breeze was wandering through this district of masonry, armoured rooms, and now deserted cages. Even at the bank's massive doors this breeze whispered, like a summons to shores far away, forgotten, and perhaps never even bespoken.

Perhaps it was trying to indicate that man had not even begun to gather the infinite possibilities of his fate on earth.

As he left the bank, Monsieur Fontaine drew a deep breath of pleasure.

A slender silhouette, its shape barely recognizable in the depths of the dark entrance way, stirred, tried to move deeper into the shadows.

"Oh! Monsieur Chenevert!" exclaimed the manager in an odd tone of voice, as though he were put out, hatefully surprised. But he recovered his usual manner, at once gruff and winning. "Good night again, Monsieur Chenevert. And don't forget: no more worries! . . . A lovely evening, isn't it?"

"No . . . Yes . . ." agreed Monsieur Chenevert.

CHAPTER VI

IT MUST have stopped raining about an hour ago. You could see how much everything had changed in but a little while; the days were growing longer. There remained a strip of light above the ridge of houses, like a sandy beach above the flat roofs and shoddy signs: to be more precise, like the coral island, his Pacific island where, could he only reach it, Alexandre imagined he might make good his manhood. Over yonder you could live on coconuts and manioc, beneath a simple shelter of leaves. Such was the colour of this evening's sky; at street corners, between the grey buildings, a deep blue lent distance and depth to short bits of alley and brief dead-ends. From these emerged an odour of sodden earth which turned the heart toward spent springtimes, rarely reminding you that this too was spring.

The moment the street lights were lit, you could see that even this very night the leaves were growing. In the daytime their delicate toil went unnoticed. But there was no doubt of it—the buds were bursting open, and the electricity made it apparent: each illuminated protuberance displayed its still-sensitive aureole of downy foliage. Pollen was floating everywhere; there was so much of it that it covered the sidewalk. Under the city dwellers' feet there lay this thin carpet of dead things they loved to trample, a compound of needles, dried fern leaves, seeds gone to waste on the concrete.

Now a strange wind had blown up. Even yesterday the wind had tried to tear off people's hats; it buffeted the little knots of people waiting at streetcar stops, as though it too had had its orders to behave harshly with men. This evening it caressed their cheeks; it soothed the shattered nerves of civil servants; it beat the fluffy locks of women's hair gently against their faces, and seemed to add beauty to their shining eyes. It was very nearly as tender as a hand smoothing a wearied brow. And it uttered almost the same sounds as the comforting, deceiving human voice when it promises that things will go better.

That the wind this evening should be so friendly and so kind encouraged man to think that his Creator must indeed love him.

Perhaps in no other city is spring so springlike as in Montreal. Elsewhere it lacks the overbearing cold, five long months of frost and snow, and in most cases, too, the blazing summer which here will follow right on winter's heels. Elsewhere it lacks this violence, this brutal harshness which, by the contrast they afford, lend springtime in Montreal its lovely power.

Here are a few, a very few, days of wonder.

Perhaps this night alone, and it will be over.

And so it happens that here spring makes people kind.

There is so little spring.

Strange fragile links are forged between men in the city; suddenly their tongues are loosened and their faces grow cheerful.

"Spring at last . . . how mild it is!" you will find yourself saying to people who might as well be Laplanders for all you know of them.

"Yes, indeed," answers the utter stranger. "How fine it is! This is the best time in the year."

Everyone seems freed of the need to be on his guard, with-drawn, long-faced, circumspect.

And so all around Alexandre glowed this rare easement of mankind.

But he knew nothing of it. He went along, his hands clenched in his pockets, his plush collar around his ears. As though Alexandre alone had not emerged from winter.

Truth to tell, he had not yet left his cage; all along the way he had tried to recapture each of his clients since ten o'clock that morning: he had reviewed the cheques, recapitulated the minor operations of the day; he had gone over it all in his head many times, from beginning to end, but without, for all his efforts, having learned when and how he had made his mistake. Because it was this that hurt him the most, that for the first time he had betrayed his professional responsibility.

And he longed, as though for one of the most important things in his life, to grasp the exact instant of his error. To whom on earth had he given that hundred dollars? To that tall man, perhaps, who had stared at him so persistently?

He raised his eyes, was surprised at the softness of the breeze, but this unexpected mildness filled him only with a sad amazement.

Why indeed did spring bother to revisit this mean world? Alexandre drew his neck back into the shelter of his collar. To jog his memory he envisioned his cash drawer here, to his right; his customers were in front of him, on the sidewalk; here was all the room needed for them to string out their lengthy queue. And the wind whispered oddly: a hundred dollars in tens, mumbled Alexandre. Or else, three twenties, three tens, two fives . . .

Shoulders lowered, he was trudging through a part of the city dedicated to listening, to understanding, to soothing pain. Here indeed were concentrated the greater part of the city's doctors. Everywhere Alexandre saw name plates shining in the gleam of the street lights. They distracted him from his reckoning; he tried to find his way back to about quarter past eleven that day . . . but the doctors' names were multiplying; now they came in tiers, one above the other, on either side of the doorways. Alexandre felt a trifle startled. How many doctors could there be in the city? One for every thousand inhabitants —perhaps more. This district seemed endlessly to offer help; it said to a man: You are not as much alone as you thought. . . . Is your stomach out of order? Why I'm a specialist in that very matter. . . . Is the heart at the end of its rope? In that case, apply here. . . . At least we can make an electrocardiogram. . . . And the plaques also displayed each practitioner's degrees, his level of proficiency. By uniting in such a solid phalanx, the doctors gave the impression of being very powerful against pain.

Alexandre turned off on Saint Denis Street . . . and kept reading: specialist for nervous disorders . . . for skin troubles . . . eczema . . . chiropractor . . . homeopathic physician . . . dermatology . . . gastroenterology . . . They had made him lose track of his figures and even, somewhat, of his sense of guilt.

Then, as he went by, the pharmacies told him of penicillin, of streptomycin; of fresh serum kept under refrigeration, of injections intramuscular or intravenous. Never had Alexandre so clearly realized how very precious is suffering. He walked along thoughtfully. The doctors kept keeping him company: former interns in the Paris hospitals . . . one named R. Darkovitch, certainly for the Jews of the neighbourhood . . . A Dr Lalonde for venereal diseases. The body was lucky. . . . Its ailments, whatever they might be, need no longer be hidden. Quite the opposite: they were welcomed, even solicited from door to door.

Alexandre went on, a little less preoccupied. You might have thought that this little man, too, his hands in his pockets, had become the prey of spring. In fact he couldn't get over the help, the thousand things there are in a single city to ease pain: complex treatments, synthetic medicines, hospitals, white beds, even mechanical devices for raising either the head or the foot of your bed. Above all, he was impressed at the idea of adjustable beds, which seemed to him a special proof of human thoughtfulness.

And he went so far, this evening, as seriously to ask himself whether it were not better in this world to be sick rather than unhappy.

A longing, the like of which neither freedom nor his dreams of travel had yet planted in his heart, stirred within him. In perspective and at a sufficient distance from him, illness attracted him almost as much as those islands: to be rid of figures, above all to be guilty no longer. Would he not himself forgive himself far more freely for being sick than for being doleful and intolerable?

For a moment he ceased raging against all the suggestions that he seek medical advice which had been plaguing him right and left for several months; instead of taking them for threats, he saw in them a concern which it would be good truly to deserve. For it went without saying that so much kindness, such unexpected forbearance here below should be earned, not stolen. He doubted whether he really deserved them. Oh! if only it were possible for him to fall ill!

But the time had not come for that yet, when he had just made so serious a mistake. He must first clear his debt, stop up a few holes, get a little ahead of things. . . .

He was passing beneath a billboard, and when he glanced up at it he learned that ten million dollars were needed for the building of a new hospital. His pretensions to sickness frightened him. What he had forgotten was the cost of care and thoughtfulness in our day. CAMPAIGN GOAL FOR SAINT JOSEPH'S HOSPITAL: TEN MILLIONS. Alexandre read the figure a second time and stopped in his tracks, bewildered. In days gone by only war had demanded millions.

And here was human suffering asking almost as much.

Why of course: the more skilful the care of the sick, the less it lay within their means.

DRIVE FOR THE JEWISH HOSPITAL . . . Still more millions!

It seemed to Alexandre that we could do without illness in this world; over and above war, it likewise ground down the citizen from every direction. How could he ever succeed in paying the price for these modern techniques aimed at the very day when he would be at the end of his tether? He decided that it would be utterly impossible for him ever to indulge himself in a long sickness.

And yet hope came back into his heart, defying logic itself which earlier had put hope to flight.

"All the same, I'm fifty-two . . . fortunately," Alexandre told himself. "The longest years are over. There can't be too many years between now and the end. . . . The time will come to drop everything. . . . Get there easily or not so easily, the end comes."

And then, as though to establish him in his views, there loomed before him a lofty inscription :

SILENCE
HOSPITAL ZONE

The city had pity. Silence, it enjoined. Only to the sick could it grant so rare a favour.

The signboard stood out prominently, even in the night, on its post along the roadway.

Never before had Alexandre so clearly understood its meaning : Silence! Here are sick people. The poor wretches are tired. Enough of noise. Enough of pain. Let them sleep.

And thus Alexandre thought to himself that for silence, at

least, as they came toward the end, people need not pay beyond their means.

A trifle heartened, he hastened his pace.

He was dreaming.

He was dreaming of the happiness, once he was almost ready to quit the world, of being nursed, understood, grieved for, perhaps. . . .

CHAPTER VII

I T WAS Eugénie who fell sick. For some time she had suffered from those disturbances of health common to a certain age in woman; natural, if you like, certainly quite uninteresting, yet perhaps as burdensome as others more capable of exciting sympathy.

Eugénie imagined it her duty to hide these distressing symptoms, which marked the end of a period in her life; yet she would have liked to have it known that she was bearing her heavy burden in noble silence. She was, however, a woman of clear complexion, her face quite free of wrinkles, her flesh still firm, and, despite her whitening hair, she preserved an appearance of health and even of benevolence arising more from her rather pleasing if undistinguished features than from any inner flame.

Living with her constantly, Alexandre noticed no great change in his wife, and this outraged her; she resented as a lack of decent consideration on his part the fact that Alexandre, because she remained plump and outwardly well, could think her spared the trials of womankind.

Her character was undergoing a change. At the period when she began to feel old age approaching, Eugénie Chenevert also felt a sharper desire for happiness. The things she had never had: an ever-manifest tenderness, little attentions, the joy of being wholly understood, gaiety, nice compliments, marks of consideration—the very things that had not been hers when she was young and still had a pretty face—these were what Eugénie Chenevert was beginning to long for at fifty.

Yet all these things—difficult enough to attain under any

circumstances—Eugénie wanted at once and without any pre-liminaries. She must be happy right away—or never.

Such exorbitant demands and other symptoms in the physical order Eugénie's doctor laid to her age. He jollied her along; he explained that time would put everything to rights. Kindly, observant, he was one of those rare men who fully appreciated this kind of ailment, since as a gynaecologist they gave him his living. He prescribed injections which cost a lot of money. But Eugénie's condition grew worse, and he insisted upon a hospital examination.

It couldn't have come at a worse time. Over and above everything else, Alexandre was the victim of a heavy cold; chapped nostrils, watery eyes, raw throat, he thought he could stand no more. He foresaw that sooner or later he was going to crack up. And suddenly that hope faded away, just as other hopes had died—his hope of being dismissed from the bank, of getting to his South Sea island, all those foolish hopes, indeed, one after the other.

". . . four or five days . . . perhaps a week at the hospital," Eugénie was saying in a plaintive voice. If she took care of it in time, perhaps it would not be too expensive. Certainly less than if she waited until there were complications. . . . Anyway, it was not her fault, and she would have been the first to want to avoid such unpleasant treatments had she been able to. . . .

Then Alexandre's wrath exploded.

The feeling that no matter what he did he could not forever surmount all difficulties, the notion that they had all conspired to belabour him at the same instant, upset him so much that he gave every appearance of having become deranged.

He strode back and forth across the carpet and glared irritably at his wife.

"This month," said he, "we've had the gas bill, the electric bill, two demands for gifts to charity, and, to cap it all, we've had to dish up some money for L'Heureux, who is celebrating his silver wedding anniversary; now they want to take another slice for the pension fund [he did not, of course, mention the lost hundred dollars]; we simply can't make ends meet," he concluded, "if, on top of all this, you have to be sick."

He walked up and down, bumping into the furniture.

He now reproached himself above all for having failed to take out health insurance for his wife as well; for having made the mistake of assuming that it would be money thrown away.

"A fine time to fall ill," he complained. "After all, I'm not the bank."

Eugénie had pulled out her handkerchief and was swabbing her eyes in outraged silence. Her gesture drove him to an even more intense irritation.

"There must be a limit somewhere. . . . There's got to be some limit," cried Alexandre, raising his clenched little fist.

Alas! the poor Cheneverts could not even quarrel in peace; because of the neighbours, they even had to muffle their rages. Far back in the kitchen there might have been less risk of being overheard, but to move into another room to be able to continue a quarrel a bit more at your ease would have made the whole thing ridiculous. To have to watch yourself and lower your voice already made the altercation sordid enough; Alexandre let his clenched fist fall to his side.

He turned around, unable to bear Eugénie's hurt looks, her resignation that so deeply wounded him. "All right," she said. "I won't talk about it again; I'll put up with it and you'll never hear another word."

What did she have to be afraid of? He was much too weak, much too insignificant to be a cause of suffering in this world. It was from others, surely, that evil came.

Now he was annoyed at his wife for having taken to herself the abuse he had intended for his debts, the higher cost of living, disastrous illness. The sorrow he had caused her suddenly made her unsupportable to him. "I'm going out for a walk," he declared, picking up once more his overcoat and small, discoloured hat.

This was his only remedy against deep emotion, remorse, and even frayed nerves. Through the tepid night, under the stars, you could see him pacing along.

He must have travelled thus two thousand, perhaps three thousand miles in his lifetime; you could even say that if he had walked in a straight line, without stopping, his ill-temper might have propelled him from the Atlantic to the Pacific. Alexandre might have tramped across the whole country spurred on by the embarrassment of having gotten himself into the bad graces of others through his face or his words. Were these drawn little features the cause of his sorry character, or his character responsible for his features? Would, for instance, a likeable face have built him up, have been more of a help to him? However that might be, to him words were disastrous. He thought, with grim determination, that he would never say another word in his life. He was done with them! Not another word; utter silence. To achieve agreement, as between man and wife, as between colleagues, friends, anyone at all, as between peoples, at peace conferences, this was the only means: silence. "Let's all shut up," Alexandre said to himself. "There's been enough talk."

Four times he circled the same cluster of houses; he was weary to the point of wishing he might lie down almost anywhere, no matter how uncomfortable, and yet he trotted along quickly, his hat cocked over one ear, his eyes blazing, and soon he struck out, away from his own neighbourhood, but in an old, familiar direction.

In the darkness of the night, not even aware of where he was going, Alexandre was hurrying toward the bank.

He felt warm, realized it was no longer winter, opened his coat.

They had had five consecutive days of spring—five perfect days—and, truth to tell, it was beginning to get wearisome; people were growing used to it, no longer paying much heed to it.

Inadvertently Alexandre turned down a little street not on his daily route, a quiet street, well suited to reflection; the windows were dark; everyone must be asleep in this part of the world. Alexandre halted under a street lamp and began seriously to seek a means of ridding himself of all his troubles at the same time.

For rest was far from being a solution. Alexandre was tempted to laugh at himself when he reflected that he could ever have been attracted by rest, a hope as little attainable, as silly as the thought of a trip to the Antilles.

In one sense the solution seemed to him wholly the opposite of what he had so far been able to envision: instead of rest, what he needed to do, and that as quickly as he could, was to set to work plugging the holes, earning a little more money, trying to find work he could do evenings.

Two or three days later, indeed, luck smiled a little at Alexandre Chenevert. He was fortunate enough to obtain some additional work.

In May he began to devote two evenings a week to the tangled accounts of a man named Markhous, a Jewish cloth merchant born in Hungary, who operated a wholesale store on the Boulevard St-Laurent. The job was not really tiring, for it also involved figures, and after all figures were as natural to Alexandre as is his instrument to a pianist. Moreover, Alexandre could attend to this task once his day was over—a major advantage, since each evening's toil yielded him a certain respite in the sense that it brought Alexandre nearer the hour of his freedom, when he would no longer owe the bank a cent, when he would have paid the fees of Eugénie's doctor, and even perhaps a few other small accounts. He was a man in whom hope dwelt stubborn despite certain weaknesses; he thought to himself that once he had cleaned up his immediate and forthcoming obligations, it was very likely that no new ones would present themselves for a good while, and he would be able to catch his breath. What was difficult was to explain these evenings away from home without divulging the business of the hundred dollars to Eugénie. He blamed them on the bank: "They need me to try to find a five-cent mistake. . . . They still needed me. . . . Oh yes! That's the way it goes!"

Finally she began to tease him: "Poor Alex! You're the first to look for work that needs doing and the last to demand your due."

Then she concluded: "The trouble with you is you hold yourself in with outsiders; and later on you work off your bad humour at home."

There was too much truth in this description for it not to goad Alexandre into uttering a few burning truths himself. He succeeded in restraining himself somewhat; Eugénie was at an age when she must be dealt with patiently and gently.

As though to punish Alexandre, she postponed doing what her doctor had told her to do. True enough, she was very fearful of the treatment; the poor woman saw in it a kind of link to marriage, woman's unjust situation, which seemed to her vaguely attributable to the selfishness of men.

"It's not worth while waiting until you get worse," Alexandre pointed out to her; "that would just make the whole thing cost us even more money."

This, in turn, wounded her by its ready agreement to subject her to a cure the fearsomeness of which seemed not to occur to her husband.

"Oh! I count for nothing in the matter," said she. "I surely might wait a little while. . . ."

And there were occasions when she would likewise say, mindful of sad reality, "Truth to tell, my poor man, you're even more used up than I am. You too are very badly in need of care. You start the ball rolling and I'll follow your example."

Nothing annoyed Alexandre more than that.

At the beginning of June it turned very hot; Alexandre hoped that the summer would pass quickly. Then at last autumn would come with its coolness! Whatever had happened to the spring? He had barely had time to notice its passage. Alexandre dragged himself from the bank to the North-Western Lunch; from the cafeteria to his cage; from there to the Boulevard St-Laurent—a tiny little round which demanded more exertion, involved greater fatigue than circling the whole globe. As he went by a travel agency, Alexandre read that this could be done comfortably in three months. Beyond belief, all the same! Occasionally he took the streetcar; but at the rush hour this was almost more exhausting than it was on foot, and hardly any faster, either. Then too, by walking through this neighbourhood, he saw new sights: Syrian faces, signs in Yiddish; strange brown visages which seemed freshly arrived from the Levant; smoked meats, strange dishes which added variety to those at the North-Western Lunch; long-bearded old men with black caps from under which protruded masses of hair. If he did not travel, at least he caught glimpses of other races—the overflow from too densely peopled lands. What multitudes there were on earth! And their peace conferences came to naught! And Markhous had no system at all.

The shop was a junk pile. A small table served Alexandre as a desk. Bolts of cloth, bundles of samples, even dried skins —and what business had these at a textile merchant's?—lay scattered upon it. As well as he could Alexandre cleared himself a space on which to stack the files of receipted bills. What Markhous wanted of him was to play up the expenditures so as to get a substantial lowering of his income taxes. Very likely he imagined that Alexandre had not yet fully grasped what a tidy little fortune this game might bring in.

"Mine friend, Shinvert," he called him. "Why you stay at de benk?" he would ask. "You should make yet a better liffing fixing reports for collector, income tax." They were now so complicated, he pointed out, that you had to have an expert. And Alexandre, sharp as he was at figures, could do very well for himself. "I dig you up tree, four oder businessmen" not big enough to afford an accountant the year round, and Alexandre would have all the clients he needed. "Leaf it to me," said Markhous, "I mek you rich. . . ."

"It's fellows like you, Markhous," Alexandre reproached him, "who force the collector to take the money he needs out of the pockets of people like me, salary-earners, who haven't a chance to cheat him out of a penny."

"Tsk, tsk, tsk," protested Markhous. "You know dat's not true, Shinvert; it's de big companies do dat."

Alexandre admitted this. He even agreed that in view of the scandalous favours he knew were granted, his desire to be strictly honest about his own taxes was a trifle ridiculous. For instance, were he to be wholly scrupulous with the collector, he would be obliged to include the little extra money he earned at this job to try to make ends meet. He was almost completely certain that if he possibly could he would avoid this excess of integrity. Still and all, this whole business of the public revenues was quite a problem for Alexandre. When he thought of widow Honorine Blanche Mathieu, for example, he recognized the injustice he would have committed in lessening even by one cent his share of the taxes which was perhaps precisely the money set aside for the poor old woman. Men having wanted charity, the law had been obliged to make it a strict obligation. So this painful compulsion did represent a kind of progress in our world.

On the other hand, when Alexandre reflected that they could go to war without his consent, behind his back, you might say; when he weighed and calculated that his small contribution, so painfully earned, could contribute to the death of someone unknown, would purchase bombs and those murderous weapons the very thought of which kept him from sleeping—then, at the moment of mailing his cheque to the collector, Alexandre would have wished he had the courage to go to prison instead. But in these days heroism was no longer within reach; long before he could achieve it, they would have brought him to see the light.

His headaches were getting worse. The light was bad in the back part of the store. Alexandre was tearing his eyes out trying to decipher the cloth merchant's writing. He really should have had his glasses checked. As soon as he had a free moment, he would see to it. Indeed his eyes were absolutely essential to him. But everything in its time. Once the debts were gone, he could afford to be sick, and once he had been sick, he'd attend to the glasses. After that there would still be the future. When Alexandre was free to go home, Markhous would detain him to recount his rise to fortune in the city, how he had landed in Montreal with only ten dollars in his pocket. Soon Alexandre was giving him three nights a week, the sooner to finish this weary task. Perhaps this year he would not even take a vacation, so as to be even more certain of setting everything to rights. He forced himself to be friendly toward Markhous; it was embarrassing to be otherwise, since—was it not odd?— this sweaty, talkative, overfamiliar little Jew seemed to have a real affection for Alexandre. He would constantly put his hand on his shoulder, clasp his fingers; he would make him little presents of candy, of still-serviceable cloth. And Alexandre, who had so often scolded Godias for his anti-Semitism, made it a point of honour not to admit that Markhous weighed on his nerves. But his effort to be friendly wore Alexandre down.

One evening when he came home he found his wife stretched out on her bed, her features pale and drawn.

He burst into reproaches: Why hadn't she taken care of herself in time? Did it make any sense to have been so obstinate? Did she perhaps think that illness took care of itself and that you could keep on just giving your poor body orders forever? Lord, Lord! now they were in a fine pickle, and what would become of them?

He did not know where to turn or what to do. He raced down the two flights he had just climbed and called Eugénie's doctor from Fred Trottier's little store, in the basement of the apartment house. There was a public telephone there, not enclosed in a booth, but simply attached to the wall behind the door. Neighbourhood people were buying bread, smoked sausage, the evening paper. Alexandre heard the buzzing of the busy signal. He hung up, but his coin did not come back. He began shaking the phone, wondering whether death might have some vague connection with this meaningless detail of a nickel caught in a faulty piece of machinery. He would certainly write the company. They had no business leaving a pay station in bad order. He would complain. And perhaps he'd have a telephone put in at home, with an eye to some similar emergency in the future. He rushed over to ask Fred Trottier for another five-cent piece. Fred, a thin little man with a big moustache, was taking a bottle out of the icebox while at the same time discussing the latest railroad strike.

"If they get their raise, we'll still be the ones to pay for it," he said. "You mark my words: prices will go up again."

Alexandre shuffled his feet. A fine time to be going into the ins and outs of childish and remote troubles.

"Unless prices can be brought down, we'll never make two ends meet," Fred Trottier continued.

Alexandre returned to the telephone and began shaking it once more; a landslide of nickels tumbled down the metal channel. Behind Alexandre a humorous voice applauded him: "You've hit the jackpot, Monsieur Chenevert."

Alexandre stood on tiptoe, stretching toward the mouthpiece, which he was too distracted to lower. He heard the far-off ringing sound, endlessly punctuated with silence, that very throb of fate on occasion assumed by the soulless intermittent drone of a number slow to answer. From that moment on, the telephone he used so infrequently would seem the very accessory of crisis. His eyes stared at an advertisement for Black Cat cigarettes. He saw Eugénie's filmy eyes, he heard her weakened voice imploring—and dreading—help. But his strongest feeling was one of guilt. He had thought himself unhappy without any real reason, he had even wished he were sick; he had offended against unhappiness, and this very instant his wife would perhaps be torn from him to show him what unhappiness truly was.

On his way down he had worked out in his mind what he was going to tell the doctor. Then, when he got the connection, he realized that he should have dialled from a less public spot. The doctor asked for more specific details. Meanwhile, as soon as it had gathered what was happening, the little group around Alexandre had become silent. Every word he uttered would be heard by these people. He fished for expressions which might be adequately informative to the medical man without conveying much to the ears of the curious. How often had Eugénie urged him never to speak of her ailments, which she had considered to be of such a nature as to make people scoff? And suddenly Alexandre had an inkling that men and women on this earth were irreparably severed from each other by the special afflictions of their sex, and that, all in all, women's afflictions were perhaps the more burdensome. The thought weighed on his heart, as though here were an injustice committed to his advantage, and one over which self-congratulation was not in order.

Dr Turcot was not long in coming. In his mind Alexandre could see the doctor's car in front of the door, the M D licence plates which would inform everyone of what was going on, the gossips at the windows, the excited hum of talk at Fred Trottier's. He became aware of how spectacular, how sadly public, sickness sometimes was.

Dr Turcot refused to commit himself to any diagnosis. At Madame Chenevert's age her condition might be serious; it was also possible that there was nothing dangerously the matter with her. In any case she must go to the hospital at once.

Alexandre went down to call a taxi. Ten minutes later he came down again, one arm around his wife's waist. "Lean against me," Alexandre begged her.

She was taller than he and, for a number of years, had likewise been stouter. All his life he had been embarrassed to go out in public with Eugénie, and even tonight, as he helped her down the stairs, he could not prevent his imagination lingering over the slightly ridiculous spectacle they presented. He had always beheld it in the glances of others; they were among those couples whom people stopped to watch pass by, with surprise, a touch of pity, and all sorts of unasked questions. Yet did it not often happen that in their time small men like him had fallen in love with sturdy, powerful women—with real women?

He installed her in the back seat of the cab. "I'm weak, poor Alex," she said piteously.

The moment they had left the immediate neighbourhood and its dull familiarity, she grew afraid and wanted to withdraw her consent. "I don't want to go to the hospital," she said, turning toward him, as though this poor little fellow could have stopped the earth in its turning.

"Come on, Eugénie!"

This taxi race to the hospital was certainly reminding her, as it was him, of the breakneck trips when Irène was born, and then the two other little girls who had died, probably of that infant anaemia now said to spring from an incompatibility between the parents' blood. In these days they would have been saved. They had decided on the name of Estelle for the first, and the second was to be called Florence. The technique now was to induce premature birth; then they drained the baby's blood and replaced it with blood of another type. More and more efficiently was science correcting nature's cruelty. And more and more people were in the habit of saying, "Oh! If only science had been as advanced then as it is now!" Probably nothing was more unjust in its own way than science.

"You won't let me die!" Eugénie begged. "I'm not old enough; I'm still young," she added.

He took Eugénie's hand and promised her: "No, No! I'll not let you die."

But he had to hand her over to strangers, sign a few forms, and go back to an empty apartment where he was left alone with his thoughts.

Then he really began to discover something about unhappiness—he who thought that on this score he had no more to learn. First—and astonishing as it might seem—his distress seemed in some sort to lighten the familiar burden of life. For by creating a new misery, it thrust aside almost all other reasons for suffering and made them insignificant. Alexandre now scarcely noticed his headaches, his heartburn. He who had imagined himself weary suddenly acquired enough nervous energy to cross the city in no time. Moreover, unhappiness cleanses the soul. Eugénie's absence, the worry she caused him, absorbed all of Alexandre's capacity for suffering. He ceased being aware of his habitual afflictions. He became, as it were, absolved of himself. He was amazed at what a man who is really put to it can do in twenty-four hours. And every evening he went to the hospital.

Eugénie was getting better. The major operation was not necessary for the time being and perhaps it never would be. Obviously Dr Turcot could not commit himself further than this. He could not promise that in two years or three years there might not be complications.

Now out of danger, Eugénie would have liked a more definite assurance: that her ailment, for example, would never recur; that she need no longer "have it on her mind." It seemed to her that she had gone through a sufficiently racking alarm so that the score should be even; she clung obstinately to an arrangement of life in accord with her own system of logic, which to her seemed just: When you have gone through "your share" of suffering, that should be the end. And she supposed that each person knew the amount he would be able to endure.

Alexandre was appalled at so childish an attitude. "You should be very grateful that you weren't more seriously stricken," he explained to his wife. "How many other women are far worse off!"

Which, under the circumstances, was precisely what he should not have said. Any belittling of her illness wounded Eugénie and after a fashion impoverished her, stripped her of any means to hold Alexandre's deep and constant attention. She already felt annoyance at the notion that she had had to be in danger to earn the right of seeing this kindly side of her husband's nature. At times his consideration made her gloomy; why had he not always been equally considerate, since at heart he was capable of being so?

But now she was a little better, and already Alexandre's attention had begun to wander from her. He busied himself with the apartment, with a spot that had appeared on his jacket; and yet one day during the visiting hours he appeared with a small bunch of flowers in his hand.

Eugénie gave a start of lively and joyful surprise. Unbelief played its large part in this outburst of joy: "Flowers, Alex! Whatever were you thinking of! You poor dear man! Flowers!"

He sat down near the bed, his face troubled; he seemed almost put out at Eugénie's pleasure. Indeed the small happinesses of others, so cheaply bought, sometimes deal us a stinging rebuke. She simply could not get over it. "Just to think that you thought of bringing me flowers!"

Truth to tell, he really had not thought of doing it. It had all happened quite otherwise. Up until this evening he had never even noticed that the other sick women in the room they shared with Eugénie each had flowers. He had not forgotten to hang the "No Bread" sign on the apartment door or to wind the clock, but he had not thought of flowers; and this evening, as on previous evenings, he might well have arrived empty-handed. Just after he had stepped into the elevator, two odd, almost abnormal, things had of a sudden struck Alexandre: first that the visitors had a preoccupied look, more noticeably so than the sick people, probably all the more evident since they were so obviously in the process of trying to mould their features into an appearance of optimism; and second that almost all of these sad men held little bunches of flowers in their hands. At first Alexandre had felt a sort of compassion. He had been moved to it by the contrast between the men's faces and these delicate sprays of colour. For him, moreover, flowers were far more associated with the country and holidays than with sorrow and illness. Nevertheless the example set by the other husbands for once led him to act in accordance with convention.

He had left the elevator and had bought a sheaf from a fellow who had set up his stall just outside the hospital portals. And he had returned to the elevator, now just like any other husband, worried-looking and grasping—he too—his flowers against his chest to keep them from being crushed. So Eugénie had no good reason for heaping such appreciation upon him. And in the back of his head he clung to a regret which in effect stripped him of any true generosity: namely the thought that he could have had the flowers cheaper had he bought them at the Bonsecours Market.

This evening, obviously proud of him, Eugénie introduced him to all the people in the room.

"Madame Bissonnette . . . my husband." She indicated a bed at the end of the room. Alexandre arose and gave an embarrassed little nod of his head. Eugénie was whispering: "A cancer; they've taken everything out of her. . . . Madame Arcand . . . my husband. . ."

Again Alexandre stood up and bowed toward a suffering head, lying flat on a pillow.

"Mademoiselle Fiset. An old maid," Eugénie added in a slightly lower tone. "Peritonitis. She moans all night."

Alexandre cast a hasty glance toward a bed the foot of which had been raised. It was sheer torture for him to be introduced in this fashion and to be abruptly pushed into so unseemly a state of intimacy.

"You shouldn't . . ." he reproached his wife. "Not so loud . . ."

She laughed, calling the others to witness. "This is no place where you can keep secrets."

Her eyes were bright this evening, and she seemed relaxed. Good colour was coming back to her, as well as that slightly vulgar, slightly noisy gaiety of years gone by which rubbed Alexandre the wrong way. With even this brief interval of separation from him, her real nature was getting the upper hand. Her nurse had helped her to do her hair. She was wearing a nightgown edged with lace which suited her complexion. All in all Alexandre thought she had an appearance of health he had rarely seen in her. The powerful support afforded us by anxiety began to be withdrawn from him. He felt himself suddenly stripped of feeling, of energy. His shoulders sagged. As he leaned over to kiss Eugénie's forehead, he became aware of a kind of rancorous envy—she at least did not have to worry where the money was coming from; she could sit back and let herself be cared for, without a worry in the world. He begrudged her her gaiety after she had caused him so much anguish.

"You'll soon be coming home?" he asked

All the cheerfulness left her face. She felt sure that above all he must be anxious to see her busying herself as before with the household chores, with keeping his clothes in order.

"Yes, indeed. I'll have to, soon."

By now she only half-wished to be back on her feet. Here she had been coddled and surrounded; she had rediscovered something of the climate of childhood: no responsibilities, no one to upbraid her, intelligent concern, the feeling of being in good hands. And last of all there were around her enough serious, more humiliating illnesses to make her own tolerable by comparison. Outside this room life seemed grey to her, too difficult, too real.

Once she had returned home, Alexandre continued for a certain length of time to bustle about and be helpful. It was only by degrees, quite imperceptibly, that they reverted to the old relationship. He rushed off to do the shopping at his breakfast hour, or when his day was over if he had been able to leave the bank early enough. And she sought hard to retain the attention her illness had brought her. At the hospital she had been astounded by the number of things she had found to relate about her life, her youth, her tastes, the moving pictures that had pleased her, and all this to strangers. She thought she might do at least as well with Alexandre. And yet evenings, sitting near him in what she liked to call the "living room," she at once encountered obstacles. Whenever an idea crossed her mind, she would think: "Here we are! Alexandre might be interested in that." And then she would no longer be so sure she had not already told him about it, perhaps the evening before. In that case Alexandre would mutter, "Yes, yes," with an air of trying to avoid hearing the rest of what she had to say. She would try to find another subject; then, just as she was about to open her mouth, the impulse would die: sometimes Alexandre's sulky appearance would discourage her; or else she would realize that what she had to say, all things considered, held no great interest. She would turn on the radio; she liked to listen to interminable serial dramas, preceded, bisected, and followed by commercials which Alexandre endured with a heavy frown, rattling the pages of his newspaper. Serious broadcasts she cut off short, twisting the dial and thus producing, out of bits and ends of phrases following each other at random, a bewildering effect. Sometimes a solemn, pessimistic voice caught Alexandre's attention. He would ask her to leave it on. Every night also he insisted on hearing the news: sure stalemates, endless parleys, rumours of war, aviation accidents, defence measures—how could he possibly be interested in all that monotonous stuff, so lacking in any variety that, from evening to evening, Eugénie had the impression that she heard exactly the same thing over and over again! At times she would look at him with a curious intensity, as though this were some stranger before her eyes.

"You're a queer one, Alexandre Chenevert," she would remark about nothing in particular.

When she saw him thus, with a certain detachment, she would on occasion likewise be aware of how badly he looked. In her own way she really wanted to do something to help him. "What good does it do you to listen to all this talk of politics and armaments? That's what keeps you awake nights."

And then again she would scold him: "You work too hard. What will it gain you in the end? It won't do you much good to stop when you have a breakdown."

He would reply with a blank look, one of those deliberately uncommunicative glances such as are most easily exchanged between people who have lived a long time together.

And she suffered too because for Alexandre she was a stranger.

Finally, after many letters announcing her arrival and then cancelling it, their daughter Irène suddenly descended upon them from Sherbrooke with her little boy. The child at once began to investigate every nook and cranny of the apartment; he pulled drawers out and threw their contents on the floor; at meals he refused to eat anything that wasn't sweet—"I want jam," he would howl. Then his chubby little hands would explore Alexandre's precious magazines and books, leaving finger marks everywhere. Alexandre contained himself; he waited for Irène to say something to the boy, but with her weary, resigned look she scarcely seemed to notice the child's misdeeds.

"Don't make too much noise," she would remark listlessly, almost imploringly. "Grampa is tired."

"Who? He?" little Paul would ask, pointing a finger at Alexandre.

He was not attractive, with a tiny, pasty face and a rather marked inco-ordination of the eyes which gave him a somewhat shifty look.

"He's not my grampa," said he. "My grampa is Grampa Galarneau."

"You have a grampa Galarneau," explained Irène, "but this one is your Grampa Chenevert."

"You look nasty," said the child.

Although he thought it silly to pay any attention to the comment of a three-year-old, Alexandre tightened his lips. This trifling episode, with Irène acting as though she were introducing a stranger to her son, had made him feel deeply uncomfortable. He tried to win the boy's friendship.

"Come on," he suggested, "Grampa'll make you a fine paper hat."

He began folding his newspaper so as to produce the traditional fore-and-aft headgear which, when he himself had been a child, had so delighted him. And little Paul, by now bored with mechanical things, since he was already the owner of a tricycle and a truck with an automatic earth-moving shovel, became at once passionately interested in the manufacture of the hat. Seemingly it sprang into being out of nothing, out of a scrap of paper. But once it was ready to wear, he could conceive of only one possible use to which to put it, based on the only sort of play he knew. Clapping it on his head, he began running from one grown-up to another, grasping an imaginary gun and pulling its trigger.

"Bang!" he cried. "I'm killing you. You're dead."

At each screech Alexandre jumped a little in his chair.

"That's not nice. You mustn't say that," Irène interrupted.

She explained that when she went to work, she had to leave

the child at a neighbour's, that he played in the street almost all day, and that, anyway, he was a hard child to bring up, being so nervous that at the least reprimand he went into a tantrum, couldn't get to sleep in consequence, and refused to eat.

"What do you want me to do?" she asked. "I can't be scolding him every minute. He'd take an antipathy toward me."

And she justified herself by pointing out that in modern books on children's upbringing you are urged not to keep them constantly under constraint. Times were changing. It was now realized, she said, that the harsh methods of other days, which were wholly repressive, were responsible for many neuroses and complexes that disfigured all a person's later life. And she didn't want to make her child into a being ruled by fear—as she herself was. . . . When she realized what she had let slip, she blushed.

In every way she resembled her father, save for his small stature, for she was tall and thin. But her slightly elongated nose, her sharp features, her high forehead, her black-circled and deep-set eyes, the harsh expression of her face all came from her father. As she was seated directly before him and in the full light, Alexandre became more aware than ever of this likeness, and it tore his soul with pity. In days gone by this resemblance had not been clearly visible. Had she been happy, Irène might in part have escaped it; but now that she had suffered some weariness and her first disillusionments, you could no longer escape the realization that she would be the very image of her father. When she was pensive, even at so youthful an age, she pinched her lips a little, just as he did. He realized that she could not be happy, and his pity became an overflowing bitterness. There she was, talking of new methods in bringing up children, or her child's happiness, as though it depended on what she did, on her wishes, on her small experience. Poor, poor child! Yet her own unhappiness stemmed from her not having listened to her father. He had not even succeeded in sparing her, while she was still too young, from a disastrous marriage. Oh, no! She knew better than he: she was in love; she would be happy. He had gotten angry; he had stormed; he had even tried gentleness, so clearly did he see what would happen. He had read it as though it were in a book already written about the future. "This lad is lazy; he'll never support you. Listen to what I tell you from my experience; you'll have to work the rest of your days." He raised his eyes to look at Irène and realized from the worried movements of her own eyes and lips that he had been all too right. A strange wrath, at once bitter and pitiful, possessed Alexandre. What he could not forgive in his daughter was that she was now miserable for lack of having listened to him.

"You're still at the Metropole Hotel?" he inquired.

She replied with an attempt at gaiety: "Yes, I make good pay. The work is not too hard. You know very well I much prefer to work outside than to keep house."

"A waitress!" said Alexandre. "You could have done better."

His daughter's occupation was to him almost an affront. For a while he had hoped to find a place for her at the bank, near him. But she had made fun of him: "Shut up in there all my life, raking in pennies like you do all day long—no, thanks!" And now she refused commiseration.

"I have a first-class job, with a day off every week."

She avoided talking about her husband, and he dared not ask. She seemed to refuse to let him think her unhappy. After a while she furnished a few reassuring details: for the time being her husband was working in a small city in the Eastern Township: he seemed to be mending his ways. If he kept his present position, she would eventually join him. The trouble was that her husband easily lost heart, moved from one job to another; she herself would not quit working so long as Augustin had not settled down.

Alexandre nodded. Then he asked, "And how's your stomach?"

That, too, she had inherited from him—a sickly stomach.

"Do be careful," he solemnly warned her. "Stomach troubles are the worst of all. Listen to me while there's yet time."

She pouted a little to express her independence. "Don't worry over me, Papa. My health is fine now that I haven't any time to worry about myself."

While she was near her father she felt that she was indeed threatened by her resemblance to him: thence came the burden of uneasiness in her soul, the feeling that her life was encumbered by that fear of misfortune so constant in her father. But at a distance, surely, she would shake off this absorption with calamity which here weighed her down.

"As a man to advise others, you set no marvellous example of good health," she said teasingly.

It was quite a business to stow everyone away for the night. There was no longer a bed in the little room Irène used to occupy, so tiny that they had finally turned it into a place to store things not constantly in use. Where else keep the books

Alexandre had bought in the days when the adventures of others could still make him happy—*Michael Strogoff, Twenty Thousand Leagues under the Sea*? Alexandre pounced on the opportunity to reproach Eugénie for having sold the other bed which might have served—one never knew—when they had "visitors." She got back at him by pointing out that if he had not bought so many books, she would not have needed to get rid of more important things. "Hundreds of books! I ask you! Squeezed in as we are here, do we have to keep every last one of them?" she appealed to her daughter. He in his turn tried to get Irène on his side: "When it comes to my things, your mother is ready to toss everything out of the window."

"Don't quarrel all the time," Irène begged.

Her whole childhood had been torn asunder by such attempts to force her to take sides, each of her parents wanting to be loved by her at the expense of the other.

Surprised, Eugénie protested, "We're not quarrelling, but facts are facts!"

Big piles of newspapers, magazines carefully tied up with string, and cartons filled with books took up almost all the space in the little room. Scornfully Eugénie shoved aside a bundle of clippings. There was not even place to set up the folding bed.

"He hangs on to everything," she complained.

"It might turn out handy," Alexandre replied dryly.

He felt as though he were threatened by a sorrow as yet unknown and fearful. The mass of yellowed paper, of books, disheartened him this evening. For a long while he had thought books of great aid to help you understand, first yourself and then others. After escape into adventure, this was what he had asked of books: to be given expression by the talent of others; in the written word he had sought himself. But once you have set out along that road, you find odds and ends, unrelated aspects of yourself, everywhere. Alexandre had excerpted, numbered, and classified hundreds of articles. But there was not enough here—there never would be enough—to contain the vastness enclosed in Alexandre's little life. How elusive and scattered was man!

"Come on," he said, doing his best to seem cheerful. "It won't be too much of a job to find a place to sleep. Follow me."

He led them into the parlour and joined two armchairs front to front.

"There's a bed for little Paul," said he.

He himself, as a child, had often slept on such an improvised affair, and never had he enjoyed a greater feeling of security, of being loved. He picked up the slumbering little boy, laid him in the hollow formed by the chairs, and covered him with his old wrapper.

"You two," said he to the women, "take the bedroom. I'll do very nicely on the couch."

He dragged the sofa into a corner and gaily set about moving the small tables and the pile of encyclopedias which he lifted with a grimace at their weight.

A mysterious lightheartedness suddenly coursed through Alexandre Chenevert.

He remembered the joyful throes of excitement aroused in days gone by when the children and grandchildren came on a visit to the elder Chenevert's home. His mother hustled about making beds, rushing from one room to another with piles of fresh sheets in her arms. Exhausted from her regular burden of work, the poor woman welcomed this additional activity as a relief from her tasks. "It's not being tired that really tires you," she assured everyone. Why, if he himself said all the welcoming words, if he this evening repeated all those actions, should he not come to feel the same soaring of the heart?

"I'm going to take my alarm clock right now, so as not to disturb you tomorrow morning," said Alexandre. "I'll not make a sound. Have you enough blankets?" he asked them, even though the heat was overpowering. "Eugénie, have you put out clean towels?"

His concern for his guests began to be irritating.

"Have you enough pillows? I could easily spare you mine. . . ."

He stretched out on the couch. He could not turn around on it, or even move very much without running the risk of falling off. Here he was even closer to the street and immediately began to be fearful that he wouldn't sleep for a single instant. After a moment or two, though, the street sounds bothered him less than the whispering of the two women. No door separated him from the bedroom; it gave on the parlour through a wide arched opening with a thin drapery stretched across it. Now to hear anyone whisper had always had a strangely upsetting effect on him, as though it must somehow concern him. He could not refrain from trying to listen, from holding his breath so as to make no sound. He heard enough of what they were saying to decide that they were not talking about him, but about themselves, and with utter frankness and a mutual understanding which wounded him. Obviously Irène was admitting a great deal more to her mother than she had while they were sitting together that evening. He caught a few words, then lost several; but from one of Eugénie's replies he gathered that Irène had no intention, even though she had assured him she had, of resuming conjugal life with her husband. Then she heard Eugénie's harrowing advice: "It's better to put up with it, my girl; believe me. I know what I'm talking about. With your father there have been times . . ."

Alexandre slid as far back on the sofa as he could, fearful that he might hear something said about him which would be all too true. Nothing could have seemed to him more out of place than to continue listening, for he recognized his wife's and his daughter's right to hide themselves from him if such was their need. But why hide from him? Why fear him who had always been so innocuous? A feeling of unbearable injury overcame him when Irène whispered, "You're the one to understand, Mama. Oh! If only you knew!"

After that they kept quiet. Some five minutes later, perhaps, from the depths of the room Eugénie's voice asked, "Alex, are you asleep?"

He assumed that she wanted to reassure herself, so as to be able to speak more freely, and emotion tightened his throat, prevented him from uttering a single sound.

Years ago, during a childhood illness, someone had asked him the same question at a moment when, under the effects of a sedative, he was no longer able to open his mouth, although he was quite aware of what was happening around him. His parents, impressed by what they knew to be the purpose of the medicine, must have supposed it capable of producing sleep immediately. He had felt their breath blowing on his face, their eyes fixed on his. The feeling that some cruel stroke, some sort of crime was going to be committed against them, against himself, alerted all his being, made him bend every effort to raise his eyelids. Clearly he had not succeeded. For he had overheard words not intended for him: "Poor, sickly kid; I wonder if this time we're going to pull him through." For once in his life he had heard others speak of him with absolute frankness.

"Are you asleep?" Eugénie asked again.

Just as on that dreadful night of childhood, Alexandre's heart was shrunk with fear. But this time the need to know what others thought of him was stronger than his apprehension. With a kind of eager curiosity he remembered that tightening of the soul when it is confronted with an intimacy not designed for its hearing. If he pretended to be asleep, if he remained immobile as a stone, perhaps he would once again in his life hear something equivalently deep. A murmuring voice reached him: "Poor man! He is asleep; let's keep quiet so as not to wake him up."

The same voice added, "You know, he's terribly tired."

Such concern, expressed at this particular moment, pierced his heart more painfully than any reproach.

Slowly he let his eyes wander over the outlandish, almost foreign aspect taken on this evening by the most familiar things in his life through the mere fact that he beheld them from a somewhat different point of view. The glow of a street light drifted into the room. It shone on the sleeping child, on Alexandre's clothes hung over the back of a chair, his suspenders trailing from the trousers, on the wallpaper's flowered design —chrysanthemums and lilies of the valley linked into patterns by streamers and, what made even less sense, here and there amid the flowers the tiny roofs of Japanese pagodas.

The hard, yellow light explored his features. Yet he was afraid that if he got up to move the sofa, he would attract the two women's attention and rekindle their need to talk. And at that moment there overwhelmed him as never before—but why? why?—his longing for a desert island.

He knew himself well enough to recognize deep down within him a real relief when he went to see their visitors off at the bus terminal. Throughout those few days, which might have been joyful, he had wished he were back in his own bed, his armchair, with his own little relaxations and his thoughts. It was intolerable to be constructed in such fashion, to feel a base stranger lodged at the very centre of his being. What was to be done? That stranger—hateful, reprobate—at least possessed the merit of a terrible frankness.

On their way the small boy thrust his hand into his grandfather's. At least Alexandre had succeeded in winning the affection of the lad, too spoiled and too lonely as he was. Yet when he felt this hand, so warm and so tiny, firmly within his own, Alexandre awoke to an anxiety as vast as the whole world. He was not a man to be easily reassured. What frightened him far more than suspicion was the obedient, gentle trust which had taught him the true measure of his slight power over the accidents of life. He walked along laden with care and, as though he might have been God, worrying over the suffering in lives sprung from him, even unto the generations to come. What would become of this poor little fellow if his own father were to turn his back on him altogether? What would become of Irène herself if her health gave out? Walking beside his daughter, holding a package in one hand and dragging a child with the other, Alexandre looked like an immigrant. And he felt that such he was after a fashion, a passer-by who bore the guilt of other lives, of responsibilities which one day or another he would have to abandon. A kind of anger shook him. "I'll not always be there," thought Alexandre as though to justify himself for an abandonment of his duties.

The small boy had drawn away his hand. "Why are you making bad eyes again?" he asked.

They arrived at the terminal. Alexandre hoisted the child onto a seat in the bus. He slid Irène's suitcase onto the baggage rack and lowered the window to give her some air. Once the two travellers were installed, he took up his post opposite them on the platform. For the moment nothing mattered more to him than to see the bus get under way, to lose sight of those two faces that forced him to feign a smile, moulded over his features like a mask and painfully held in place as though by taut threads.

The driver clambered in. The motor growled. With a preoccupied glance that suddenly added years to her age, Irène made sure that she had all her belongings around her. Then the pain of having been unable to spare his daughter unhappiness became so intolerable to Alexandre that he almost ran beneath the huge wheels to say a last word to her; it seemed to him he must surely have words within his command true enough and strong enough to mend everything, to wipe clean the slate. She herself leaned her head out through the window, her face pinched with emotion. So many people in this world succeed in expressing their affection only through anxiety. Amid the racket of the coughing motor and the screech of tyres, they both cried out phrases which made an incongruous chorus.

"Poor Papa! You don't look well; try to take care of yourself. . . ."

And, from him, "Be careful . . . you're none too strong. . . ."

Now, at the end of the platform, he was nothing more than a little man alone, who might have saved himself the trouble of waving his hat, for the bus was drawing out of sight and it was wholly useless to continue gestures of farewell with no one there to receive them. The heart's best things seemed fated to be used up on regrets, to be dissipated, like the brooks, the springs, the rivers, like all the earth's cool, living waters in the bitterness of the ocean.

In a moment he was jogging toward the streetcar, his head lowered, fearful of being late at the bank. He searched his pocket for a ticket he knew he still had, and, not finding it at once, he imagined in the distress of his emotions that he had lost it too, when he had pulled out his glove a moment earlier —or perhaps the evening before, when he had taken a handkerchief from his pocket.

Life was becoming unbearable to him, a compound of unbelievable spite; the pettiest of worries were beginning to overshadow those that really mattered.

And so his almost constant heartburn, his more and more racking headaches began once more to harass him as much as his desire for security.

He finally made up his mind to go see a doctor.

Dead and buried, too, was his great, delightful dream, that dream of a serious illness which would be his last, of a stay at the hospital, of true rest.

More modest and more reasonable was what he wanted now : just a little relief, a few pills, perhaps, which would do him more good than remedies of his own devising.

And he said to himself, trying to get the courage needed for this great, distasteful step, "If I've nothing to gain by it, I certainly have nothing to lose."

CHAPTER VIII

E HAD shined his shoes and put on a new shirt; he walked into the consultation room looking as neat as a pin, but his face was drawn with exhaustion, like so many small men who dress with special attention when they go see a doctor and who, at a photographer's, always look uneasy. He introduced himself, adding a little to his stature by standing on tiptoe.

"You certainly don't know me, Doctor. My manager, Monsieur Fontaine, suggested my coming to you. Chenevert," said he as he sat down. "Alexandre."

The doctor pulled a sheet of fresh paper from beneath a pile of prospectuses, brochures, and folders.

More and more nowadays doctors' offices are getting to look like travel agencies, with all the mass of advertising that daily floods their mail. Most of the pharmaceutical products presented therein are backed up with a barrage of anatomical drawings in three or four colours, vermilion for the blood, green for the bile, mauve for the nervous system; to suggest the menopause, a reproduction of an autumn landscape . . . complete with falling leaves. There was a wholly captivating assortment of such on the doctor's desk : products to regulate the blood pressure, to activate the bladder, to relieve insomnia. Certain preparations had more subtle ends—relief for depression, violent pain, irritation. The blotter the doctor had just picked up explained how to "entice sleep by . . ." Alexandre had no time to read further, for the doctor was drying the name he had just written down. He had spelled it Chênevert, with an accent. Underneath he wrote in the details : the age of the little man in his best suit, his weight, his matrimonial status, the diseases he had had, what he looked like.

"Whooping cough?"

"Yes, whooping cough too."

And so began Alexandre Chenevert's "history." A bank employee for thirty-four years . . . emotive, irritable, highly nervous . . . had had the whole roster of contagious diseases . . . His father sickly, gloomy; lived to the age of eighty-two, however . . .

"Ah!" said the doctor from time to time, as though on the trail of an important clue and well satisfied with details that showed he was headed in the right direction; and his pen scratched away at top speed, sometimes recording the patient's own expression :

". . . poor mother, she wasn't very robust either, but she wouldn't give up. Her bad heart was the end of her. . . ." Two sisters dead before thirty. . . . Patient says he has been just dragging himself around for the last few years, judges he has been worse since. . . .

". . . Since when, precisely?"

And into Alexandre's history entered the incident of his professional mistake, which was once again to count against him. Was it not bad enough that it had been recorded in the report to the head office of the bank? The best thing for his peace of mind would have been to let the whole business drop into oblivion. But he was confronting a very skilful man, who now asked, "What brings you here? What's your trouble, exactly?"

"Exactly . . ." repeated Alexandre, drawing his chair closer and now more at ease. For if there was a subject in all the world which he knew, it must surely be that one. After all he was the only one to know it by direct contact with the source material. And yet his first explanations did not seem to please the doctor.

"A pain in the pit of the stomach? Is it really a pain? Is it not rather a burning sensation? . . . You realize the difference between a pain and a burn?" asked the doctor in a tone which brought Alexandre down a peg.

"Perhaps it is only a burning sensation," he said apologetically, as though a trifle dissatisfied.

"Perhaps? Aren't you sure?"

"I think so," said Alexandre, suddenly uncertain of the value of his own testimony.

They moved on to the headaches.

"Where are they centred? In the back? At the forehead? On one side only?"

"It's as though a hand of iron were gripping my skull," Alexandre explained.

Then, after having committed himself with so specific an answer, he felt a scruple. It was often like a small hammer pounding away at his right temple. He had suffered from headaches just about all his life; it greatly vexed him not to be able to speak with the precise assurance so long an experience should have afforded him. And so many exact questions tended also to befog his mind with doubt. Had his head really made him suffer? Of course everyone suffered from headaches very likely. But, less inclined to complain than he, they attached no importance to them.

The doctor was entering everything in his records; already he had a good half page inscribed against Alexandre. Curious as to what had been charged to his account on the ledger, the latter leaned forward a little.

From time to time, to help him in his task, the doctor would dictate to himself in an almost inaudible voice, mingling tag ends of phrases with a reflective humming sound. Alexandre, who had a sharp ear, caught: ". . . an intimate acquaintance with purgatives, laxatives, medicines of his own choosing . . . has always been . . ." He was strongly tempted to protest on behalf of the simple truth. Occasionally, like everyone else, he dosed himself according to his own notions. At first it had been perhaps once a week, and then a bit more often. . . .

The doctor picked up his sheet of paper to read it over. Here, in summary, was how Monsieur Chenevert appeared to him after a half hour.

"A slight, thin man, sickly-looking, seems older than his true age. . . . Admits he has already, *at some time or other*, consulted another doctor, who found nothing the matter with him. . . . Frequently contradicts himself. *Dreamy*. At present complains of his stomach. No sharp pain in the epigastrium. Unlocalized headaches. Distressed by his throat . . . by the insensitivity and ill manners of our times. . . . Distressed by his neighbours, by their radio, by the propaganda which *has the upper hand in everything*. We no longer know, he states, where we are going these days. . . ."

"Take off your coat," the doctor requested.

When Alexandre was behind the screen which hid the examination table, the doctor began asking him questions of a more personal sort.

There then followed an embarrassed silence. Alexandre had perhaps just come to realize that in a doctor's vocabulary all is technical, even including the most fearsome of life's secrets. Behind the screen he began to murmur that "fortunately, he wasn't much inclined that way nowadays . . . that it just wasn't as important to him as it had once been. . . ."

Approaching him the doctor applied his stethoscope and asked. "Why *fortunately?*"

He palpated the thin body, bereft of beauty. And he pointed out, with a sort of deliberate indifference, that "at Monsieur Chenevert's age it was not counter-indicated, and that, practised within reason. . . ."

Alexandre's pinched face turned away. Beneath his protruding ribs, his heart pounded rapidly. The patient's eyes retained their obstinate, inaccessible expression. How clearly he realized that men did not like what they called love. That most embarrassing of subjects between men they approached with half-utterances, with false carelessness, or else with a vulgar leer, never easily and comfortably.

". . . beneficial in keeping the nerves on an even keel," added the doctor, without further elaboration.

Alexandre hastened to change the subject.

"The worst of all," said he as he hastily slipped back into his clothes, "is the business of feeling so sleepy when my work is at its most demanding. If you could do something for that, at least . . ."

"We'll certainly do something about that," said the doctor, who always used the plural pronoun when he saw that a bit of reassuring was needful.

We seemed to produce the desired effect.

His immediate problem was how persuade his patient to agree to undergo laboratory and X-ray examinations. He considered them the only almost certain methods of medical investigation. But they were more expensive than two or three visits to his office. For this very reason the doctor often found himself facing a minor problem of conscience: to begin treatment after a clinical examination alone and remain fairly sure of being paid; or else to require tests which often would exhaust the patient's means. Moreover, to those whose illness he guessed was principally due to worry, he did not suggest them without a certain hesitation, since, were they to reveal no serious ailment, these expensive procedures seemed to such people a wholly useless outlay of money. Yet the fact remained that it was wiser to go into things thoroughly at the very beginning, and the doctor said so to Monsieur Chenevert. "What's the use of waiting until some serious and easily recognized disease sets in? Medicine consists as much in prevention as in cure. . . ."

"Obviously," said Alexandre, overcome by so much logic.

His mind was far from made up.

He did not think he was in bad enough health, he explained, to make X-rays worth the trouble. He seemed less fearful of the expenditure than of not being sufficiently sick to allow himself any such disbursement.

"Haven't you health insurance?" inquired the doctor.

Yes, Alexandre had a policy, but not the most expensive, the most serviceable. The insurance he carried paid only if he were hospitalized.

"These insurance companies do strange things," said he; "to prevent their customers from cheating they force them to spend more than is necessary and take up hospital space needed for the seriously ill."

The doctor at once agreed with him. He loathed those companies which now went as far as dictating terms to a doctor, even occasionally setting the amount of his fee.

"All the same," he suggested, "couldn't you take a week's vacation for this complete checkup?"

No, that was impossible; Alexandre resisted any such idea. If the worst came to the worst, he could get a half day here and a half day there . . . perhaps. But he would have to state his reasons for asking, and right at the moment, he had no desire to ask any favours.

"Later on, perhaps . . . I'll look into it . . . I'll study it out . . ."

"You don't have to work so hard at it," interjected the doctor, a trifle out of patience. "I'll phone the hospital; we'll try to get you through early in the morning, so that afterward you can appear at your office, if you set so much store by it. In any case," he said, "you'll be freed of anxiety. . . ."

It was not that he lacked sympathy for human beings. But he was plunged up to his neck in the sufferings of others, just as Alexandre was up to his neck in figures.

A few days later the doctor received detailed reports which became part of the Chenevert case history. They did not tell him much he had not seen during the clinical examination. At least they disposed of certain possibilities for error; among others the diagnosis of a gastric ulcer, for the moment he had laid eyes on Monsieur Chenevert with his puckered mouth and his bad colouring he had thought, "An ulcer . . . very probably . . ." So that was a false alarm. Even though certain erosions of the mucous membrane were substantially invisible in radiographs.

The little man returned; he seated himself as he had the first time, his hat on his knees, his forehead drawn with wrinkles. He stared at the photos on the wall. One showed a smiling young woman surrounded with smiling children. He averted his eyes as though his gloomy mood had suffered a reproach from this invulnerable good humour.

The doctor had extracted the Chenevert file, now quite substantial. The greater part of the tests gave negative indications; at times it's an expensive matter to reach so consoling a conclusion.

It was nonetheless obvious that the poor man was ailing in every department, everywhere at once and in so many small ways that it was becoming terribly hard to be of any use to him. Yet there was nothing genuinely serious . . . as yet.

The doctor told him this, with a sort of fleeting, little smile. "Indeed your stomach is rather on the husky side, to have put up with all it has. . . ."

But Alexandre seemed to draw therefrom only a meagre satisfaction, almost a certain discomfiture.

So the doctor had returned to his scribbling: ". . . sulphate of magnesia, bile salts, belladonna . . . passion flower . . . valerian . . ."

The pretty names of flowers, and others less enchanting . . .

There were good grounds for prescribing charcoal to absorb gas, emollients, vegetable gelatins; a few unobnoxious powders for the stomach . . . so many other products, synthetic or natural . . .

It was while working out such lengthy and complicated prescriptions that Dr Hudon suffered the worst from his practice of medicine. Confronting a complex of functional disturbances and lacking the power to strike at the root of what was wrong, he had to alleviate ten various effects at once, and take care not to aggravate one by what he did to relieve another. How to begin? With the nervous tension that disturbed the digestive functions? With the faulty functioning of the organs which added to the strain on the nervous system? With malnutrition? With low spirits? Some said, "Care for the body which, if it is always sick, inclines the mind toward melancholy." Others, even more sure of themselves: "Begin with the soul which, by affinity, makes ill the body." Twisting his fountain pen in his fingers, the doctor was trying to unravel Alexandre Chenevert.

His eyelid flickered frequently. Deep furrows crossed his forehead and marked the passage of contradictory thoughts. The mouth bore the expression of someone who has just scolded himself for insufficient reason. Sitting straight on the front edge of a straight chair, Monsieur Chenevert seemed absorbed in exhausting interior argument.

He had to be made to sleep.

To calm him; if need be, to stupefy him.

Gardenal or the barbiturates, thought the doctor. Or else one of those new sedatives combined with a stimulant to offset the former's depressive effect.

The best thing for Monsieur Chenevert, though, would be to sleep without the aid of poisons.

The doctor glanced at his watch.

He had three or four more patients left who had come seeking his advice. And today there were a few house calls he could not put off. He really should try to get a little writing done on an article which might be useful to his reputation. And he thought of his wife; at home he had turned into a mere bundle of nerves and could not stand any talk of illness or the least fatigue.

Suddenly he felt fed up.

He was still young, at the beginning of his forties, but he had always lived tensely; during his impoverished youth, straining toward the profession which alone in his eyes could satisfy his personal ambitions for public esteem and comfortable circumstances, coupled with the pride of being wholly at the service of others; once he had become a doctor, straining over his patients, whose loyalty he wished to keep, but without such tricks as needlessly repeated visits to his office, each the occasion for prescribing a palliative to afford the delusion of improvement. Now an almost constant bitterness, while making him see that his own motives were not quite so lofty, disfigured for him the motives of others, of all mankind. Stern, often exasperated, his face was nevertheless sympathetic, with its brown, attentive eyes, so filled with weariness. Tiny wrinkles which crowded his temples seemed to stretch those eyes, as though Dr Hudon were continuously facing a tiring problem.

He made up his mind: another quarter-hour; he could surely

manage to grant another short quarter-hour to Monsieur . . .
he checked the heading on the case history—to this Monsieur
Chenevert.

"Do you smoke?" he asked. "How much?"

"Eight to ten," said Alexandre, referring only to those rare
days when he limited himself to about that number.

"Too much!" the doctor exclaimed. "You'll also have to cut
out coffee . . . perhaps a little very weak tea."

"No more coffee!"

Yet it was surely good, strong, black coffee and cigarettes
that kept him going. He bowed his head.

"What was that?" he inquired politely, overcoming his distraction.

The doctor repeated: "I was asking you, Monsieur Chenevert, have you any troubles? Are you an unhappy man?"

He pursed his lips, his fingers twisting the brim of his hat.
Under the smooth dry skin of his hands, the bluish network of
his veins grew more prominent. His eyes flamed with challenge

"No . . . not that I know of . . . no."

The unhappy were those poor wretches who had no country,
who had not enough to eat. . . . He longed to ask the doctor
whether he also had read last week in the *Echo* that three men
out of four on our planet were undernourished. No, he could
not see that he had any right to be unhappy.

"On earth," said Alexandre "in this world of ours . . ."

"Have you worries?"

He tried to think of some. He didn't see that he had anything
to worry about. Certainly there must be people with worries
of a different order than his—the millionaires . . .

"Your relations . . . with your wife . . . are cordial?"

"I get along well with Madame Chenevert," said Alexandre
with a tone of dignity that cut short any further exploration
of the subject. "She's a fine woman."

"With your daughter?"

"She pays her own way," said Alexandre distractedly.

"Does your work at the bank upset you?" continued the
doctor. "Figures all day long; I should think it would get tedious
. . . in the long run. . . ."

He thought within himself: absolutely sickening; never
could have stood such a life.

"All those faces trooping by your wicket, the constant neces-
sity of being polite, helpful . . . the strain of all that may well
have been too much?"

"There are all kinds of people," Alexandre began to explain, "but generally, in my experience, there are more decent people than otherwise. . . ."

He did not see how, if he were unhappy in some respect, he would be better off. Or the doctor in a better position to care for him. As a sick man, there was always something to be done for him, always pills to be given.

"I live my life; what more can I do!" said he with a certain irritation.

"But do you really live your life?" the doctor reproached him. "You look to me like a man who is always in a rush."

"No, I have things pretty well arranged; I've very rarely late."

And yet it was perfectly obvious that this poor man must do everything wrong: eat quickly, with one eye on the clock, in the depths of some noisy restaurant; then, having gulped the last mouthful, rush back to work, go to bed with his head full of figures; get up tired, struggle through to another evening . . . Dr Hudon enfolded Monsieur Chenevert in a glance vexed beyond endurance. Of a sudden he realized how this man could so greatly plague him: it was because his name, indeed, was legion.

Every morning at a set hour he walked down a thousand staircases at once, running from every corner of the city toward bulging streetcars. He crowded into them by the hundreds and thousands. From tram to tram, from street to street, you could see him standing in public conveyances, his hands slipped through leather straps, his arms stretched in a curious likeness to a prisoner at the whipping post.

An hour's—perhaps over an hour's—travel morning and evening to add to the length of his working day.

A bite grabbed at the edge of a lunch counter. And the little man covered the sidewalks with his hurried, overburdened, sometimes sullen multitude. He disappeared behind store counters, into offices crackling with racket and the clatter of typewriters, beneath piles and piles of paper work—reports, ledgers, registers, applications . . . far and ever further and further, from his pristine unconcern.

Dr Hudon saw perfectly the meaningless, the inevitability, the lopsidedness of the human misery of his times.

"But do you imagine," he broke out, "that I can cure you all by myself?"

He had spoken rather sharply. Often enough, these days, he caught himself ill repressing his impatience.

He wondered what was coming over him.

Then his very wonder made him smile at himself.

For of course he himself lived a crazy life; meals gobbled in haste at irregular hours, his sleep often interrupted, his responsibility for decisions on which could depend the lives of others —responsibility: that was what wore you down the most. Yet, after all, he could hardly do other than live the life that was his life.

What did he have left to live? At most a few years to tie up the loose ends, to assure himself a summer home for those visits to the country which had become absolutely necessary to assuage his weariness; to look after his children's upbringing and his wife's security; to provide for the future.

At the moment life seemed incredibly short to Dr Hudon.

He continued gently, "There's not much sense to living the way you live, Monsieur Chenevert. Take that business of the hundred dollars. Can't you forget it, somehow?"

He spoke in a conciliatory tone which forced Alexandre to acquiesce with the whole of his suspicious, absorbed face.

For the money had been repaid him. Yes, indeed, it was just as silly as that: he had loaded himself, in order to repay the whole debt, with an overburden of work which had laid him low. Then a certain Simon Coutu, on his return from a trip, had noticed a hundred-dollar item he could not identify credited to his account, and he had immediately notified the bank. So Alexandre was back where he had started; or more precisely, he was now richer by one hundred dollars, since he had made up the deficit. Richer, though, had little meaning: for he was in the process of spending that very money on X-rays and care he might perhaps not have needed had he not nearly killed himself to earn it. Still he had not the least intention of admitting that he had been a man to worry his head over absolutely nothing. The whole story was too improbable.

"At night," asked the doctor, "when you don't sleep, what do you think of? Any particular subject?"

"No," said Alexandre, "I think of this, and that . . . of silly things. . . . It doesn't prove anything."

A little provoked, the doctor tapped his desk with the point of his pencil. He had greatly exceeded the fifteen minutes he had thought is reasonable to grant Monsieur . . . no, not Monsieur Dandurand . . . but Monsieur Chenevert. The prime difficulty in his way of life was to stick to a schedule. Yet within a few years he would most certainly have to bring more order into his life, he would have to lighten the daily load. In a word, live better, more abundantly, at the expense of a smaller number of suffering beings. No, that wasn't it; what he wanted, simply, was to take on some, to drop others. . . . But he was no better suited with this way of stating his ambition. "Drop some? The more dubious cases? The sick people who consume too much time?" He tried to define his objective in yet other terms: "To be finally settled in my career, settled in life," said he to himself. And this formula, as he gave it his irritated attention, seemed the most farfetched of all. As long as suffering existed, would it ever allow him a personal life?

"You have your faith?" he inquired.

Alexandre winced. He said, as though accusing himself, "Yes I have my faith."

A ruddy-faced priest had one day asked him the same question, and almost with the same tone of reproach which implied, "Well then, why don't you sleep?" And perhaps, thought Alexandre in great dismay, his insomnia was indeed proof that he had not a true faith. Eternal punishment, the misfortunes of the innocent in this world—perhaps the faith did not require you to keep them constantly in mind, especially as they concerned others. The saints, however, don't seem to have been people who slept like tops. . . . He begged the doctor to repeat what he had just said, explaining, "I was distracted . . . something else on my mind. . . . You were saying?"

He thought he had heard some words relating to sport, but he suspected that his ears had misled him.

"I asked you," the doctor continued, "if you shouldn't like to play golf."

"Golf?"

"Yes, the game of golf."

"No," Alexandre dismissed that suggestion.

"What about bowling, then?"

That inspiration had struck the doctor on the spur of the moment. As he scrutinized his patient, with his narrow chest, and the sad seriousness of his eyes, he had appeared to him the very embodiment of all those little men you see, after their working hours, in dusty bowling alleys so dedicated to the game that they finally come to excel at it and dispense with heaven knows what other exacting ambition wholly beyond their reach.

"No," said Alexandre, annoyed.

The doctor made a gesture of discouragement. He thought he had really struck pay ore.

"It's a fine distraction, they tell me. You throw a ball at a lot of pins. It's easy enough, but it seems to stop you from thinking."

Alexandre looked at him, quite perplexed and a trifle offended: what? take all that trouble to prevent yourself pursuing the only activity that matters, the only rational activity?

His raised eyebrows, the movement of his thought, so easy to follow in his wrinkled forehead, and the movement of his lips were tiresome in themselves, even to someone who had been watching Alexandre for only five minutes. Out of patience the doctor raised his voice a little: "But somehow you've simply got to learn to relax."

Himself at the end of his patience, Alexandre seemed to catch sight of a quite harrowing conclusion.

"So, then," said he, "there's nothing the matter with me; I'm not sick? Nothing wrong?"

"Nothing!" replied the doctor with that kind of abruptness which served him as charity. "You're worn out. You're headed for a fall...."

"Oh!..."

He would not have believed it, though, at any time along the way.

"You're on the edge of disaster," the doctor warned him. "No one can live indefinitely as tense as you are. You think too much. You let things weigh too much on your mind. For heaven's sake," he said, "you carry the whole world on your shoulders!"

It was impossible for him not to recognize himself, however little; Alexandre's suddenly widened eyes seemed to ratify the doctor's keen insight. Then his head sagged between his shoulders. He admitted, "All in all, there's some truth in what you say."

"Do you think you're obliged to carry the world on your shoulders?"

So stated, the question obviously broke through his defences. "No."

"After all, it's not your world ..."

"Not mine, altogether, no ..." Alexandre assented, though still clinging to a mental reservation.

"Don't hang on so obstinately, then," the doctor advised him.

As though these words might serve him as a signal for his departure, Alexandre slipped to the edge of his chair. He excused himself. "I've taken up a lot of your time."

He had all the while been very much aware of the impatience of the sick people who were waiting their turn in the outer office. The glances that had followed him to the threshold of the consultation room had clearly said to him, "Try to get through quickly." One woman had even said out loud, "I have a train to catch." She must by now be furious at Alexandre. He had a knack of being aware at some distance, even through a partition, of other people's constraint.

"Well, then," said Alexandre, as though he were at the bank and he wished to settle a bit of business : "What do I owe you?"

Meanwhile the doctor was just getting around to the question of fresh air, moderate exercise, and—above all—emancipation from the daily rounds of anxieties.

". . . if at all possible, a change of scene . . ."

Alexandre had pulled out his ancient leather billfold.

". . . a visit to the country . . ."

The bank notes were carefully sorted out according to their value, just as they were in Alexandre's cash drawer, and carefully secured with a rubber band.

"What does it come to?" he asked.

The doctor waved one hand irritably. "There's no hurry."

He could not get used to taking in cash, directly from a patient, as though he were running a service station or a grocery. Above all when he was trying to sell the idea of peace of mind, of relaxation. At heart he had remained too sensitive for his trade. Such expressions as "How much does that cost?" "What do I owe you?" wounded him perhaps even more than the sight of money. Alexandre was fingering his roll of bills, his eyes withdrawn, so absorbed in his mental arithmetic that he was oblivious of his moving lips. And the doctor felt a certain acrimony toward Monsieur Chenevert.

"You can come back later. We shall see."

But Alexandre clung to his purpose. He explained, "I pay my debts as I go along." He had withdrawn two bills, but he ostentatiously kept the billfold open, his hand lingering over the money remaining there, probably fearful lest—if the fee should prove to be higher—he give the impression of having failed to foresee this, or of finding reason to be surprised at the greater sum.

The doctor glanced elsewhere; on such occasions he was tempted to be as embarrassed for strangers as though they were members of his own family. Before Alexandre could extract a third bill, he stopped him. "That's quite enough."

He stood up facing Monsieur Chenevert, looming so high above him that he at once had to look down, and even to stoop over, in order to be able to make out beneath Alexandre's glasses the little man's lowered features. And used as he was to human ills, Dr Hudon felt a deep compassion surging within him—a very annoying feeling the novelty of which never seemed to wear off.

"At least you'll take a vacation?"

"I'm on vacation right now," said Alexandre. "I requested my holiday a little ahead of my turn, so I'd be free for the

X-rays and tests; I thought it would work out better that way. So I'm on vacation."

"Don't tell me," said the doctor ill-humouredly, "you call that a vacation!"

He pocketed the bills given him by Alexandre. "Keep careful track of your medical expenses," he suggested. "You might at least get a deduction from your income tax—you know that, don't you?"

"Naturally," said Alexandre, with the implication that that was not the sort of detail he was likely to forget. "But," said he, "it's only four per cent, and you can only claim the deduction after a pretty high minimum expenditure."

Upon reflection he added: "Nowadays the best plan, if you want to get the full benefit of the collective security idea, is for everyone to be sick at the same time—I mean, of course, in a given family. It would have been more advantageous for me if I had gone to the hospital. Then you can make everything count," said Alexandre, "medicines, injections. The more it costs, the better off you are . . . in this connection, of course. . . ." He gave signs of being a little happier about life. "This year," he remarked, "my wife was rather ill. So, by totalling everything I've spent, I'll get a small reduction." He thought for a moment, glancing at the ceiling. "Social security, after all, is a good thing." Then growing sad he added, as though in apology, "But it makes one spendthrift. You'd say their idea is to force us, to push us into wasting money. . . ."

He looked more tormented than ever.

"Where on earth are we ever going to end up—this notion of making others pay for each person's security, of encouraging us to take as much advantage of others as we can?"

"There are people who wouldn't be bothered by your scruples," said the doctor.

"We don't know what we're headed for," Alexandre elaborated.

Now that the consultation seemed to be over, he was getting a certain enjoyment from a conversation that was turning into interesting channels with a man the likes of whom he did not run into every day.

"You're too thin-skinned for this world," the doctor reproved him. "You seem made to suffer. That's not wise."

"I'm not as bad as all that," said Alexandre emphatically, as much upset as though he had had a compliment he dared not consider justified.

His lip began to tremble and he turned toward the door. Under the heavy hanging designed to muffle the sound of voices he fumbled for the knob. Suddenly he was overwhelmed by his having encountered a real sympathy in his behalf.

The doctor stepped forward a few paces. He wanted to put his hand on Monsieur Chenevert's shoulder. There came over him a burning desire to save this man—with or against the will of God he knew not. Medical motives so often remained ambiguous.

"Go, Monsieur Chenevert," said he. "Go away. Shed your excess baggage. At least once in your life do what you have always wanted to."

This time his tone alarmed Alexandre.

"You think I should? You really believe it?"

He raised his eyes toward the doctor, less intractable, still highly perturbed, yet shaken all the same.

"Yes, yes," the doctor insisted. He seemed to be pleading: forget about other people; just try to be happy yourself.

"You truly think . . ." Alexandre began.

All his defences seemed ready to crumble. His mouth softened. He turned away from the doctor. But deep within the averted face there was kindled a glow of resolve : that yearning —yes, that yearning—to be happy he no longer was able to hide, yet it must still be hidden . . . did you betray such a weakness to a stranger?

He got hold of himself a little and extended his small dry hand toward the doctor.

"You are very kind," said Alexandre. "I thank you."

CHAPTER IX

HE MARCHED off in a state of confusion, a bit ashamed and still a trifle irritated into the bargain. Ten dollars here . . . twelve dollars there . . . a blood count . . . an analysis of his digestive fluids—and all that merely to have someone tell you that he needed to be happy. Every last fool knew that. You might say that man was born with this notion in his head, and most likely on the verge of death he still clung to that poor little idea.

He covered a certain distance in high dudgeon with himself,

embarrassed by the whims that had been put in his head. "Be happy!" he jeered.

He began to realize, though, that his case had differed a little from the cases of others. To him, Alexandre finally became aware, permission to be happy had been freely granted. Even more, it had been urged upon him by a person with proper authority and, if you looked at it that way, as a medicine.

Considered as a medication, happiness—he had to grant—was less selfish, less preposterous. He thought it over.

"It makes sense."

When you came right down to it and reckoned the sum total of what consultations, prescriptions, examinations cost, happiness seemed indeed the cheapest cure.

"Yes, indeed," Alexandre ingenuously told himself. "Look at the Eskimos, the South Sea islanders; they scarcely possess clothing to cover their backs, but it seems that they are happy, and it costs them nothing."

It was the realization of such facts in the practical order that, when it came to a decision, best melted Alexandre's resistance and quickly—very quickly—set him off on the road to his personal happiness.

Now he cast aside all doubt; little by little progress was being made in this world, since at last it was coming to be recognized that happiness is beneficial to man. This probably had been known in an earlier day, but not scientifically as at present. These days it was being put on the list of stated essentials.

"It's a sign of the times," thought Alexandre, glancing up at the sky.

He became aware that it was summer, almost the end of summer. But was not summer most precious of all during those threatened final days? And at fifty-two was not happiness more necessary than at twenty?

He reached Saint Louis Square and let himself relax on a park bench. It was pleasantly warm in this little area of green surrounded by cool stone houses. "This is a little corner of Montreal I've always rather liked," Alexandre naïvely confided to himself. The heat penetrated his hands, which gradually unbent and finally came to rest, quiet and open, upon his knees, now comfortably spread apart.

In the interests of honesty, he tried to tell himself that he had no more right to pamper himself than had, for instance, that poor policeman glued to the asphalt in the sun's glare, and signalling so continuously with his arms that the mere sight of it began to fatigue Monsieur Chenevert. Then, as, when you got down to it, he had been perfectly free to do all his life, he looked at something else. Perhaps it was bad to keep telling people that they had the right to be happy. Such a relaxation of barriers might one day produce a strange confusion—no more policemen on street corners, no more miners, no more spinners or weavers at their unhealthy trades.

Alexandre jumped spryly from his seat. He jogged across the square and hurried over to the other side of the street, risking collision with any car that might chance to pass. He came to a newsstand. He bought an evening paper. He opened it in haste. For the first time in his life he paid no attention to the headlines, to the large type, never wasted—understandably enough—on pleasant news, but reserved for matters of international moment. The whole vast human herd, always at loggerheads over oil, cotton, secret treaties, suddenly left Monsieur Chenevert indifferent, bored. He turned straight to the classified ads.

Camp to let. Sainte-Thérèse. Good fishing. Rowboat.

Why had he never before appreciated how peacefully inviting were these paragraphs? Here was a good sample:

At Sainte Geneviève: a log cabin. Two rooms. Stove. On the old Saraguay Trail.

You could almost see the simple old Indians passing in single file along this shady forest highway, bows and arrows hanging from their backs.

Far from the beaten track. Camp at Val Morin.

All this had served, maybe, as preparation for Alexandre's perfect joy when his eyes lit upon the following lines:

Small trapper's cabin. Inexpensive. At Lac des Isles. Address your inquiries to Etienne Le Gardeur, at his farm four miles from Saint-Donat. We can certainly get together.

Everything about this suited Alexandre.

His eye had first been caught by the word trapper. And then he liked the sound of the family's name: Le Gardeur, a name which inspired confidence and friendship, while at the same time conveying a notion of protective guardianship. And then there was everything implied by that "We can certainly get together," a formula you would hardly expect in the modern world, a sentence which in itself seemed almost wildly fanciful, delusive; yet there it was, all spelled out.

With that red pencil which he used at the bank to point out

the place where you signed something, Alexandre underlined the item.

Then he slipped the newspaper under his arm. He gave his hat a friendly little tap. He looked toward the far horizon.

The marvel of it all, when you really thought it over, was that, beyond being astonished at himself, he should have discovered he was a man like any other, who longed for happiness, and who at last yielded to that longing.

CHAPTER X

THE NEXT day, at a little earlier than his usual hour, he clambered down his corkscrew staircase bearing a heavy object which banged against the cast-iron steps. Fred Trottier popped out onto the threshold of his basement store. On the other side of the stairway was a cleaner's shop, advertised by a large, multicoloured sign: TWENTY-FOUR HOUR VALET SERVICE. MINOR REPAIRS. With his steaming iron in his hand, the cleaner stretched his head toward his sidewalk-level window, half-concealed by the sign. No slightest irregularity in the habits of the strangers who live so close to them escapes the residents of such a quarter. Through their windows the closest neighbours ascertained that the unusual sounds they heard this morning were caused by a suitcase the little man in 8846 was dragging down the stairs. This piece of baggage was yellow, tired-looking, old-fashioned, but of real leather, one of those ancient valises that make people think, "In its day that must have been a very handsome bag."

Alexandre had bought it for his honeymoon and not without qualms, for it represented an expenditure way beyond the ordinary. But to have gone off on his wedding trip with a shoddy papièr-mâché bag had seemed to him to place his whole married life under the aegis of niggardly penny-pinching.

On occasion the fortunes of life so arrange matters that extravagant purchases prove economical and that one has reason to congratulate oneself a hundredfold for having done at least one silly thing. "My suitcase is still as sturdy as ever," thought Alexandre. "That's what comes of having bought a good piece of luggage."

At the foot of the stairs he turned back to acknowledge a last greeting from Eugénie Chenevert; in her wrapper, and clutching its cotton material in heavy folds across her chest, she was leaning down over the banister.

"Alexandre Chenevert," said she with a certain solemnity, "take care of yourself! Don't run foolish risks. Be careful what you eat. Don't read until after midnight . . . and let me hear from you."

She gave the impression of reading mentally from a list of recommendations prepared in advance.

"Yes," replied Alexandre, "you have a good vacation yourself."

She was to go to Sherbrooke on a visit to their daughter.

"Give Irène my best," said he.

"Certainly," she rejoined. "And don't forget to put on your woollen underwear if it's cold up there. Don't take any chances."

Alexandre patiently and gravely promised. It was the first time since their marriage that each was going his separate way, and this great happening required that they display to each other a politeness and concern quite out of the ordinary. Eugénie went back in.

Fred Trottier, leaning against his door jamb, inquired, "So you're taking your holiday apart this year?"

"That's what it looks like," Alexandre cut him short, for he had never liked to encourage familiarity, or account for his minor comings and goings.

"Have you a special place in mind?"

"None," said Alexandre picking up his bag once more.

"Just stopping when you feel like it?"

"When I feel like it."

Behind him the curious voice persisted, "For long?"

Alexandre hauled his suitcase to the streetcar stop, despite what Eugénie had said to him in her proud fear of the neighbourhood's comments: "It looks terrible to be taking a streetcar when you go on a trip! At least you might take a taxi." But he knew where to draw the line. For going to the hospital or funerals, a taxi was in order. Or when you were leaving on a major journey, for instance a voyage to Europe; but on this occasion, on his way into the woods, a taxi was not at all indicated.

Alexandre hoisted the bag first onto the step and then into the interior of the streetcar, despite the large number of passengers and the objections of the conductor. But Monsieur Chenevert had no intention of letting himself be robbed of such an expensive piece of baggage. He sat down toward the centre of the tram, his yellow bag at his feet. The passengers who stumbled over it looked with curiosity to see what sort of person could be its owner. And they beheld a little man with wrinkled eyebrows and a drooping mouth, pale, emaciated, who certainly looked as though he badly needed to go somewhere.

He arrived at the bus terminal a good half-hour early, and had plenty of time to congratulate himself once more for not having paid any heed to Eugénie, who scolded him for leaving too early, for always leaving too early, for wearing himself to a frazzle always trying to be ahead of time. Already at the Rawdon bus gate travellers were more numerous than at Alexandre's wicket on a Saturday ten minutes before closing. He took his place with the others under the grey vaulting which made them all look sallow. The air which reeked with exhaust gas was also torn by instructions barked over the loud-speakers—"Platform Number One . . . Platform Number Six . . ." Alexandre's group comprised a compact little island isolated from the other groups on the concrete platforms. Some thirty people surrounded him, a few sitting awkwardly on their bags, others standing, and holding tired and whimpering children, yet others plagued with the worry of watching badly fastened packages burst open, almost everyone worn out by having got up too early and by the mass of little last-minute details they had had to deal with. They were pale-faced, weary, yet very cheerful, and it soon transpired, from random conversations, that almost all of these exhausted people were on vacation. Was it not the fifteenth of August, that midsummer holiday which opened the doors to the country for thousands of city dwellers with two free weeks before them? In the heat, the hum of voices, and the racket of loud-speakers, Alexandre had the impression of being, among refugees, himself a refugee, and that all of them together were awaiting a return to their native soil. That home they all yearned for—was it, for the others as for him, merely some small, unknown patch of greenery?

Good nature disappeared the moment the autobus drew into place, since you could not fail to see at a glance that the crowd was too large for everyone to find seats. There was a scuffle. Out of patience, the conductor vainly cried, "There's room! There'll be plenty of room!" No one believed him. They were in no mood to believe anything. A heavy-set woman, who had certainly arrived after Alexandre, was manoeuvring to filch his place. He looked at her severely. "Madame," he expostulated, "if you were set on having a good place, you should have done like the others and come ahead of time." But he would have had to protest in every direction at once against the rudeness, the thrusting elbows, the unabashed jockeying for position. The peace that was their goal made all these people outrageously bellicose.

Frowning and dragging his bag inch by inch, Alexandre shoved with the rest. He got through the door. He sank down onto a seat at the back of the bus, just above the rear wheels. The curved floor beneath him left him no place to stretch his legs, but what did that matter? He was better off than those who were left standing, their heads almost touching the low ceiling. What would they see of the countryside, poor people! His eyelids began to close. The night before he had scarcely had a wink of sleep, so overexcited had he been at his resolution to go away, and worried too at this new aspect of his character, this act of the will which chilled his spine, as though he were committing a perhaps dangerously foolhardy thing, which might cost him dear.

He heard the lament of the streetcar bells, the rasping brakes, the bicycle sirens. At first the city's voice only stilled for brief intervals; then it died down almost completely, came back to life, and gradually was still. Sky had begun to show between the buildings, turning then into great patches of blue.

And now they were skirting the Rivière des Prairies. Telephone poles flanked the road, their wires strung over narrow fields; there were, as yet, only occasional clumps of skimpy trees; on the other side of the river a suburb stretched its neat rows of houses. The grass was not yet truly green.

To the left stood the penitentiary. But Alexandre happened to be looking out on the river side.

And he who essentially knew no other world than that of the city, its lampposts, its street numbers, was now quitting it, astonished, disturbed as though he were being released from prison.

What space, what light, what freedom!

TWO

LE GARDEUR led the way, clearing a path through the raspberries and wild roses, Alexandre following as best he could; he kept stumbling, worn out by too much air and sun. Here he was—he who had thought the home of solitude to be in some faraway Pacific Isle—headed into a forest of his own country, less than a day's journey distant, with the feeling of an adventure beyond recall. The brambles tore threads out of his brown suit, which he reproached himself for having subjected to the ordeals of such an expedition. For indeed Monsieur Chenevert had set off in his best clothes; as he struggled through briary swamps and clouds of mosquitoes, he still looked as though he were on his way to his bank. And yet, after such an escapade, how ever could he go back there, even find his way back? His very reasons for suffering had been, as it were, stripped from him along the way, had become trifling, meaningless. Here whom could he touch, whom could he move? Alexandre had reached that stage on his voyage where what you feel is not yet an illusion of beginning anew, but much rather of coming to an end. Occasionally from a thick clump of bushes, from a tangle of tall grass, there would emerge just his tiny visage, furrowed with weariness, emotion, and a tearing impatience to discover whether what he here would find would at last be happiness.

They came to a cabin built of rough planking. On one side a succession of peacefully contoured little hills, on the other a vast area covered with spruce. The valley thus defined opened upon a small lake, and no other dwelling looked upon it, no travelled road led to it.

The sun was on its way down; over the most distant vista of the lake it cast a showery glow, sulphur yellow and purple. Elsewhere the sky was suffused with a diminished light just sufficient to illumine the woods which enclosed this wild bit of countryside. Over all reigned a silence that long held Alexandre captive. The peace of the valley smote him like a reproach. Vain was your restlessness, without purpose your anguish, without merit your suffering, all of it useless sad silence to this spent man. And besides, have you really suffered? nature asked him; unable in this place to assert that he had, Alexandre bowed his head; he felt that in all the world there was no man more naked.

"How quiet it is!" he remarked in a sort of wail.

With a push of his knee the farmer shoved in the door. It creaked on its hinges. Alexandre breathed in a musty, stuffy smell. He could not yet clearly make out the interior, cocking his head a little to one side in an attitude of suspicious curiosity. The farmer pulled aside a scrap of curtain stretched over the small window set in the door, and the cabin sprang to life, yet so small that Alexandre, used as he was to confined spaces, could not help a stealthy glance of disappointment. Never would he have thought it possible that, if anyone were to take the trouble to build a house, he could have built it so tiny. Naturally it was only a single room, and yet a complete dwelling, with stove, door, and windows, so that it conveyed to a solemn Alexandre the impression of poking fun at all domestic organization. In such close quarters, would it be possible for him even to think—such was his odd fear. Too much space outside, not enough inside; the curious law of living alone put him out of countenance. And yet he already felt better here, safer than under the overwhelming sky. Throwing a hasty glance about him, he realized that one of his life's deep needs was beginning to be satisfied. For was it not of this sort that he had desired earthly possessions—things unimportant, very humble, cut to the essential, little cumbersome to him as a mere traveller toward another world?

"Yes, yes," said Alexandre, "I think all this will do me very well."

"Fine! Fine!" applauded the farmer, who had watched with a certain anxiety the reaction of the city gentleman.

His mind now at rest upon this point, he set about listing the facilities of the place: "Your cooking equipment," he remarked, tapping a small black frying pan and a chipped cup hanging from the wall.

He leaned under the bed and laughed as he pulled out a basin in which reposed a clean towel and a cake of soap. "That's to wash with," said he. "My old lady has thought of everything. She's filled your lamp with oil, and there's stove wood alongside the house. Anyway, if there's anything missing, just holler!"

Finally he took a chair and made himself at home, explaining: "We've been put in this world, the way I look at it, to give each other a helping hand. Isn't that a fact, Monsieur Chenevert? . . . Chenevert . . . Seems to me I've already run across a man with that name. . . . No, I guess it was Boisvert. You're from Montreal, eh? Quite a town, quite a town! You came by bus, of course. Lots of people. The world certainly is full of people these days!"

He was a square-built, heavy shouldered man, dressed in coarse blue work clothes who, between questions, tried to put new life into his pipe by three or four long, sucking draughts. His hair was a bundle of reddish hemp, and under heavy eyelids of the same fibre, gay eyes were wrinkled in a perpetual smile, which allowed you to see in their deep blue only a constant crackle of curiosity. Etienne Le Gardeur was certainly as Alexandre had imagined him, except that he had neglected the likelihood that he would be so talkative.

On his way in, Alexandre had already had to put up with half a hundred questions, commingled with bits of life history which he was the last man in the world to have solicited—for instance, how he, Le Gardeur, had left the Lake Saint John region to settle here, and the labour of clearing he had undertaken. In the midst of all this, he had begun the history of the cabin, which had been erected by a Russian he referred to as the Character. And here he was beginning all over again:

"My Russian character—just imagine—was camping out here in your cabin when I bought the land. There was plenty of room for the two of us, as you can very well see, but do you think that Russian could stand living within a mile of a Christian family? Not on your life! Off he went, with his fishnets, his snares, and his woollen bonnet, and can you give a guess where he is today, Mister? . . . It's always been my opinion that the Russians are the strangest characters of all. . . ."

With a weary gesture, Alexandre indicated that perhaps that was true. His sympathies were beginning to turn definitely in the Russian's direction, who had certainly been driven into the depths of the wilderness by such a stream of loquacity. To have come so far, thought he, only to be forced to endure this discrimination between races of people, so belittling to man. He shifted from one foot to another. The day's emotions had worn him out. Indeed the only thing that kept him going was a vast, impatient curiosity: even here, would he be happy? For him there could be no question of pushing on still farther, like his predecessor.

"Strange people, all these foreigners," Le Gardeur continued, but with less animation. "Very strange; not one bit like us . . ."

In his narrator's joy, he had barely noticed before that he might as well have been talking to himself, so little encouragement did Monsieur Chenevert give him. Now, though, everything about his tenant seemed to him stiff and unfriendly—the withered little smile with which he greeted humorous remarks, the eyes travelling back and forth behind the glasses, "like a rabbit looking for cover in the woods," Le Gardeur told himself. Quite nonplussed, he felt loath to leave his tenant with an unfortunate impression. For an instant he wondered whether it might have arisen from his not having shown enough cordiality. Both he and his "old lady," ever since they had put the advertisement in the paper, had lived on tenterhooks and—it must be admitted—with a feeling of friendliness toward the guest who might come their way. Le Gardeur did not know how to break away. He seemed to be going, and then returned, announcing without conviction, as though he could not resign himself to Alexandre's lack of enthusiasm, "Perhaps you'd rather be by yourself. Some folk prefer their own company. So I guess I'll be telling you good night."

But he repeated his offers of service : "Whatever you could possibly need. Why are we in this world, if not to help each other? That's what I always say. . . ."

"Yes, yes," said Alexandre.

He heaved a sigh when Le Gardeur finally closed the door behind him. Yet only a little later, when the silence proved that the farmer had really gone, he had the feeling of having been abandoned to his fate. No sound. Not a voice. Only a great, silent reproach. He stood on the threshold of the cabin, a tiny man, his hat perched on the side of his head. In his hand he still held one of his gloves. And in all his life nothing had ever made him feel so alone as this landscape so deeply at peace and foreign, in its way, to his cares as a human being. Only the crows were stirring at this hour, and they fitfully perched on the sparse tops of spruce trees. One of them cried out and flew over the valley, beating its sooty wings.

Alexandre wandered off toward the lake; but after five or six steps he hesitated, and changed direction toward the woods, soon again coming to a halt. He had made only a tiny circle around himself. Then, stripped bare, he surveyed the vastness of the world as it had been made ready for him. Night was coming. The valley took on a grey hue of abandonment. From its centre, the lake cast a reflection like an old, pock-marked mirror. This evil radiance seemed to give the human consciousness a glance at once indifferent, without pity, and cruelly frank.

"It's beautiful, it's very beautiful," murmured Alexandre, his heart in anguish.

Suddenly the light faded. And already Alexandre was in another world. The edges of the lake had lost definition and were confused with the shadow of great fallen trees. These vast masses of shadow suggested grotesque and bewildering forms to Alexandre's imagination. He thought he could make out a mammoth bear, rearing on its hind legs and advancing toward him with a great knotted stick in its paw. He walked toward the monster, forced himself to touch it, and it turned into a huge gnarled tree with a hanging branch.

Near him twigs cracked.

Alexandre jumped, became exasperated at so many silly apprehensions. "It's some little animal of the woods," he told himself.

Then, above his head, the clouds spoke to him out of the void about the unknown. Voices of distress, long sighs whispered through the air; the invisible which had been uttering its plaints seemed to chuckle, very high up, above the treetops.

"The wind," said Alexandre to himself.

He entered the cabin and lit the lamp. And he heard a very odd, fragile sound, which had even followed him indoors and persisted when he forced himself into complete immobility. At last he realized that this disturbance was the sound of his own breathing.

He tried to smile at his terrors.

He unfastened his tie and lay down on the cot.

And then, without any further possibility of subterfuge, he knew that he was in the presence of her who had called him, seduced him, deceived him, whom he sometimes thought he loved, and whom in very fact he had never encountered—solitude.

What manner of thing was this?

On spring evenings, because there was no one who thought as he did, he had imagined he was alone; but now he saw it; what he had taken for solitude was good and comforting: at least the streets were illuminated; all night long the electric lights burned there; bits and snatches of radio music stole from open windows; you could glance inside dwellings and share in the lives of strangers; and to the sound of Alexandre's footsteps there responded the footsteps of thousands of other men who perhaps also thought themselves alone.

At other moments, in these same streets, elbowed and pushed aside by others, he had complained that he lacked solitude. Oh foolish and human pretence!

Even absorbed within her, Alexandre could not succeed in seeing what she was. A good? An evil?

He slept even less than in the city.

On the ceiling shone the light of his lamp, and in the air current set in motion by this tiny bit of heat, a fragment of spider web trembled, a tenuous fragment that even the lightest breath would have torn into nothingness.

Greater and greater grew the impression of emptiness around Alexandre.

Solitude seemed to be absence; absence of everything—of men, of the past, of the future, of unhappiness and of happiness —an utter stripping. Yet, at the centre of this absence, there was something like a glance, which overlooked no thought, no action of Alexandre Chenevert's. Was it God Who in this deep night, far in the dark bush, had again sought out Alexandre? What could be the reason for such unswerving attention? What could God want with Alexandre who was on holiday? On whom the doctor had urged rest. Here God reigned in His most ambiguous aspect.

Those dark stirrings, those clouds, this exhausted creature in this unfamiliar place—all tonight seemed to dread Him.

Close as he was to his happiness, Alexandre was very near to forswearing it, to setting out at once on foot toward the Le Gardeurs' and asking them for hospitality and succour. Yet what man can protect another against God!

As soon as the sun had risen, Alexandre hastily left the cabin.

Perhaps, in the open light, he hoped at last to wrest from solitude her secret.

But now her visage was benign, soft, and pleasant. The dew shone upon the grass, woven into a carpet of numberless little insect webs. Alexandre had to touch it, to see it dissolve at the tips of his fingers to understand that the mere condensation of water could yield this extraordinary effect. The shadowy masses on the other side of the lake were nothing more than beneficent trees, varieties which Alexandre, who was not utterly ignorant of botany, readily recognized—maples, pines, a few mountain ashes, larches, the spruce family above all. The scent of their resin was in the air. As for the mysterious reach of water, yesterday a snare to his consciousness, it was merely a small lake, about a mile long where it stretched the farthest and, at its broadest, scarcely a quarter as much. Alexandre's eyes could easily take it all in at once.

Moreover, in the morning, solitude spoke the consoling language of indifference. The trees bent over, told Alexandre that they lived for a time, died, were replaced and that this was all for the good.

The beauty of this cool morning, which already spoke some hint of autumn, said as much.

Here there was no trace of pity left . . . what rest for the weary!

Alexandre grew soothed, cut down to the measure of passing things.

He watched the grass at his feet as the wind flattened it into long paths; birds flitted to and fro, a score of species, exquisite, the like of which he had never seen, even in pictures; distant clouds drifted by; and he identified himself with a secret understanding between the heart and the innocent, tractable elements of creation. Was he himself anything more than one of these green and supple reeds? And yet autumn was already beginning to wither them. The valley lay in the sunlight, level almost throughout its length, save at one or two places where slight rises allowed Alexandre to envisage it as a whole—calm, happy, spared.

At the coming of night, his soul began to be uneasy, but rather at memories of the night before than at any expectation of the unknown. Suffocating a few brief hours before, solitude had become familiar like life itself, and like it something you could make your peace with.

"How strange," thought Alexandre. "One grows accustomed to everything. I wonder whether there is any kind of life to which men, in the long run, cannot adapt themselves?"

He noticed that he was an almost constant source of astonishment to himself. Here was Alexandre's first pleasure in solitude: to discover within himself as many promises of the unknown as he would in a stranger.

That night he slept much better, yet not altogether perfectly. His sleep had too long been fitful. It still weighed upon his bemused conscience as time stolen from all those on earth who continued to suffer and to labour.

Alexandre Chenevert dreamed. He was at the Savings Bank of the City and Island of Montreal. His gooseneck lamp was lit, the great ledger was spread before his eyes, and he was doing sums. But at the bottom of each column his memory lost the figure he must carry over into the next. So he would begin all over again. And abruptly, instead of dollars and cents, what he was adding up were the Chinese. "Don't miss a single one of them," Monsieur Fontaine kept insisting. "It's very important that not one of them be missing. The collector of income taxes has asked me to balance them up, to the very last man. You know—for the use of God the Father." But it was hard to keep the book up to date. "You can't imagine," said Alexandre, "how quickly the Chinese die, how quickly they replace themselves, what with their famines and their revolutions. I'd have to have an adding machine to keep count of the men alone, and is it absolutely necessary to keep track of these Chinese? There are so many of them. One of these days they're going to spill over the whole world. You know, the yellow peril! Would it not be more humane to let them die of their hunger, since later on we'll have to wage war against them?"

His lips, his hands, his head were all shaking. Lying in profile against his pillow, outlined by the dull glow from the rectangle of the little window, his face betrayed its suffering.

Then someone came and carried off the book, closing it and hurling it far into the lake. There was something like a slight plopping sound. Almost at once the ripples in the lake died away.

And then it was all over. Alexandre slept as it befits a man to sleep.

CHAPTER XII

HE WAS quitting this world, his eyelids quiet, his arms gently stretched along his sides, like a drowned man whose face is turned toward the sky. Over his relaxed features there played only a reflection of water and the glow of the moon. He was floating down a long river of forgetfulness, and he himself was this river, free and sable. He no longer had any least recollection of any task, required or interrupted. He was delivered from God and from men. No longer was Alexandre answerable for original sin, nor yet for those weapons of our day so dangerous that men journey to test them on desert islands. Had there been, in times gone by, Chinese who died by the thousand in lands too arid? A scheme to make barren Palestine fruitful? Alexandre had forgotten. No longer did he know a person on earth; he knew not even who he was. His lips parted slightly; he looked at peace. Alexandre Chenevert? What was he doing in the world? It must have been a century since last he set foot in the bank. The door to his cage must have been left ajar; the papers had blown away: precious registers and account books. Melted away, the man with the beaked nose . . . Alexandre had no more past and—even greater freedom—no future.

Without a goal, inert and swept along, he floated.

Under the ruddy moon, between the spruce trees, the lake sent against its banks a ripple of wavelets, a drowsy song, which murmured an accompaniment to Alexandre Chenevert's deliverance. The blunted brain registered just the right number of images. The colours were beyond compare, the depths so lovely to explore in this watery abyss through which he journeyed.

The intoxication of sinking between secret shores, more thickly green than the night! How ravishing the blue fronds which curled about his limbs and then slipped by! The quality of the silence in this muffled land! The unutterable absence of all life, except for the water's even and continuous murmur. Even the trees here did not tremble or grow, but were fixed fast in high, stylized branches, which for centuries on end had held their pendant flowers. In brown inlets, the water stood stagnant, bearing great petaled cups of moss. Oh! The matchless release of the man asleep!

Who has not realized through experience that sleep tells the truth about us? In sleep a human being is finally brought back to himself, having sloughed off everything else. Bound hand and foot, fettered with fatigue, he at last drifts toward the caverns of the unknown.

Some men have returned therefrom with poems fully written, or with equations solved.

As he slept, Alexandre smiled a little. Once his hand sought to rise, as though to catch at some alluring object. Then it slumped back, yielding, full of trust, unconcerned.

His forehead became pale and smooth. Inert and unsullied flesh, without crease or wrinkle.

Alexandre was asleep. A thin branch, impelled by the wind, knocked at the window and then drew back. There were moments when this frond impressed its delicate shadow on Alexandre's face. For six hours on end he had been sleeping.

Through sleep God permitted His creature from time to time to believe that he was free.

Meanwhile Alexandre's eyelids began to flicker feebly; then they came to rest and remained tight-closed. Air bubbles came up to burst on the water's surface and stirred a little the circles of pollen. A wind trembled through the airy boughs. This paradise which Alexandre's long distress extracted from his subconsciousness possessed that frozen wisdom and refinement one finds in Japanese prints.

Just as though God had decreed the earth's revolution, as it circles round the sun, merely not to have to behold suffering, at least for half the time!

To Him, too, there is perhaps something pleasant in beholding a man asleep, with his hands open at his sides, his feet joined together, and his head nestled in the pillow.

But now a bird was whistling a few scattered notes through Alexandre's slumber. And the sleeper, whose memory had begun to function once more, knew that the bird's wings must be spotted with bright red. The first signs of life were beginning to break into this silent country through a slow passage toward conciousness. Before he was quite aware of himself, Alexandre perceived the freshness of the morning. The bird's cry became more distinct, closer at hand. As gently as a long, supple, and ultimate wave washes its froth and flowers ashore, sleep laid Alexandre on the threshold of the day.

He opened his eyes, and without the least shock, knew at once that this was an August morning in the country.

He raised an elbow to the pillow; on the window sill a squirrel watched him, nibbling a bit of bread.

Alexandre dared not move.

He felt a gentle pleasure at finding himself robbed by this graceful beast. Life seemed to him innocent.

Whether it was an illusion of sleep or—quite the opposite—a very lucid perception on the boundary of the world of dreams, at the instant when he awoke Alexandre thought he perceived something like a presence which unfastened itself from him, a vague form which regretfully drew away.

A feeling of childhood swathed Alexandre.

And so began the most beautiful day of his life.

Some few men, when you ask them to single out the days when they have been happy, can hesitate between three or four. As he opened his eyes, Alexandre knew that this day would be the best.

It alone was such as all life should be.

CHAPTER XIII

VERY LIKELY the benign presence had not withdrawn very far from Alexandre. He had no reason to seek it in one place more than another, in this quiet countryside, or even on the face of this earth. For Alexandre had a very settled notion that Heaven can only be at some great distance. Somewhere way beyond the clouds was where his imagination placed the presence that filled him to overflowing. And who could it be if it were not God once more? For who else would have taken so much trouble with Alexandre and would so constantly have sought him out? This contentment, seeping through the valley, pierced him with a certainty of God such as he had never yet experienced.

He jumped briskly out of bed.

For twenty years, thirty years, he had suffered from city noises—barking dogs, slamming doors, clanking milk bottles. And now within three days he had grown used to waking naturally.

Another thing, and very odd too : normally, when he talked to himself, it was with bitterness, to say something derogatory about himself or about others. And now the thoughts that crossed his mind were joyous thoughts—you might almost call them trivial.

He had become a stranger to himself, and living with this stranger was far easier, a thousand times pleasanter than living with the old Alexandre.

He washed and dressed with care, just as in days gone by, when through cleanliness and discipline he tried to arm himself for a worthy, undeviating life.

Already the sun had generously invaded his tiny domain. This morning he found it sufficiently ample and very adequately furnished. Was it the Russian or was it Le Gardeur who had made it so comfortable? Someone well acquainted with Alexandre's tastes could have done no better. Everything you needed was here : an old and rusty cast-iron box stove, one of those stoves you know on sight has many a night warmed a man and his thoughts; a bucket to draw water—from inside the cabin you could hear the spring murmuring—a narrow bed, two sets of shelves, a deal table.

Alexandre looked with pity upon men who burdened themselves with the building of costly stone dwellings, not to mention country houses, which they then proceeded to hem in with iron fences, ending with gatekeepers' lodges.

He was lathering his hollow cheeks, constantly turning around, shaving brush in hand, to cast a glance of understanding at the stove and the tiny collection of pots and pans.

Gradually he, Alexandre Chenevert was reaching the conclusion that he was happier than the greater part of mankind.

He became aware that he was hungry.

To feel hunger and satisfy it—here was a pleasure he had almost forgotten.

He puttered about at the stove. He had suddenly felt a longing to eat potatoes seared and stewed with salt pork, a dish for which he had yearned for some time, but one which, since it upset his stomach, he had flatly dismissed as unrefined. Today he seemed none the worse for it; quite the opposite, he was less uncomfortable than after his ordinary meals of dull vegetables and milk puddings.

Then, no longer hungry, and spared his habitual discomfort after eating, Alexandre felt free.

Even yesterday he had clung to his practice of dividing his day into a schedule of drudgery; he had felt obliged to do such and such a thing during the morning, something else in the afternoon. He was the slave of time.

From now on he would let his impulses rule.

With his hands clasped behind his back, he set out to circle the lake on foot. His bearing put you in mind of a city dweller strolling through the streets, but of one who, instead of other pedestrians and billboards, was scrutinizing trees, a bustling anthill, a hornets' nest. It soon occurred to him that there might be occupations better suited to the day's heat; a slightly acrid odour emanating from the water powerfully attracted him.

He looked for Le Gardeur's rowboat and found it tied to the root of a willow which leaned out over the lake.

And then it was that Alexandre discovered what morning is : the time for decision, for letting yourself go, for enthusiasm, the time which restores to man the full bloom of his will; a setting-forth, a fresh journey !

Awkwardly he tried to row a few strokes, but succeeded only in slapping the water with the flat of his oars. No matter— he was moving away from shore. He had a feeling of adventure and even—a joyful thing—of a certain peril. For Alexandre had no notion of how to swim; and indeed he had not much idea of how to manage oars. But in the morning, does not everything seem easy to learn? He progressed a little further toward open water. Then he had to ship his oars to catch his breath. A gentle current and barely perceptible breeze continued to propel him. And Alexandre attained a joy beyond belief. Something happened to him better than anything yet vouchsafed: he felt young.

Not as he had at thirty, naturally.

Nor yet as he felt at forty.

All the same, Alexandre had the delight of having shed a few years from his life. He no longer felt their weight. He still retained the wisdom, the lessons those years had taught him, but neither their weariness nor their wear and tear.

He started rowing again; almost at once the bottom of the boat struck a rocky shoal. He took advantage of this halt to light a small corncob pipe he had bought at Saint Donat. At the time he had told himself that smoking such a pipe could not be as harmful as cigarettes. And now he was pensive, basking in that self-gratification of a man who thinks it in order to grant himself a favour, as a reward for being happy.

Here is what you might have beheld that day in this remote corner of the world:

First, a sheet of water quivering with light; at its centre, barely stirring, a rowboat. In it a man sat quietly, his legs spread apart.

He was smoking.

An ancient straw hat with a frayed brim shaded his face. His pale neck was exposed by a light sport shirt which made him seem youthful.

From time to time the man cupped the bowl of his pipe in one hand and drew on it mightily. He was wholly surrounded by blue smoke, quite distinguishable in the clarity of the air.

The rowboat rocked him in its cradle.

The man glanced first at one bank, then at the other, both equally free of all intruders. And at that moment he loved all his fellows on this earth.

What other good thing befell him? In truth, nothing of extraordinary moment. He grew hungry and he ate. He was thirsty and he drank. He felt a natural, wholesome fatigue, and he lay down under the branches of a pine tree, his old hat pulled over his eyes. He thought thoughts, welling up from within him as on every other day, but they were no longer his enemies. Very few people would have seen in this something to make a man thank God that God exists. Yet for Alexandre here was a gift from Heaven which he received with thankfulness.

From joy to joy the day carried him on toward evening. And then he discovered the night.

It was like a moment of motherly concern. Night bade the birds fold their tired wings, close their beaks so long busy with pecking after food. It stilled the anxious trembling of the aspens. It wandered here and there, unseen and full of heed, like a lonely woman seeking to pledge and share a secret.

A pail over his arm, Alexandre made his way toward the spring, which he could hear and which thus served him as guide through the woods.

He placed his feet in the spoor left by some large animal. In the clearing flooded with moonlight, the water shone and ceaselessly laved some curly greenery. Alexandre marvelled at this delicate stream. He turned his face toward the distant point in the heavens where he still situated his Creator, and he did not fail to thank Him. But when he had scooped up water in a cup left at hand for this purpose, since he was neither ungrateful nor stupid, he recognized that the ingenuity of man played a large part in his well-being.

He needed a little light. With a wholly automatic movement he struck several matches. But before even two of these little sulphur-tipped wooden sticks had been consumed, he realized, in the blackness of the trees, their fabulous usefulness. The most trifling invention, beginning with the pail, here bore witness to man's brotherhood.

Never had Alexandre felt upon his forehead and his lips so comforting a night. His eyes lingered on the stars, seeking out the best known. That one must be Saturn. There was the Great Bear . . . the North Star. Bits of human explanation, wrested from this overwhelming universe, warmed his soul. Indeed the discovery of the world by a man leaning upon century after century of civilization dazzles the heart.

It roused in Alexandre the most solemn astonishment. He stumbled in the tracks the great beast had left behind it. At almost every step the water slopped over as he moved along, scanning the sky through the black branches.

Now Alexandre suddenly noticed a glow which seemed to be coming to meet him through the forest.

"Who could that possibly be?"

Then he became aware that it was he who was approaching the light, and that it shone from the lamp burning in his cabin.

Never before had he thus approached his tiny dwelling, by night, drawn near the bright windows which seemed to betoken gentleness, the attraction of earthly security.

For that matter, never had he approached in such fashion

any lodging he had ever had. At first he would recognize them by the street number; then, thanks to a certain corkscrew stair-way, some tiny store in the basement, Coca-Cola advertisements, he would know that he was home; later on, habit alone would carry him there, at set hours, tired, indifferent like an old horse returning to his stable. Never had a flame of his own greeted him, at the day's end, with a real and symbolic bit of fire.

And it delighted his soul.

"My flame of light," said he to himself, savouring the idea.

Didn't people say, "See how the lights flicker in that valley"?

No other image seemed to him a more vivid expression of shelter, earthly continuity, the little comforts of this world.

He walked at a brisk pace toward his true dwelling, and no one recognized better than he what folly it is to bind one's heart to temporal things.

Until now he had thought of it as "the cabin."

This evening he began to say, "my cabin, my lake, my God."

It was not cold; you could hardly even call it a cool evening, but Alexandre made a fire.

For the moments while, over a scrap of paper, tiny twigs smoked before catching fire, he looked anxious. Yet little by little the wood caught flame, and the rays of the fire flickered over Alexandre's features. Stooped a little, he watched it like some great novelty. He pulled up the cabin's only chair. He sat down near his stove as a man sits near a friend, his legs slightly straddled. The branches crackled and Alexandre listened, his head bent.

Here was the history of the world ever since men's first efforts to make it more liveable. There was a time, the fire said, when no one knew me. Can you imagine so sad a thing : not a fire anywhere on God's earth !

Then there was a human being who one day whiled away the time by rubbing one stone against another; he saw a spark spring into life. In order to recapture this brilliance, this fleeting colour, he began once more to knock his stones together.

"I was the first friend of men," said the fire.

"It was around me that they first began to gather together. Before that they remained distant, each going his own way, all of them snarling and afraid."

Alexandre had placed his feet on the projecting front of the stove. His features, as they bent over, were suffused with a red glow which at moments illuminated them to the depths of the eyes. His pupils took on a dreamy quality, a friendliness no human being had ever seen in them before. It must indeed have been at a fire's warmth, he reflected, that the hardness of men began to melt.

And then—ultimate benediction within a single day—it began to rain. Alexandre listened to that delicate sound, so pleasing to the ears, of raindrops against the windows, against the door, upon the roof of a good tight house, alone in the midst of the forest. Only a single crack through which the water might enter would have been enough to dispel the comfortable impression. But Alexandre's little house was sound; it very adequately defied the rain.

He felt for him who had built it that same deep friendship aroused within us when we behold a lovely tree along a roadside, friendship for the unknown person who long ago planted it there.

Within one day alone, how many joyful impressions can make their impact upon a human heart when it is free to give them welcome!

For not yet had Alexandre reached the end of his contentment.

He heard a scratching at the door.

"What can that be? At such an hour!" he asked himself, more surprised than frightened.

He went to open the door, but the first glance he gave his visitor was none too kindly.

It was the little black farm dog. Twice already he had trotted through the woods as far as Alexandre's cabin. He had stopped short on a flat stone and had lavished every sort of hint that he would like to be invited further. He had whimpered, his muzzle laid against his outstretched paws, while his eyes followed the man's unresponsive movements. His tail thumped upon the ground; obstinately he proffered his affection.

Alexandre had picked up a stick to threaten the intruder. "I want no dog here," he had informed him.

And he had continued gathering other bits of wood, but more for the purpose of getting a supply for his fire. The timid little black form had streaked off among the trees.

But this time the dog had screwed his courage not only to the point of returning, but actually of scratching at Alexandre's door.

"What do you want?" he asked him.

Blacky sat on his haunches to plead his case, his eyes timorous. He was one of those unsettled, fickle beasts, seeking affection indiscriminately, from tramps, along the highways and byways. Alexandre never suspected that in the person of Blacky he would be admitting to his home friendship under its most delusive aspect. He opened the screen door.

"What's your name?"

The dog wriggled in, twisting and dragging his after-end, so overcome that his whole body doubled itself into a half-circle, and he seemed to be backing away from rather than advancing toward his friend. Beyond any imagining had he been attracted to Alexandre's tiny light, hidden deep away in the woods.

"You silly little animal!" said Alexandre.

He went to get the dog some of what remained from his supper. Stuffed with the leavings of the farm, Blackie pretended, purely through politeness, to taste a morsel, while giving the man a devastating glance out of the corner of his eye. To his own surprise, Alexandre extended his hand to caress the damp coat. His austere affection, embittered by so many disappointments, really was coming back to life in a most curious way. This morning it had gone out to the squirrel who had stolen some of his bread; this evening it welcomed a dog whose humility was almost abject. But in animals the defects of men suddenly made Alexandre grow tender.

"Come on now! Lie down and keep quiet!"

He resumed his place near the stove. He must have dozed a few minutes erect on his straight chair, his chin slumped against his chest. Then he awoke and noted with a certain joy that he was not wholly alone; the dog at his feet was explaining to him with his eyes: "Yes, indeed, I'm here with you. We're always a bit more at our ease when there are two of us. Even a dog knows that much."

Then—was it thanks to his companion or to some old book read years before?—Alexandre's heart seized upon that ancient human dream, the dream of Robinson Crusoe!

He yielded to it.

Might he not tame the squirrel who had come to pilfer some of his bread? Perhaps a crow next—picturing it as a garrulous pet, following him wherever he went. It did not seem impossible to him to become a beekeeper, perhaps a settler, and live here without wrath and in goodness all his life. As for clothes, it ought to be possible to learn how to make them out of elk skin. No longer would he have any need of his fellow men; to no one among them would he be debtor. From thenceforth, how could he continue harming anyone, even God? Such was his dream that evening, in the glow of the dying fire.

The next day he awoke less happy, already a little distraught. As in other times, his first thought was a sort of mental calculation; how many days of his vacation had he already used up? How many had he left? It pained him to see the time passing too quickly now.

He went out onto his porch. Humble as it might be, the cabin possessed certain elements of luxury: two windows and a sort of small balcony built of rough planks supported at either end by two frail posts. Of the whole domain, it was this porch Alexandre liked best of all.

From it you had a wonderful view over the lake. And on it you were more at your ease than in the open, for the light roof over it protected you against the sun. Then too, there he was in his own home.

Yet this morning the small balcony facing the lake, the chair he had installed on it, his doorstep, all made him heartsick, so perfect was it here. The thought that he did not possess this happiness forever made of it a misery. From the way he looked at his porch and his wicker chair, you would have thought that Alexandre wanted to assure himself of their being his until he died.

"I still have a week," he told himself.

But what did a week amount to now!

He surveyed everything around him with almost as much mistrust as affection. Then abruptly the expression of his features slipped from hesitancy to determination. Alexandre put the padlock on the door and went off in the direction of the woods where he knew he would find Le Gardeur busy felling trees.

He came to a field in the process of being cleared, sprinkled with those mauve flowers which grow so profusely with their fragile fronds of flowers everywhere in Canada where the forest has been cut and gathered into piles of brush. Seeing him moving along through the stumps and swarms of black flies, the farmer came to meet him, wiping his hand against his cotton garment. The sturdy fellow tramped amid the flowers and called out cordially, "Oh! So there you are! I had almost made up my mind to go root you out and see if you were still alive."

With his wife he had discussed at length the peculiar individual who had come to them, his supplies bought in advance, who had refused to stop off a moment at their house and who ever since repelled every attempt at neighbourliness. Had he done some evil in the world that he should be so unsociable? Never had the Le Gardeurs thought it possible they could run across anyone more misanthropic than the Russian, and yet they had to admit the facts. Then, too, the other man had been of foreign blood, which up to a certain point could explain his shyness. "But a French Canadian, just like us!" Le Gardeur kept repeating morning, noon, and night. "What could we have done to him?" He took as a personal affront such a barrier of solitude erected between two people of the same tongue. At times he had a half-notion that the cabin might be responsible for the kind of individual it sheltered. "Two strangers," he had explained to his wife; "you'd think that that cabin is fated to harbour strangers." However the sight of his tenant at last seeking him out for the purpose of being sociable soothed Le Gardeur's sensitiveness.

"Well, Monsieur Chenevert, is there something I can do for you?"

"As a matter of fact . . ."

What Alexandre really had to say was far from any possibility of blunt statement. True enough, he had always lived on illusions, but he was used to the rigour of figures, and if they were to convince him, his illusions must bear reality's stamp of approval. And in translating his idea into words he hesitated lest he give it a twist which would compromise its worth. From his cautious sentences, from his prudent queries, it ultimately emerged that he wanted to know whether "a man could wrest his livelihood from these woods? A city man, for instance, without any training at roughing it?"

He had been at much pains to avoid indicating what he had in mind.

He had said it explicitly: "A man, let's say any man in general."

"Oh! So that's what's on your mind!" said Le Gardeur.

And he started laughing, as though at a riddle that was really too easy. To him who had lived happily, well-fed, comfortable and cheery, among his hills, there was not the least doubt that a man, any man in general, could make himself a living there.

"Well, I'll tell you something, Monsieur Chenevert," shoving his cap onto the back of his head; "it's in the cities that I'd think it hard to make a living. Pale, thin folk, people only half alive— that's the city, when you get right down to it. But here!" he added, taking in the countryside with a sweeping gesture.

To find himself so sure of his subject restored the farmer to his natural good humour.

He took Alexandre by the arm. "Come, Monsieur Chenevert; come along with me, I'll show you a sight worth seeing, just in case you haven't seen it yourself yet. Come along, now, and let me really show you something!"

CHAPTER XIV

THEY CAME to the western end of the lake. They were on a point of land which stretched out far into the water and was clothed in young willows stirred by sunny gusts of wind. The lake bottom was of white sand and fine pebbles, and the water so clear that a quick glance might have judged it rather shallow.

"The lake is twenty feet deep here," said Le Gardeur. "Come close, Monsieur Chenevert. Don't be afraid; the footing is good and firm. Take a look. You'll see enough fish in there to last out Lent for a heap of Christians."

Alexandre looked fixedly at the spot indicated by the farmer. Droplets of water on his glasses obscured his vision. He took them off, wiped them carefully, put them back on, and then the bank teller's eager eyes beheld a multitude of shadowy forms, some brownish, others slightly roseate, drifting over the pebbles.

"Grey trout, sunfish, speckled trout—there are all sorts in there," said Le Gardeur. "I don't think you could fish it out if you tried. And if you've a mind to, Monsieur Chenevert, try your luck. My own lines and poles are right here handy."

He lifted a light covering of branches and uncovered a complete if rough and ready fishing outfit.

Alexandre's old straw hat leaned toward the rich store of fish. He saw flashing through the water bluish backs and streaks of silver which enchanted him. His liking for beauty and for security was satisfied at once in both its objects.

"There are hundreds . . . maybe thousands of them!" he exclaimed.

"Sure enough," Le Gardeur agreed.

And he gave proof that in his own season he could meditate, reach conclusions, philosophize.

"What I say is, the good Lord piles it on; do you follow me, Monsieur Chenevert? When He furnishes something, He does a thorough job of it. And don't get the idea that He's only provided for our fast days. Do you want a bit of meat? Well, then turn around quickly, but don't make a racket. Over there, above the ledge, do you see something moving in the branches? A moose, Monsieur; that's a moose."

Alexandre keenly searched the woods in the direction indicated by Le Gardeur's outstretched arm.

"A beauty!" the farmer elaborated. "They always come along the heights. Right at that same spot last fall I killed one which must have weighed about fifteen hundred pounds. My wife canned a lot of it. We sent some fine cuts to her relatives down near the city. We ate it to our heart's content."

"Our heart's content!" Alexandre repeated.

It seemed to him he had never heard an expression more to his liking.

"And you can see that it doesn't cost much," Le Gardeur continued. "A rifle, a couple of cartridges, a short walk through the woods, and there you are with meat for the winter."

The frail desk worker, stumbling through the undergrowth alongside the nimble farmer, asked, "How do you go about it? Is it difficult?"

"It takes a bit of practice," stated Le Gardeur. "You find yourself cover in heavy growth. Naturally you move against the wind. You take your stand behind a tree. You wait for the animal to come down to the water. Then . . . bing! you shoot him straight between the eyes."

"Oh!" said Alexandre, paling. "That must be hard. I don't think I could do it."

"Monsieur Chenevert," returned the other defensively, "if you didn't kill the deer and moose in woods like these, they'd certainly make plenty of mess here!"

"What's the lake called?" asked Alexandre.

Le Gardeur scratched his head, then he quite simply admitted, "We all call it just 'the Lake.' But wait a moment; I think it has a name. If I remember right, the prospectors christened it 'Lac Vert' . . . I think that's it . . . something like that. Yes, I believe it's 'Lac Vert.'"

This was very likely true. North of a certain latitude in Quebec nature had been seen by simple people who loved it without romantic overtones. Bodies of water were called "Round Lake," "Red Lake," "Lone Lake"; above all were there hosts of "Green Lakes"—"Lacs Vert."

This commonplace name was not displeasing to Alexandre. It was easy but not at all vague. The lake was in fact green. Wholly green. The deep green of the surrounding forest.

Meanwhile Le Gardeur continued to enumerate the region's advantages. To do so seemed to afford him great pleasure—the pleasure of sharing without being thereby any the poorer. Moreover Alexandre's docility as he stood beside him, the delight he took in listening to the farmer's explanations had entirely obliterated the latter's earlier feeling of being slighted.

"Not to mention the fruits, Monsieur Chenevert. There are almost too many of them. Strawberries, raspberries. Further back, behind your camping spot, there are cranberries. And apart from these, there are blueberries to burn. The children gather them by the bucketful, and in no time at all. And then there are partridges."

"Partridges too?" Alexandre avidly inquired.

"Haven't you heard them in the little thicket east of your cabin? They make enough racket, heaven knows."

"I did hear a noise occasionally, something like a small motor . . . I didn't know what . . ."

"A partridge, Monsieur, when it's beginning its flight . . . There's no better small game."

"And firewood?" asked Alexandre. "There's enough of that?"

"Enough? Monsieur Chenevert, are you joking? Just with the dry dead branches, you'd have enough for your camp all winter."

"Ah!" said Alexandre, with a look of deep satisfaction.

He had thought of every detail, and then informed himself concerning each, like a man who, before buying a domain, carefully checks its possibilities, and he was quite won over. Residence on this earth suited him. In every respect—at least in Canada—the Creator had furnished and equipped it; and although He had made it hard to kill certain animals, above all the deer with its gentle eyes, no one could say that God had been lacking in consideration for man.

"The good Lord has been generous to the Canadians," commented Alexandre.

"Right!" Le Gardeur exclaimed, laughing. "But first of all He gave it to the Indians."

"Ah! And what you say is certainly the truth," said Alexandre disconcerted, if not, indeed, even more disappointed.

"Are you thinking of settling down here for good?" asked Le Gardeur, who could no longer contain his curiosity.

"No . . . that is . . . well, no."

That was not the big point. What mattered was that Lac Vert should exist, and that Alexandre should have seen it with his own eyes. Later on it would always remain his property. To believe in an earthly Paradise—that was what he had so deeply needed.

"I won't promise I might not come some time later on," he concluded with an expression of sober joy, but unsmiling.

"Because if you take a notion to live here, I'm sure we could get together, Monsieur Chenevert," the farmer suggested. "At first—and no bones about it—we found you a bit strange. We thought you were a little on your high horse. But you're all right, when a man gets to know you a bit better. . . ."

"Perhaps . . . I'd like . . ." began Alexandre, and then grew silent.

The two men had set out along the ill-defined path that ended at the farm. Cows browsed around the stumps. A duck pond reflected a patch of sky and the tail of a white cloud. An empty hay cart, its shafts resting on the grass, cast a square shadow in an open space flooded with ruddy sunlight. And, their combs held high, two fine Rhode Island Red cocks were strutting about. The whole landscape pierced Alexandre's soul. It seemed to him he had found the spot where he would like to die.

They went on a bit further; the house came into sight.

It was the Canadian dwelling, as in the land's yesteryears. A big lean-to on its side served as kitchen during the mild season. The main body of the building was topped with a steep-pitched roof, which flattened out a little before coming to rest on the balustraded porch. Small attic windows looked out on the cleared area, and on those same purple-spired flowers Alexandre had seen on the land freshly claimed from the forest. The house had never had a coat of paint, but the wood, because of its fine quality, had decayed but little and had acquired a grey-blue tone, very ancient and cosy. Alexandre had looked at it with distaste when he had arrived. Today it pleased him. Ceremoniously he extended his hand to his companion.

"Le Gardeur," said he solemnly, "I congratulate you. You are the salt of the earth—of those who live, you understand—without filching a thing from any man."

A bit worried over this compliment, all Le Gardeur could do was laugh : "Ho ! Ho !·You're laying it on a bit thick !"

Then the person he described as "my old woman" came bustling to the kitchen doorstep. She might have been about forty at most, a woman of ample proportions, her sleeves rolled up over round arms, a lock of hair streaming in the wind. Two young children were hiding in the folds of her skirt; three or four other curious little heads peered out from behind her.

"Good-day ! Good-day ! Monsieur Chenevert," she called out in a shrill and affable voice.

Blacky, who pretended he no longer knew Alexandre, had started barking.

"Rover ! Will you shut up !" cried the farm woman

Le Gardeur seconded the order, but with more emphasis, "Stop your damn noise—go lie down !"

From the kitchen you could also hear the rumble of the cream separator, which was being cranked by the eldest daughter. In the midst of all these noises, Alexandre crossed the threshold and found himself in a large, bright room full of children, cats, saucepans, and light. On the floor a varicoloured oilcloth shone almost as brilliantly as the windows reddened by the sun.

In Quebec hospitality often finds expression in this way : in distraining the visitor, exclaiming over him, exuberantly and completely taking possession of him. Before Alexandre had had time to turn around, a generous rocking chair had been indicated to him, he had been offered a drink, and he had been constrained to stay for supper.

There are doubtless other corners of the globe where a stranger's arrival provokes a like commotion, other places where, as soon as he has crossed the doorsill, he becomes the prey of an eager need for hospitality—at lonely crossroads, in solitary huts of Provence, in the tents of Tibet, this may be so. It may even be that foreigners have as many virtues as we have in this country. But what distinguishes the welcome of rural Canadians is that it finds its expression in terms of command. Thus Edmondine Le Gardeur settled matters : "You'll stay for supper. And you'll spend the evening."

To all the embarrassed protests he tried to make, he received the same categorical reply : "Will you please sit down !"

Since he was already seated, Edmondine's command must be taken figuratively. It indicated a refusal to accept any excuse. Alexandre no longer dared budge from his chair. He was completely self-conscious. He feared he had endangered the good effect of his holiday by venturing too quickly among human beings. Surely they expected that he would be friendly and likeable. Never had Alexandre been aware within himself of any capacity for neighbourliness.

Perched on the edge of his rocker, he said by way of excuse, "In cities, you can live for years without even knowing your neighbours. To the right of where I live, for instance, there's a family named Patenaude, but for the life of me I couldn't tell you just where they work or what they do, either the father or the children."

He had turned toward Edmondine's kindly countenance. It was to her he was furnishing his explanation. For if Edmondine was awesome in her commands, she was not in the least so in her face, which was moon-shaped, open, and smiling.

"Are you really telling me the truth!" she cried. "Are you serious? I've heard tell that that was the way it goes, but I could scarcely believe it. You hear that, Etienne! Not even to know one's neighbours! Why, it must be boring enough to kill you...."

After the meal, a sort of calm descended upon this noisy household. The younger children were sent to bed. The cats were drowsing on the plaited rugs. The fire in the stove was burning low. In her own fashion Edmondine gave expression to the hour's restfulness: "How pleasant it is," said she, "when evening comes. I love it, especially when we have company."

There was not enough daylight for them to see each other distinctly. Their features remained blurred. Their voices came out of shadow and met as though they were disembodied. Edmondine herself had sat down. All though the meal, rushing about, dripping perspiration, darting back and forth from table to stove, she had chattered endlessly. Now, having blown off her steam, she spoke with less shrillness in her voice.

"There's nothing in the world I like better than company. It's the only thing we lack here. In every other way we're so happy."

"You are happy?" echoed Alexandre.

Never before had he heard a human being admit to happiness.

"Yes, thanks be to God, we surely are happy!" Edmondine averred.

"Ah!" said Alexandre, extraordinarily relieved at heart, "how good it is to hear someone say so."

In a certain sense, it was the most beautiful avowal he ever had received in all his life. Up until now, whoever could have been tempted to make Alexandre this gift? Rather the people around him would have hidden such a thing, even could it have been true. He loved Edmondine for being happy and for telling him so. Just as God must be pleased when, amid the lamentation and cries which mounted toward Him, He somewhere heard a human voice saying, as did Edmondine that evening: "Yes, how happy we all are! Just think: here's winter on its way and I have three hundred jars of preserves in the cellar."

"Three hundred!"

"Yes, there must certainly be three hundred, eh, Etienne?" Edmondine appealed to her husband.

The farmer was on the point of dozing off.

"You must know more about that than I do, Mother. That's your department."

"Very close to three hundred jars anyway," Edmondine resumed. "Peas and string beans, tomatoes, strawberries, beef, poultry, moose. And apart from all that, we have our potatoes, our cabbages, our carrots, our turnips; we're always a bag of flour and a bag of sugar ahead. Then there's the salt pork, Monsieur Chenevert. When autumn comes we kill the pig; we salt it away. All winter long we have enough to eat. We smoke the hams. I have onions, parsley, pickles, rhubarb . . ."

She couldn't stop, perhaps aware that she was giving her visitor pleasure by this display of wealth.

"We have the wool from our sheep for stockings and the children's knitted clothes . . . our cows, our geese. I make my pillows out of goose down. Then in summer I have flowers as well," she said.

"Zinnias, sweet peas, stocks, poppies . . ." one of the small girls began to enumerate their kinds; obviously she shared her mother's delight in listing their goods.

"Don't forget the sunflowers," prompted another little girl.

One of the boys, sitting barefoot on the floor, where he could enjoy the coolness, was playing the harmonica, but very low, so as not to interfere with the conversation. It was a tiny trickle of music, so feeble that at times you lost it completely, when a gust of wind seized upon the heads of the trees in the forest so near at hand.

"You may play, Albert," Edmondine encouraged him. "Play something nice for Monsieur Chenevert."

Albert having launched into a shrilly repetitive series of notes, his mother raised her voice: "We have music, too. All the children are talented."

When Albert had finished his piece, she begged him, "Play some more. Play another tune."

To Alexandre it seemed that the young musician kept repeating exactly the same series of notes, monotonous, melancholy, and without any marked melodic line. So he was rather surprised to hear Edmondine express her lively approval. "That's the 'Hunchback's Reel,' the one he plays best."

· Two or three times the boy stopped playing, and then began an air as like as two peas to the one he had just finished, but Edmondine distinguished carefully between them: "The 'Hanged Man's Reel,' Monsieur Chenevert. . . . And this is the "Miss Souris Waltz.' Are you fond of music, too, Monsieur Chenevert?"

It was one of the rare occasions in his life when he had the gentle and captivating desire to smile. He said, "Yes, I like music."

"Fortunately we have our music," Edmondine responded.

Two or three cats had taken to chasing each other around the room. Suddenly Alexandre felt something clawing his ankle; almost instantly a silky ball curled on his knees and was already beginning to purr. He began to stroke it.

"There are times," he said, "when I think I'd like to have a cat. Would it be a great sacrifice for you to let me have one?"

Edmondine burst into roars of laughter; it took her several minutes to catch her breath.

"A sacrifice!" she finally succeeded in saying. "To have one less cat?"

"How many have you?" asked Alexandre.

"Far more than makes any sense," said Edmondine, still laughing. "But of course they aren't all house cats. There are six of them who come inside. But in the barn . . . How many can there be in the barn?" She seemed to be putting it up to her children as though it were a riddle.

"Ten," cried one childish voice.

"No, eleven," another corrected.

"Tiger Stripes has just had a litter," one of the children pointed out.

"Not again!" sighed Edmondine.

Another child was ticking them off: "Show-Off, Dirty Face, Sparks, Black Tom . . . I think there are thirteen of them . . ."

"You understand," Edmondine apologized, "every spring I tell Etienne, we must try to find all the litters and drown them. . . ."

"Well hidden in the hay! Do you think that's an easy job!" protested Le Gardeur, whom they had thought asleep.

"Later, when they leave the hayloft," continued Edmondine, "their eyes are open and they're cute and roly-poly. You can't find the heart to kill them. . . . Play some more, Albert. . . ."

When Alexandre departed, the whole family saw him out-doors. Etienne Le Gardeur, recovered from his sleepiness, was apologizing. "When my eyes begin to close on me, I'm not very good company. But see to it that you come back . . . some evening . . . whenever you feel like it. The door is always open."

There was almost as much hubbub around Alexandre as at the moment of his arrival.

Rover was barking.

"Will you shut up!" almost all the children cried at once.

Edmondine called sharply after Alexandre, "We'll be expecting you. Come again, do you hear? Come again."

He turned around and gave her a formal salute by lifting his hat.

He no longer had the least doubt that he—a stranger to all these people—was liked by them. But for what earthly reason?

How and why, indeed? This evening he had said nothing, done nothing deserving affection. So this seemed to him proof that the old Alexandre—grumbling, lonely, unsociable—was at last dead. Another had taken his place, one who effortlessly, naturally, attracted people's fellow feeling. But how unjust this was, all the same, toward the first and impoverished Alexandre!

Behind him ran a shadow—humble, repentant, not yet daring to make known his presence. At last it came close and brushed Alexandre's legs. It was Blacky, or rather Rover, who seemed to have followed to explain his behaviour.

The path lay clear in the moonlight. Moreover, Alexandre was now quite without fear, even alone in the darkness and the forest. God almost continuously walked at his side during those days. It was as though He had forgiven Alexandre all the sins committed since the beginning of the centuries.

Better still: Alexandre knew deep within him that this evening he, of his own accord, on behalf of happy Edmondine, on behalf of one single happy being, could at last forgive God for the suffering so freely scattered over the four corners of the world.

An utter lightness of heart swelled his soul.

Evening after evening, though, Monsieur Chenevert was expected at the farm and never came.

And these good people began once more to ask themselves: "Could we have done something else to upset him? And yet he seemed happy, do you remember? All the same, could we have offended him?"

When there wasn't the least trace of mist, Edmondine would see the lonely man's lamp shining far off among the trees. It stayed lit very late. One night Edmondine, having got up to attend to one of the children, saw—very visible, very clear— the sharp point of light winking at least a mile away from her.

What could Monsieur Chenevert be doing at such an hour?

To what mysterious business could he be attending when he should have been getting his rest?

So frail, sickly, and pitiable had Alexandre appeared to these folk that they worried about the dire tasks which, without comprehending them, they imagined the little man capable of imposing upon himself.

And what, indeed, could Monsieur Chenevert be up to!

CHAPTER XV

H E WAS writing a letter to the editors, a message which would go far beyond that in his communication published years ago in the *Sol*. Never had so great a project sprung up in his heart, like a summer wind over rich harvests.

It was on the evening of his return from Edmondine's house that the idea had come to him, as he was looking at the stars.

In one brief and glorious instant Alexandre had received the revelation that here at Lac Vert men, more even than God Himself, were his constant helpmeets and support.

What pleasure could living in the forest have given him had not their concern dwelt there in a thousand forms?

What would he have done without their milled grain, their handy tinned goods, his predecessor's stove?

The fancy had struck him that you must be the product of an ancient civilization to be able to be as happy as he was in solitude. How could he even have existed without the aid of others: the white bread and vegetables, fruits of Edmondine's toil; the supplies bought at the village grocer's? And, if you went to the very bottom of the matter, Alexandre became aware that he owed gratitude for the tea he was so fond of to some unknown Chinese. Thus he realized once for all and with tenderness that he was in the debt of thousands of men, even of men no longer living. Were there not also the books he had brought with him, the authors of which—perhaps long since dead and buried—still whiled away Alexandre's long evenings? Ink, pen, paper!—he also would record his findings!

For such was the undertaking that had exalted his soul: to discharge his obligation toward others; to give them the best in his power to give.

Now what could this be, if it were not the voice of his own experience? Of all the gifts exchanged on earth, it was still the gift of thought which stirred him the most.

Joyfully had he entered the cabin on that evening. He rubbed his hands together in happy anticipation of what mankind—as yet wholly unsuspecting of what was to come—would receive from Alexandre Chenevert.

From remote Lac Vert he would make men hear his words. He would write. If possible he would shed light. There must be a great number of people puzzled and sorrowing as he had been himself. To such Alexandre would point out the way. He would say that God wants our happiness and that men are rarely as bad as they believe themselves to be. At last he, on whom others had heaped so much, in his turn would do some good. He would tell how peace comes, and then hope. . . . It would be—how could you describe it?—very beautiful, moving, and absolutely sincere.

So far all this was still locked within Alexandre's heart.

Upon the white sheet of paper there was nothing.

At least not much except a series of erasures.

But this evening he had made up his mind to get done with it.

He pulled the small rough-hewn table into the middle of the cabin. On it he placed the lamp, sharpened pencils, paper.

He sat down with his back to the lake, facing the wall, like a man in prison.

To put off the moment he feared, he lined up his pencils in another order, took off his glasses and began carefully wiping them clean.

Nothing came to him. That is nothing except tag ends of phrases which seemed to trace back directly to his nickel newspaper, to the catch-lines in the streetcar ads. Such platitudes were far from what he expected of himself; take, for instance, "Silence soothes the nerves. . . . Our worries fade away when we stand face to face with our mother, nature. . . . Go deep into the wilderness if you want a cure. . . ." It struck him that he was expressing himelf in the tone of an advertising copy writer, and he was the first to feel that this moves no one. It seemed as though the hollow mood of propaganda had branded him with its mark.

He got up and paced from one end of the cabin to the other. This amounted to taking three steps from wall to wall, with a little care to avoid bumping into the table. Once again wrinkles of frustration had come to furrow his brow. He had gone back to smoking : a saucer on the table was already overflowing with butts. No matter; he would break all the rules if he must in order to bring forth the very best that was in him.

For beauty was in him; no power on earth could have torn from him the poignant certainty that he possessed it in his heart. All he lacked were the words. And why was it that so deep, so sincere an emotion should not call forth the means of sharing it with others?

He was trying to bring to rebirth the mandate he had received while he was on his way back from Edmondine's. At the time he had not sought it or even wished for it. Gratuitous, urgent, the task had sought him out. Why, now that he had set about it, did it elude his grasp?

There had been a moment when his letter had seemed to him, if you will, ready-made, from its friendly salutation to its "Yours sincerely, Alexandre Chenevert." In less than half a minute the trick was done, his letter written in the slightly long and solemn phrases he found so much to his liking, and then slipped into an envelope and addressed to:

The Editor,
Le Journal,
Montreal.

And now it was all gone. Alexandre thumped his forehead: that skittish skull should at least restore to him what it had once so clearly held. Would he never, never succeed in extracting from it a single thought to do him honour? Suddenly he trembled with impatience. He seemed to recognize an inner surge, like that which thought, when it comes to life, conveys to the whole person tense with hope.

He rushed toward the little table. His three long evenings' labour had at least taught him the quickness with which you must capture thoughts that deserved retention.

He dipped his pen. Leaning over the sheet of paper, he shook with fear as much as with determination. Alas! under his very eyes, bulging with helpless amazement, he saw his own thought escape him, seeming to scamper down into some hole from which he was morally certain he would never succeed in dislodging it.

An implacable obduracy toward himself then took hold of Alexandre. He would write his letter, and that was all there was to it. He simply would not tolerate any such self-betrayal. He would stay at that table, with the paper in front of him, as long as might be necessary to dig out the lovely sentences which could properly speak in his name.

Unhappy Alexandre!

He set to work: "Dear friend and fellow citizen . . ."

As this brought him to a full stop, Alexandre nibbled his pen, looked inquiringly at the wall that loomed in front of him, changed the position of his paper, and began once more: "Dear friend and fellow citizen . . ."

Most infuriating of all was that his mind continued so active, but to no purpose for the end he strove for. Even had he wanted to slow down its functioning, he could no longer do so.

"The greatest supplies of oil were in Iran; God consisted of three persons; the world was one and indivisible; autumn was coming . . ." All he had managed to do was set in motion a senseless sequence of ideas. Yet his pen began to scratch the paper, and quickly, too, with a sudden ease. He wrote, "We have the pleasure to transmit herewith a copy of your current account, as of November, and showing a balance in your favour of $100.25 (one hundred dollars and twenty-five cents) which we have again placed to your credit. We request that you verify it and let us know . . . let us know . . . let us know . . ."

"What kind of silly fool am I ! . . ." exclaimed Alexandre, hiding his head as though he were ashamed.

It would seem that the only sort of prose which was sufficiently natural to him was precisely the sort for which he had no use.

A great desolation flooded over him.

How on earth did they do it—those people who were able to give a just expression to sentiments which rang true for themselves and for all men? How ever did they go about it, those authors of volumes in which he had recognized himself better than in the original?

He opened a book to calm the acute vexation of his failure. But he was far from discovering in it his usual pleasure. From now on the beauty of the world would always be a reproach to him, for there would be an abyss between the happiness of receiving it from others, and that of being himself its instrument.

A few minutes later, however, Alexandre stirred no longer.

To what goal had so much determination, discontent, rebellion brought him? The pure air, weariness, the late hour had got the best of Alexandre who, slumped over his sheet of paper with all its scrawls and erasures, was fast asleep.

CHAPTER XVI

HE BEGAN to get bored at Lac Vert. He had given up his Herculean efforts, and once again his appetite was good; he slept well, too, a real sleep in which he no longer tried to fit together puzzles of words and phrases. He realized that there was no sense in being unreasonable and continuing profitlessly to torture himself. His cheeks seemed to be filling out, if ever so little. When he looked into the tiny mirror while shaving, he thought he could truly say he had gained a few pounds. The less you meditated, the better it was for the nerves. "Consider the Eskimos, the Polynesian tribes . . ." Alexandre would say as he used to, but no longer with any wish to resemble them. Were he, like them, to reach the point where he no longer worried about anything, certainly he would achieve perfect health. But what use would that be if it meant centring your life on meaningless activities —bringing in wood, warming up your food, and day after day going through the same tedious drudgery to get water? When the ripe fruit fallen upon the ground exhaled a sweet, warm smell, he no longer troubled himself about the unlucky people in the city who would have taken joy in such abundance. He was slipping toward indifference, retaining just enough clear-wittedness to believe that he had been more worthy of esteem in his earlier state. Good health seemed to him to have a humiliating aspect.

And even happiness, happiness such as he had witnessed at Edmondine's, he began to hold in scorn. At bottom, of what was this happiness compounded except mere sufficiency? The Le Gardeurs were happy because they had need of no one in this world. "Because I lack not vines, nor a hearth, because I am not sick, I look upon God as my benefactor." Basically, for what did the happy man give thanks if not for inequality on earth?

Alexandre doubted whether he hungered for happiness.

A bit later and he was appraising the quality of the landscape surrounding him. Toward day's end, the sun never cast the same light on Lac Vert. Sometimes it was sulphur-coloured, conjuring up for Alexandre the idea of a shipwreck which left only a faraway shadow on the indifferent water; and then again the loneliness was livened by a green glow of uninhabited lands. Around an inlet bordered with fine sand stood a growth of white birches, their bodies sparse and vibrant. Of all trees, Alexandre now preferred these, and their endless plaint. He loved their sorrowful whispering.

Yet soon he wandered amid the trees no longer noticing them, grown weary of them : everlastingly smooth trunks and speechless boughs. Was this oppressive monotony, then, the distinguishing mark of peace?

One evening he happened to be on the shore of a sheltered cove. This spot had become a place of escape for him, whence he could plunge with avid heart into the past. And there, on that evening, Alexandre found the city again. In place of dusky banks, he perceived the swarm of lights by which cities reveal themselves in the fullness of the night. Homesickness for the crowded lives there, for the intermeshed lives, startled him, more compelling than any longing he had ever felt in all his days, like a longing for eternity.

He thought of the shop windows bursting with provisions, of an abundance such as the poor Le Gardeurs could not conceive. He dreamed also of the newspapers and magazines piled high on the sidewalks, bearing tidings of all the world. There was life, that endless, stirring, brotherly interchange.

His memories continued to grow more beautiful.

And so he found himself moved once more to write, but to people he knew, first of all to Godias. He described his accommodations to him; into his letter he slipped a drawing which showed the cabin and its little porch closely flanked by trees. He suggested to his fellow worker that some day he should try out the experience of solitude. Alexandre's preachy tone broke through a little. He proposed, "We might journey together into the woods; it seems to me we should complement each other nicely. The Russian's cabin is small; it might be possible to rent a larger one in the region; or else two, side by side." He kept writing : 'You should . . . We must . . . Take my advice . . .'' And he exulted : "At last I've found peace."

He also wrote Eugénie. His best moments, toward the end of his holidays, were precisely those when, already severed from Lac Vert, he was with his own. Then he envisioned Eugénie as she had been twenty years before. "My dear Eugénie," he told her, "you'd hardly recognize me. I've certainly improved. . . ." He was concerned to warn her of the transformation in him, so that it might not embarrass him too deeply when he saw his wife face to face. "We shall begin fresh. Our life together will be easier. . . ." Alexandre addressed her as though she were someone who had also gone away to get a new set of nerves. He said that she might expect him back soon.

And what did it serve for him to remain here? Merely through boasting of his happiness he felt he had already lessened it. Moreover he was better; he was cured. What could a few more days in the country profit him?

Alexandre was restless.

Two days before the end of his vacation, he left Lac Vert. And thus it happened that he entrusted to himself the delivery of his letter to Eugénie.

Perched on the high seat of the wagon alongside the farmer,

he travelled the four miles as far as Saint Donat. The morning was exquisitely fresh. But only intermittently and already under memory's guise did Alexandre's heart quicken at nature's beauty.

It upset Le Gardeur to see him go, still so thin and stoop-shouldered.

"What you really need is six months here, Monsieur Chenevert."

Alexandre shook his head ill-naturedly. He explained, "They're expecting me at the bank, you know, Le Gardeur. . . . I can't overdo it. . . . I have to earn my living."

And this was indeed what hurried him on—the job he must return to, his wish to do what he must in the world.

Little by little he had resumed his city man's look, serious, a bit tense, and superior.

Before climbing aboard the bus, he said good-bye to Le Gardeur. At the last moment he had turned down the little cat proffered by Edmondine, remembering just in time that Eugénie did not like cats, that the poor animal might be unhappy on the third floor in the midst of the city, and that in any case the bus company did not permit the transportation of animals in its vehicles. In vain had Edmondine proposed a sturdy box, pierced with air holes and disguised as a package; Alexandre had refused.

He extended his hand to Le Gardeur. He acted like everyone else at the end of a holiday. He scribbled his address on a scrap of paper. He promised he would write. Suddenly a doubt began to undermine his self-confidence. Yet all the same he said, his grey eyes uncertain of the efficacy of his intentions: "I will come back, Le Gardeur."

CHAPTER XVII

THE FARMSTEADS grew more numerous and the villages somewhat closer together. The bus took on passengers at the summer hotels and along the highway. The air began to be noticeably odorous. Some of the travellers wanted the windows opened wider, others complained of the draughts. Still in the open country, a billboard suggested smoking PLAYER'S MILD cigarettes, CANADA'S MILDEST.

Alexandre had begun chatting with his neighbour, likewise an office worker. He held a job at the Montreal City Hall; his doctor's advice had been three months' holiday. But how could he manage that? Only one of his daughters was married. As he put it, a man's life seemed to consist in leaving the country in order to make enough money in the city to be able to return to the country to recover the health he had lost in the city. His name was Lavigne. His wife had been a "little Lajoie." And he certainly had good reason—this chap named Lavigne—when he had furnished so much information about himself, to be put out at his companion's behaviour. For, after having seemed fairly cordial and after having tolerated the extraction of a few items of a personal nature, Alexandre, with no apparent reason, had turned uncommunicative. He had stopped answering questions: "You say you work for a bank? What bank, may I ask?" His blank face seemed to want an end of talk.

Chertsey . . . Rawdon . . . Sainte Julienne . . . The bus was moving down the slope of the Laurentians. A statue of Christ loomed up along the road. Electric wires linked it to a Hydro-Quebec pole. On its back you could glimpse a full-fledged installation: a network of twisted cables, lighter lead-lines, and what was probably a fuse box. Alexandre wondered whether there was not likewise a meter, keeping track of the number of kilowatts the Christ might consume when it was illuminated at night; whether the Christ lit itself up automatically, or whether—what seemed more likely—someone in the neighbourhood came at a set hour and pushed some button on the electrical system. Long after they had passed by, the electrified Christ continued to bother him. Then he began to feel sorry for the saints in their niches on the church façades along the way, each with its aureole of electric light bulbs. More and more posters, now, in praise of Seven-Up. A small barn all by itself in a field announced in every direction, "The pause that refreshes . . ." A succession of shanties passed by: shanties haphazardly thrown together, cottages of fake brick and fake stone—in a country richly endowed with fine wood. Their garden plots were full of chickens, dwarfs, and Grecian vases made of pottery or concrete. At the entrance to a prosperous and charming village, Alexandre made out a legend strategically placed on an embankment flanking the highway: "Begging forbidden in Saint Esprit. . . ." Pelletier let it be known that he was a licensed grocer and butcher and extended his "welcome" to visitors. . . . Madame Aldude served LIGHT

LUNCHES, HOT DOGS, HAMBURGERS, and FRENCH FRIES. . . . Joe Latendresse was a Funeral Director. . . . And there was no better heel than the long-wearing Cat's Paw. . . .

They crossed the Milles Iles River. Under the bridge shining eddies sparkled. After that there was a little more country, but the fields were smaller and they were enclosed with barbed wire. Here and there, alone in the stubble, there still stood a few tall birches, transfixed with light.

On their left flowed the powerful Des Prairies River, on their right lay the penitentiary enclosure. In the watchtowers guards surveyed the prisoners at work, guns held at the ready. Is there anything sadder than to have to admit, on your way back from a holiday that penitentiaries are perhaps indispensable? In the distance could be seen something like a cloud of stagnant smoke, that greyer, more pensive colour of the sky above great cities, forewarning you of them even when you are still miles away. High factory chimneys caught the eye, blackened spires, billboards which, from now on, were propped on roofs. They prated of two hundred rooms with running water . . . sixty rooms with private baths . . . Beauty-Rest mattresses . . . six hundred other rooms . . . fireproof . . . Vulcanizing . . . used parts . . . The Pius XI Garage, Regd. . . . A few dust-laden trees struggled for existence; vaguely-defined fields defended themselves pitifully, spoiled by real-estate signs : Fine lots for sale. The public was requested not to dump trash there, and it was precisely at these spots that mounds of rusty tin cans sprouted.

Houses began to follow each other in regular sequence. Then they became linked together, a long, uninterrupted front of brick and windows; a solid block which, at street intersections, turned into a tiny commercial centre. There you saw a drugstore, the receiving counter of some dry-cleaning establishment, a place where beauty awaited the human face; often a branch bank. Then the same thing all over again, exactly the same, at the next street corner. Sometimes this little business district included a moving-picture theatre, with posters of an amorous nature. Some corners had their funeral parlours; there vividly green ferns summoned the eye. Quite frequently next door to a gas station stood some little grocery store; boxes of corn flakes were stacked within, just about as cans of oil were piled at the neighbour's.

The bus was making progress with difficulty, having to slow down constantly. The driver kept sounding his horn.

Alexandre poked his head outside. It was a bright day, and since here the sun encountered a great multitude of nickel, aluminum, and other smooth surfaces, it produced a rich and shining brilliance.

Amid the cars, against a truck's enormous double tires, he saw the silhouette of a youngster mounted on two slender wheels and pedalling strenuously. The vulnerability of the child, with his bare hands, his frail back, his exposed face, made him hateful to Alexandre. The youngster threaded his way through the cars until he reached the bus and grabbed it with his hand in order to get a tow; all the while the little beggar was whistling! The heavy vehicle brushed his clothes, and intinctively Alexandre looked away. But in a flash the small delivery boy had slipped off, as agile as a monkey. For a brief moment he darted ahead of all the traffic, which seemed to be pursuing him. The Saint Donat bus made a difficult turn. Alexandre glimpsed a conglomeration of wheels and hand signals made by automobile drivers to show which way they were going. The bus driver struggled to turn his steering wheel. At last the vehicle glided in under the high vaulting of the terminus.

Loud-speakers were announcing imminent departures; people were rushing along the platforms. Indeed it was still the vacation season, for it takes a good while to empty a city and then bring back its population. There remained a few fine summer weeks to portion out. Alexandre stepped out onto the concrete, into the full, evil-smelling blast of all those humming motors.

He moved with great care to steer his valise clear of the packages and umbrellas. He pushed along, muttering, "Excuse me . . ." to each person he passed. . . . He was utterly routed, in the midst of strangers. The revolving doors spun round; the big hand on the clock jumped forward a minute with an audible click; and already what seemed like a wholly new set of faces surrounded him. He had the odd sensation that he could not feel more a stranger in Moscow or Paris. What was happening to him was worse than loneliness : it was like a frightful misunderstanding. He laid down his suitcase and passed a hand over his forehead. "Come, come," thought Alexandre. "I've lived all my life in Montreal; I was born here and here I shall probably die." He felt the full impact of the city's terrible lack of concern for him.

He went out onto Dorchester Street.

Cars were passing in tight ranks. Alexandre noticed a gap and made a dash for it. An automobile was bearing down on him. Brakes screamed a long cry of rage. A harsh voice barked at him : "Hey, you! Can't you look where you're going?"

Alexandre clambered back on the sidewalk. His heart was thumping like an angered animal's. "You should be careful," a pedestrian reproached him. He had trembled for Alexandre's wretched life, and his fear had left him with the need to scold.

Alexandre was recovering his equanimity. He waited with the others for the red light to go out and for a green glow to take its place, telling him he might start across with the human tide that at intervals thronged over the pavement. Still worried about Alexandre, the man who had already spoken to him, thinking him from the country, warned him the moment they both reached the opposite sidewalk: "Never cross on a red light. In Montreal that's not allowed."

Alexandre accepted the advice. With a tightening of the heart he felt the need of laying claim to some spot that was home.

"At Lac Vert, we don't know anything about traffic rules," he explained.

He continued on foot to Saint Catherine Street. Workmen were repairing a section of asphalt. Each time a streetcar passed, they moved out of the way and then returned to work for a moment or two. They had just time to lift their picks again and dig them two or three times into the pavement when another train demanded right of passage. Repairing the least little thing in a city seemed to Alexandre to require almost absurd efforts. The weight of his bag was stretching his arm; in spite of himself he glanced at the newspaper headlines. He had lived very well without them for several weeks. Why this sudden and furious curiosity about disasters?

. . . A tornado, somewhere in Texas, had done two million dollars' worth of damage. . . . Another peace conference had ended in stalemate. . . . The railway strike was not over yet. . . .

He passed a sort of lunchroom; sitting at tables toward the rear of this hole-in-the-wall, taxi drivers were munching sandwiches while they listened to the news. Rioting had broken out in Tel Aviv at eleven o'clock . . . twelve dead . . . bombs had been planted in hidden places. . . . Jaws moved in time with the announcer's voice. These men chewing words rasped out by an invisible loud-speaker, the announcer closeted in a soundproof studio to talk about Jews in Palestine—this farfetched relationship between human beings—utterly bewildered Alexandre. He raised his eyes aimlessly above the roofs, looking for the sky, and he read in the heavens:

DRINK PEPSI-COLA

He lowered them once more to the street. A small truck was shooting by, its body covered with a screaming poster :

Read the Avenir du Pays! *It* tells the *Truth*!

In front of a Baptist church a poster advertised a sermon on a text from Saint Matthew . . . and added, "Come to church . . . prayer is all-powerful. . . ."

At the corner of Saint Catherine and Peel a young girl almost forcibly thrust a folder into Alexandre's hands. It was signed, "The Witnesses of Jehovah."

At this intersection there is a special newsstand, stocking papers from almost all the world's major cities. There are even some in Yiddish . . . strange-looking small letters disturbing one's equanimity. Do they conceal something you should really know about? Headlines danced before the eyes : Ten Jehovah's Witnesses arrested . . . Nationalization of Industry continues in England . . . Only free enterprise can restore prosperity . . . DO YOU WANT TRUTH?

Alexandre had reached his streetcar stop. 83's, 3's, 3A's—they stood there in a serried rank, heavy vehicles painted a nasty yellow, a nuisance to traffic.

Alexandre had raised his hand and waved it as his car drew near. Then he had done what the others did. He had started zigzagging through the autos whose drivers were sounding their horns in an effort to pass the trams. At last the doors—thank God!—opened for Alexandre. Shoved by the crowd, he slipped first his head and then his body inside. But he still had to push in his suitcase, which was preventing the doors from closing. He succeeded in dragging it toward him. His hat had slid over onto the side of his head. He could not set it straight; he could not move at all. Then he dimly realized that in everything he had just struggled through, there was still nothing so far out of the ordinary for him; every day of his life before Lac Vert he had done almost as much. Astonishment spread over his face, now pale with weariness. Were then all his life's habits bad and abnormal? He hesitated before so amazing a revelation. Of course he was wrong, of course he would see things in another light within a few days, when he had become broken in to his regular way of life.

He surrendered himself to the advertising which, from one end of the tram to the other, above the seats, lavished advice, threats, and warnings. Yum-yum gelatin desserts were beyond compare . . . and the only *ism* for Canadians, announced a distillery, was Patriotism. . . .

The motorman kept pounding his sole on the bell pedal.

Clank! Clank! Clank! The thin, tinny sound wore on the nerves. Sudden jerks threw Alexandre onto the feet of a man standing beside him and toward a housewife laden with parcels, who cast outraged glances at him. "Use both entrances! Step forward!" the conductor shouted exasperatedly in French. Then, in English, "Step inside if you please." He was instinctively more polite when he spoke English. A friar sitting in front of Alexandre kept his head obstinately lowered. A recollection that he still had his soul to save shot through Alexandre's distracted mind. All other toil was vain and without consequence. Yet salvation seemed to him something unlikely, an individual solution, in lonely glory at the end of a torturing promiscuity.

He swung on a hand strap. He half-opened his stinging eyelids. Never before had Alexandre believed that other men were as sensitive as he. But, at sight of the weary faces surrounding him, he concluded that the others were just as unhappy. Two folds of bitterness creased his mouth.

He was about to close his eyes again, escape from what was around him, but he saw a poster over which he might well have reproached himself for the rest of his life had he neglected it. It showed a group of tragic-faced children. Almost a group of skeletons. Beneath it he read, "Are you going to let Greek children starve to death?"

And Alexandre, as though the appeal had been addressed to him personally, shook his head. He immediately took out his address book and found a pencil. He wrote down the address given at the bottom of the advertisement, and made the following note, to help his own memory in case it should fail him: "N.B. Don't forget the hungry children."

For how could he sleep again if he neglected this appeal?

Yet two streets further on, he had time to absorb a poster affixed to the planking around an excavation. Boldly outlined, an old man, a woman with a disconsolate face, skinny children besought Alexandre. The drawing was accompanied by words in large type: JEWISH FEDERATION OF CHARITIES. Then Alexandre turned away his head and lowered his eyes. How could he have found the wherewithal to give even twenty-five cents each to all these organizations which were suddenly thrusting their palms toward him? The league against cancer, crippled children . . . the Salvation Army, vacations for the poverty-stricken sick, Friendless Youth, all of them had that day chanced upon an open, defenceless heart, and were making the best of it.

Give, Alexandre read and understood, blood to the Red Cross

. . . your mite to Catholic Welfare . . . at least some old clothes. . . . GIVE GENEROUSLY . . .

In the end he had got a seat. Beyond the streetcar windows, he often saw, at street corners, new bank buildings designed to suit the current taste, namely with fronts entirely of glass, the effect of which was to make banks like Alexandre's seem very old and wholly out of fashion. He felt that, like his savings bank, he had been left behind by his own day.

Near him stood two men, surely the only ones aboard this crowded tram who looked at peace and happy; their conversation concerned their forthcoming holidays. Alexandre heard farfetched and pleasant words: rivers full of trout . . . a lake far from everything . . . a log camp . . . sunset . . .

He tightened his lips. Nothing, perhaps, could wound him more to the quick than these two men's hopes. He came very close to warning them: "Listen to me! . . . Above all, don't go away . . . never, never take a vacation. . . ."

Just above his eye level the insolent picture of a young girl with full breasts extolled the resiliency of Elastex brassières.

He got off the streetcar. The corkscrew stairways twisted up the façades of the buildings like fire escapes. Alexandre knew that he was back home. 8838 . . . 8840 . . . 8842 . . . Almost in front of his door stood a delivery wagon filled with cakes, tarts, and buns. Painted pink, it bore the name, "La Patisserie de Ma Tante." The ancient horse which served as its motive power was straining against its harness; it was trying to push the bottom of its feedbag against the ground in order to be able to lick up the last elusive handful of oats.

Misery seemed to him to be so much everywhere and at the same time that Alexandre hurried over to the old hack and at least gave him a hand in his struggles.

He watched the poor animal's oblique, mournful eye, too besotted to be grateful. Then he picked up his wedding valise once more and trotted up his stairs to avoid meddling Fred Trottier, who would certainly be after him with questions. He reached the top. He did not call out, as he joyfully had planned to, "You there, Eugénie!" But he thrust his key in the lock, and when it turned with a dry and oh! so familiar sound, it seemed to him that this pointed bit of steel had made its half-turn within his very heart.

At first Eugénie could find nothing to say. Merely, "Ah! It's you!"

He seemed to suffer just as he had before he left. Nor did it seem that he had really put on any weight. Looking at him with compassion—and with a certain irritation, too—she remarked: "It doesn't appear that your holiday has done you much good. Poor old chap! And the crazy notion of going all by yourself into the woods!"

He never gave her the letter he had in his jacket pocket, that lovely letter, now a little mussed, which began with the words, "My dear Eugénie, you're going to find me a changed man. . . ."

THREE

W HAT FEW years he had left to live at least were in an era of progress. The average life span was longer: fully three or four years more than in the preceding century. It was true that in return Alexandre paid more to the government; taxes, taxes on all sides, and the cost of living was soaring. Nevertheless this century was good for men, almost all of whom wanted, first of all, to live a long while, and secondly—if that were possible—to be happy.

He had grown thinner since his return from Lac Vert. His staring eyes upset those who did not know him. What could be preying upon this poor man? His blood pressure was going up. He had very little patience. And Dr Hudon said to him: "You can't continue like this; it can't last."

And yet it did last. For months and months. His stomach powders, and especially the pills aimed at his sympathetic nervous system, helped him a little. The only thing left to try was the sedatives. These tiny tablets did to some extent withdraw Alexandre from his day, from himself . . . or from others. . . . Really tiny pellets, very hard to pick up, since they rolled between your fingers; occasionally they would even slip down into the cracks between the floor boards. They befogged his mind's anguish—and at the same time his memory. "A very, very good thing!" Dr Hudon acclaimed. But this good effect was not lasting. Alexandre's powers of reflection won the day. He realized that he was busy earning money to buy more and more medications which in turn helped him to earn his money. Once again the life of the Eskimos began to appeal to him.

"What you should have is a month, perhaps two months, of rest," Dr Hudon would thoughtfully remark. "Couldn't you find some small, very easy job, which would not tire you?"

Always such quite impractical suggestions as that, to which Alexandre would reply, "I've taken my vacation; I'm just back from my vacation." Or else, "What easier job could I get than the one I know already and have done all my life?"

He grew querulous. "At my age I most certainly can't learn a new trade." And the only ones which might have tempted him were those of the lumberman or trapper.

"You wouldn't get very far as a lumberjack," the doctor permitted himself to comment with a smile.

Alexandre did not think so either, but he did think that he would stop bothering the doctor over troubles that were certainly tedious to bear, but still not necessarily serious. Are not the minor daily pains and aches almost always a guarantee of long life?

Heart disease was still killer number one. After that came cancer. But tuberculosis was on the way out. The average age of the population in Alexandre's day was higher than it had been in his father's, who had died at eighty-two. The government, moreover, talked of supporting the aged after they had passed their sixty-fifth birthday; and thus could hardly be said to have anything to gain by keeping old people alive. To encourage age, longevity, the worn-out, thought Alexandre—was not that against the principles of economy, and hence a step toward true progress, which, on certain days, seemed to him above all to consist in prodigality?

He found himself in a generous world which forced him to busy himself with security—after which security would busy itself with him, would take him in its tow; but meanwhile his tiny pittance was often used to pay for the government's huge follies.

No longer did the sedatives adequately prevent him from thinking; for days on end the pills did him no good; then, as though they operated by delayed action, some fine morning Alexandre would perhaps have a terrible time getting out of bed; he would have to drink several cups of coffee, one after the other; he would come home in the evening very much overwrought, and he would then have to take several more tablets to neutralize the effect of the coffee. Finally he sent the sedatives packing. When you came right down to it, had he not always known better than the doctor? What would have been right for him would have been a stimulant as powerful as a kick in the teeth!

And truly it surpassed the realm of the possible to see a man as peaked as Alexandre still moving under his own steam, let alone working. All the same, among the million and a half inhabitants of his city, especially at the times of day when you could really take a look at them—on their way to or from their offices—Alexandre's face was not a sight to stop anyone dead in his tracks. There were a fair number of others fully as pale, nervous, and tense. What distinguished him from the rest was that he took so seriously an age he did not seem fated to have to endure for long.

"Will they succeed in avoiding war?" asked Alexandre.

Would we see the day when the Russians and the Americans destroyed their atomic bombs, and then shook hands? Would we ever see so sensible an event take place on earth—sensible as eventually all men would, sooner or later, meet each other in eternity? The closer he drew to his own end, the more Alexandre worried over the state in which he would leave the universe.

"He's a man who enjoys wearing himself out," said Eugénie about her husband.

It was the moment of the Nuremberg war-crimes trials. A small city, said Alexandre, once famous for its toys. But Göring escaped punishment by taking cyanide of potassium. And was it not significant, Alexandre pointed out to Godias, that all the tyrants of the day should have died violent deaths? Hitler, Mussolini, Göring, Goebbels? He saw a photograph of the man who had done away with himself in one of the big American magazines.

"It's the first time in the world's history," said Alexandre, "when those responsible for war have been brought to trial. You'll see, Godias," he added rubbing his hands, "that men will think twice before declaring war, now that they may be hauled into court when it's over."

"Phooey!" said Godias.

The latter was not a bad fellow; indeed he tended to be on the charitable side, but he believed all men's efforts to achieve peace childish and doomed to failure. In this he was not alone. What was so terribly lacking all round Alexandre was faith in the usefulness of human undertakings.

Yet never had so much money been spent to establish confidence. President Truman had just signed a European aid treaty authorizing the expenditure of $400,000,000 on behalf of Greece and Turkey. The cost of living was still going up, and when Alexandre had to buy himself a suit, he paid ten dollars more for it than the previous one had cost, even though the cloth— Alexandre realized that at the first glance—was less sturdy. The same story with shoes and shirts; the dollar was now worth something like sixty cents, and for all that Alexandre kept paying his full share for the public expenditures—for the aged, the sick, national defence. He would not have sulked had he been certain that this was not money thrown away. If peace could ever be won, it would never cost him too dear. But now he had his doubts, and others around him doubted even more seriously. Could peace be bought? Would President Truman's billions be enough? Deeply disturbed, Alexandre sounded the opinions of four or five people chosen at random. They had all reflected for a moment or two, some openly laughing, and they had all replied no, certainly not.

He even put the question to Monsieur Fontaine, one evening when they happened to leave the bank together, for did not Monsieur Fontaine represent a fairly widespread opinion?

"Yes," said Monsieur Fontaine, with assurance. "I believe we have a real possibility of consolidating peace, but on condition we spend every spare penny on preparing ourselves, arming ourselves to the teeth. We must be the stronger, Monsieur Chenevert, if we want peace."

Such was about the tone of the greater part of what one heard on the radio. A man influential in the country's affairs said over the air: "We want peace; we are pacific and peaceable people who intend to show the world that we wish to live in peace . . . and that is why we are building ships of war."

Alexandre was very irritated to see his money used in such fashion by the "big shots." Yet he believed that he understood how put to it they were to know how to act. That was why the Big Three were almost always meeting in some corner of the globe. They exchanged views through their interpreters. Could you really ask any more of them—those poor Big Three, at their age, weary as they must surely be, and perhaps even ill, for Roosevelt at least had started off on his last journey in very poor health—could you ask any more of them than constantly to be setting out to travel across the sky?

Whenever he heard an airplane roar above the city, Alexandre would throw his head back a trifle; he would follow it in its flight and keep thinking of Mr Churchill who smoked cigars that were far too strong.

He prayed Heaven to come to the aid of the great men.

He had read that Mr Roosevelt, because of world affairs, had had to give up his holiday at Warm Springs, where the medicinal waters did him so much good.

Alexandre hoped that God would credit this to Mr Roosevelt's account.

But had God ratified the Yalta agreement?

Did He concede that His earth be divided into zones of influence: "To you, Monsieur Stalin, goes Poland. To me, South Korea. . . ."

Alexandre began to wonder; if they were less sure of Heaven, would not men set themselves more seriously about their tasks on earth? If they were absolutely alone, they'd have to get out of their difficulties somehow.

But he thought of this with dread and circumspectly, refusing to admit that he thought of it.

Henceforth he was himself too close to his own death to put himself in God's bad graces.

So much the worse for the others, Alexandre said to himself. Let them fuss with *their* war and *their* peace and *their* security.

By severing himself from *them*, however, he had not the impression of being thereby a closer friend of God.

He was now truly no more than skin and bones. His piercing eyes, eager for bad news, devoured the whole of his face. His vision was growing dimmer; whenever he made an effort to recognize old customers, Alexandre contracted his eyebrows so much that he looked churlish. Even the widow Honorine Blanche Mathieu was now a bit afraid of Alexandre, and one morning he was stupefied to notice her going to Godias's cage rather than his own. He found it hard to forgive her, and one day when he saw that he was going to meet her on the street, he hurried across to the opposite sidewalk.

It was bitterly cold. The winter was severe. This wind was more savage than any wind had ever been before. Just cleaning the snow of one storm off the city's streets cost a million dollars. And Gandhi was assassinated!

At first Alexandre insisted on denying the news when it was broadcast over the radio. "No! No! It just can't be possible!"

Seeing him so overwhelmed, Eugénie hit upon words she thought would console him, and at the same time shame him a little: "After all, he was no relative of ours!"

True enough, but now you could expect every sort of excess and violence, Gandhi no longer being here to condemn them with one stern look! A tiny slip of a man, feeble, sickly, Alexandre reflected tenderly. Oh! it was not always the sturdy ones who brought the most to pass in the world—far from it!

They had looked a bit alike; others had also noticed it: the same hollow mouth, the same piercing eyes, but Alexandre had never claimed his eyes had the same quality; his own were sunken rather than deep. It was certainly his own best self which today they had killed for him.

Abruptly Alexandre pushed aside his toast. After all he could not eat at the moment when Gandhi had just breathed his last. Perhaps he would fast for two or three days, in commemoration of the Mahatma—in order that at least someone in North America should in some slight fashion continue the work of the peacemaker.

"Are you crazy? Are you really out of your mind, Alexandre Chenevert?" Eugénie tried to reason with him. "One fasts for

Our Lord; one doesn't fast for some Hindu. Poor old man, have you reached the point of thinking that you can work without eating? And you, who already look like a scarecrow."

Out of respect for Gandhi's memory, Alexandre made the extra effort required to master the terrible irritation aroused in him by his wife's stupid attacks.

At his wicket, free, unhampered, he felt that he was of use to the world. He already was hungry; and certainly this was nothing compared to what he would feel a bit later, but he would continue to suffer as a protest against violence, war, and murder. Why had he not earlier understood that his role in life, as Gandhi had pointed out for him, lay in meekness?

Moreover, apart from the pangs of hunger, his stomach was better than usual. No burning sensations and—it went without saying—no heaviness. He was astounded that he had not thought earlier of this variety of treatment. Would it not be providential all the same had chance led him to this beneficent discovery?

But the figures were beginning to look foggy to him. Repeatedly he took off his glasses and examined them suspiciously, as though they might be the cause of the figures' blurred dance. Faces withdrew instead of coming closer; they melted away into an odd haze. Then a rushing stream began to roar inside the bank. Alexandre almost took a header into his papers. Horror at what might have happened led him at the accustomed hour to the North-Western Lunch, so that at least he might get a bite to eat. But once he got there, he almost found the odour of the food enticing, and the cooking seemed to him better than it had been the day before. He ate a very good meal, and rather sadly reflected that he would always be free to resume his protest on the morrow.

Alas! he was soon to become aware that Eugénie was perfectly right; in his case fasting was not feasible, even dishonest. In the bank's pay, he owed his employer an unimpaired effort; for indeed he was now being kept on only through charity. Gandhi seemed to him favoured indeed, since he had been able to fast without doing any harm to any boss or any company. In brief, fasting was a vocation for the chosen few, which required a certain position of means, a certain independence.

Dying of hunger was not within the reach of all.

It remained for him to die gradually. At about this time he began to predict to Eugénie that he hadn't much time ahead of him. Nevertheless—and more than ever—he interested himself in reading whatever had to do with the progress of medicine. Thus diabetics could live indefinitely with insulin. Pneumonia was a mere nothing, thanks to penicillin. The times gave you the impression that illness and death, much more than war, were the enemies of mankind. For war, men were making themselves ready, but tirelessly and with all their strength they were out to kill disease. Especially the more painful diseases. You might have said that medicine wanted to permit the existence only of tranquil death. We were on the eve, Alexandre read, of discovering the cause of cancer, or at least an effective treatment for it; medicine did not always have to know the cause of an illness to come to its aid.

Now Alexandre weighed only 119 pounds. He faced a dilemma : if he ate, he suffered; if he did not eat, the result was the same. He had come to fear eating, just as some people, because of their stricken hearts, fear emotion—joy almost as much as sorrow. Would it not have been possible to succeed in sustaining him with little pills which would not upset his stomach? Could not this century, with all its fine progress, do that much for Alexandre? Oh! to be able to avoid eating!

And so things continued until the day when, apparently of its own accord, his stomach went back approximately to normal.

Then the world took on a different hue for Alexandre. Of a sudden he began to notice, as though he were just back from a trip, the state of the weather, and the news in today's papers seemed better to him.

From one decent night's sleep, from the fairly quiet digestion of a meal he drew such satisfaction as very few men have known in an entire lifetime.

More joy even than in his youth he had felt at being young and carefree.

Astonishment at all this filled him with ease.

Come, come! There's nothing like ill health to make you appreciate life!

You must suffer in order to understand, and is not understanding the greatest of all riches?

God wrought well when he made his world, Alexandre reflected.

During this interval, he was as jolly as could be. He asked his old clients all about how things were going with them; he greeted the ladies by bowing from the waist behind his wicket, and begged them to take care on the icy sidewalks. If in return, someone charitably remarked to him that he wasn't looking a bit well, he thrust the subject aside, wrinkling his forehead in disagreement. "A man mustn't fuss too much over himself, always be worried about his indispositions."

One day when he was thus "in his good mood," as Eugénie put it, he was bold enough to enumerate the advantages of winter for the benefit of Monsieur Fontaine who, distrustful of the condition of the streets, seemed uneasy and even a trifle put out. The pavements were covered with a thin coat of ice, more than sufficiently slippery; it made driving exceedingly dangerous, but, to balance this, the trees and buildings coated with frost turned the city into a sheer fairyland, as though it had been rebuilt during the night of precious materials, easily shattered, white, and shot through with gleaming sparks. It was a day made more for pedestrians than automobilists.

"What a sky! What colours!" exclaimed Alexandre, whose heart always beat a bit harder the moment he forced himself out of politeness to say a few words to his manager. "Let them say all they want against our country," said he, "on a day like this it's worthwhile living in Canada."

"You think so?" was Monsieur Fontaine's rather dry comment. "I find it a bit on the tedious side."

And as he walked away from him, Alexandre said about Monsieur Fontaine: "Poor fellow!"

He felt at ease when he entered the noisy, warm atmosphere of the North-Western Lunch. He broached serious matters with Godias, trying to prove to him that the world, all in all, was doing pretty well.

The times in which they were living, explained Alexandre, were obviously superior to the vaunted past. There were far more humanitarian enterprises than in the old days. He named a scientist he had heard about, a Russian—yes, indeed, the Russians also had their scientists, their mighty brains; Alexandre stated that it was the absolute truth; he had read it in the *Digest*—a Russian, then, who was thought to have discovered a serum of longevity, or "that's what they say," remarked Alexandre, who did not want to commit himself too far.

He explained that he thought he had understood this much: growing old, what was called the process of ageing, was only, according to Bogomoletz, the exhaustion of the conjunctive tissue. By re-establishing the activity of this tissue, one could delay the process of ageing. No longer was growing old an absolutely necessary thing.

Godias yawned widely, and Alexandre tried to make himself more interesting. Indeed he knew the name of another scientist, this time a German called Lorenz. He had seen this in the *Digest* also. Lorenz believed that a virus must be the cause of cancer.

Lorenz wanted only five years more to act on the authority of the cures already effected.

"Don't go believing everything you read," commented Godias, a cigarette hanging from his thick lower lip. "How on earth can you know how much truth there may be in it?"

Alexandre shrugged his shoulders, but without too much irritation, thinking in his turn, "Poor, incredulous Godias! When you come right down to it, he's the real pessimist!"

Thus on such good days he was open-minded, acceptive toward ideas. He thought peace possible, under international supervision.

His quiet soul left his sympathetic nervous system and his stomach at rest; or perhaps it was rather his sympathetic nervous system which had ceased affecting his consciousness. In general the betterment lasted no longer than a day.

Afterwards, utterly stripped of so delicate and just an awareness of things, Alexandre sank lower than ever.

He reached the point of asking himself whether God, after all, knew human suffering.

After his awareness, the day before, of such ample support —so happy it was impossible to charge that happiness to his own credit—he now felt himself too lonely to be convinced that he was still understood by God.

Of course God knew men's sufferings in part. But did He know what it was to suffer without nobleness?

To suffer stupidly, meanly.

He suffered in a godlike way, which was a very different thing.

The days were incredibly harder for Alexandre to bear than the run of mortals could even conceive.

He was mistrustful.

When you came down to it, what good would ever come of preventing men from growing old? They would merely have a longer time in which to fleece one another, and nothing more.

Peace was no longer within the realm of possibility.

They were scolding each other at the Chaillot Palace. In Paris, Alexandre specified. The conference had started out fairly well, all the delegates being agreed that what was pressing, now that everyone had the bomb, was to protect oneself against it.

Leaning over his small radio, his forehead troubled, Alexandre made a motion to Eugénie that she should keep silent. Vishinsky left and slammed the door behind him. The most appalling thing about it was that neither one side nor the other seemed really to take into account one Alexandre Chenevert, who was listening at the other end of the world.

"Poor men." Less and less did Alexandre understand them: weird beings in whom he no longer recognized himself in the least, the very least!

Come to think of it, he was alone among—how many inhabitants did the terrestrial globe now encompass, was it thousands of millions, or merely millions?—alone in such a seething mass; did that make any sense at all?

Meanwhile the delegates concerned with the Rights of Man, under the chairmanship of Mrs Roosevelt, were labouring to define our rights:

First: every man has a right to freedom, to security.

Second: every man has a right . . .

Alexandre was quite confused at the thought that Mrs Roosevelt herself was busy in his defence.

Eleanor must be sincere.

In fact the great sincerity of almost all these efforts to assure him peace was really what saddened him. They were now supplying Berlin by airlift. "Imagine what that must cost," he complained to Godias. He had contributed a dollar to one of the huge hospitals they wanted to build in his city. But at least two or three others were needed, one of them for children. There was also a lack of insane asylums. The peace conference had come to naught in Paris, but the various delegations had moved with their stacks of files to Lake Success, and everything had begun all over again. There was a possibility that the atomic bomb would now be used as a source of domestic heat. An association had been founded to come to the aid of Europe's unfortunate children. Then there began to be circulated through the city the first pamphlets giving advice on the best possible way to protect yourself against the atomic bomb. First you must throw yourself flat down on the ground. Second you must hide your face. Third avoid scattering fragments of glass . . .

Meanwhile thousands of employees in the city were required to undergo a free radiographic examination of their lungs.

Even in the streetcars, people were warned against tuberculosis and against cancer too.

> Have yourself examined in time . . .
> Cancer progresses by stealth . . .

More and more Alexandre's eye was drawn in that direction. The warning was often issued by insurance companies. In such cases it was not too worrisome. But the government also, without a thing to gain by it, begged him to go have an examination . . . at the least possible hint of danger.

And yet from week to week he said to himself, "Let's wait a little while." For years, now, he had had to get up during the night, through a "purely nervous" habit, the doctor had said. But during the day it was becoming necessary for him several times to leave his cage. The eyes of the other employees followed his comings and goings with surprise; then they all pretended to notice nothing.

Alexandre perhaps had the impression that if he could only postpone being seriously stricken for a few years, perhaps even a few months, medicine within the interval would be in a much better position to come to his assistance. Was it not unjust to perish at the very moment when medicine was making such great progress?

He saw even greater justice on the way. In the end would we not see the lead mines, the iron and uranium mines, exploited for the good of all? And why not also a solution for the common good of the problem of age, of hunger in India, or suffering on this earth? A justice so complete that no one in the world would any longer be happy!

Again he postponed going for a checkup. He was too young to be stricken with what he feared. Not altogether fifty-four— that was not old enough. And then they were so pressed with work at the bank these days because of the fourth teller's illness. Alexandre thought it was more becoming to wait until his colleague had recovered.

Moreover, his symptoms were becoming less acute. Thus he had no longer had to leave his cage during working hours; quite the contrary. But when this happened, pain came.

It was late, very late, when Alexandre made up his mind once again to take a seat in Dr Hudon's consultation room.

The doctor had some trouble recognizing him. "I've taken care of you before? . . ." he was about to ask, but little by little memory returned to him, memory slow and ill at ease.

"Oh! . . . yes . . . Monsieur Chenevert . . . if I am not mistaken!"

There are times when you have the impression of talking with a man who seems almost to have passed the boundaries of life. It leads you to lower your voice and also to a greater deference. "And how are you, Monsieur Chenevert? You're holding your own?"

The solemn eyes continued to accuse him.

"This way . . . Monsieur Chenevert . . . good; lie down, please."

He was once again on the hateful examination table. Not even a year and a half earlier, he was at Lac Vert; and there he must have been in fairly good health, since he went around on foot for hours and enjoyed a hundred innocent pleasures. In less than eighteen months, a man could not lose this much ground. . . . Back there a big pine tree stood at a little distance from the others. When there was not a breath of wind anywhere else, there was always a slight breeze in this pine. Even on the calmest, most soundless days, Alexandre would hear a distant noise, soft and very pretty. Was it the sound of rain or a small waterfall? No, not quite. At last, today, he was to have the satisfaction of identifying this remembered thing: it was like the passage of a little country train, far in the distance. A small, lost railroad train was wandering through that foliage for the joy, perhaps, of a single human heart.

The doctor's hand was palpating a very noticeable area of hardness.

"You must have suffered a lot from retention of your urine," said he.

"Recently, yes, it's been bothering me especially that way."

"And from headaches, too?"

"Oh! headaches . . ." said Alexandre. "I've had those for so long a while. . . ."

"But more violent ones?"

"Perhaps. I couldn't exactly say. You get used to things! . . ."

"Dizziness?"

"Once in a while."

"Other pain, perhaps?"

"Nothing much; except, during the last few months, a little pain in the hip. I thought it might be rheumatism. . . ."

The doctor felt deeply vexed. Why had this man not come for frequent checkups? Was it possible that he himself, at the last clinical examination, had neglected to investigate certain things? Hastily he looked into the Chenevert file. At the first consultation, during the month of August, he found that already then, "the patient had to get up during the night"; but Dr Hudon ascertained that he had connected this habit only with insomnia. He had concentrated especially on the gastric disorders and the sick man's excessive nervousness. His forehead in his hands, he meditated, from time to time casting a glance at the file; after all the last consultation was already more than a year ago, an interval perhaps sufficient for the appearance and the development of the present symptoms.

"But you must have suffered a great deal from retention," he repeated as though he were accusing Alexandre Chenevert.

"A little . . . I thought it might be a passing thing. . . ."

"You'll have to enter the hospital immediately," said the doctor.

"I was afraid it would be that way . . . I suspected as much . . ." Alexandre admitted. Yet he still dared ask, and a trifle insistently, "Couldn't I wait another week or two? It's very difficult," he explained, "to leave the others in the lurch at the worst time in the year . . . just before Christmas. . . ."

The doctor smiled briefly but quite inflexibly. "As soon as possible. Day after tomorrow if you can manage it."

"Oh! As quickly as all that!" said Alexandre.

He was taken by surprise. Despite so long a premonition of the worst! Despite so many efforts to strip him of his capacity for dread, for astonishment!

The doctor watched him with deep dissatisfaction. He confided to him, a little in reproach, a little by way of defence: "I should sooner have expected from you some complication of the stomach."

"Me, too," said Alexandre with a kind of regret.

That was what struck him as the most sneaky: that the illness did not strike where he might have expected it. What indeed had it served to have suffered from his stomach for years if this organ was not to kill him in the end?

How account for his indignation—this sickness which the doctor had just found in him was the very last Alexandre would have chosen!

Once again, along the streets of the city, as he glanced up he recognized man's solicitude:

Take care of yourself in time . . .
At the outset, cancer is curable . . .

"Tumour . . . tumour . . ." Alexandre Chenevert said to himself. Was not that the word that human charity almost always used in place of another, too unfeeling?

The taxi was waiting at the foot of the staircase. The expense, this time, seemed justifiable. The chauffeur, standing near his car, was beating his feet to keep warm; the snow was falling on him in big, hurried flakes, which he almost joyfully shook off by abruptly stretching out his arms and shaking them; he went about it with the quick motions of a man who has no fear of exceeding his strength. Alexandre came down the steps, this time helped by Eugénie, who insisted on holding his elbow. And he tried to free his arm, thinking that he must present a pitiful sight. The chauffeur came toward them to take the wedding suitcase.

For a moment or two Alexandre kept his eyes fixed upon it. It seemed to him that the suitcase itself had been the bestower of the emotions he had known whenever he had sallied forth, carrying it in his hand; that it was the suitcase which had taken him along on their little excursions, then to Lac Vert—which had always taken the initiative, and which again today urged him to flee by the first train. . . . Very few people died on the railroad. . . . It was rather in airplanes . . .

The moment he understood that this man was sick, the chauffeur became even more attentive and kind. He covered Alexandre as he sat on the back seat with a heavy woollen robe. Before putting it into gear, he let his motor turn over for a minute or two. Very soon a pleasant warmth pervaded the car. The goodheartedness of men already surrounded Alexandre. It worried him, as the clearest danger signal he had yet received. He eagerly turned around to cast a last glance behind him. What indeed did he hope to see in his street, in front of his house?

The taxi ground into motion, awkwardly found its way into icy ruts. Under the fresh snow there was a hard, slippery surface.

"Be careful," Eugénie begged.

"Don't be nervous," said the driver patiently, smiling at her in the rear-view mirror. "I'll get you to the hospital."

The car gathered a little speed.

Greetings began to rain upon Eugénie and Alexandre Chenevert.

MERRY CHRISTMAS . . . SMOKE SWEET CAPORALS . . .
MERRY CHRISTMAS . . . DRINK COCA-COLA . . .

Daylight was coming to an end. And the snow, minutely stirring in the air, still obstructed visibility. In a hardware store window, room had been made for a small crèche. The child Jesus was alone with Mary and Joseph among the electric accessories suggested as gifts. Further on, along the great avenues with their overflowing shops, you could better recognize the advent of Christmas. Not a window which did not call to mind the fact that the time had come to think of one's neighbour. Guileful in its season, the advertising, without going into detail, insisted, "Don't forget *him*. . . ."

Santa Claus was playing his part in the show. He had now become a creature of commerce. Even a bank announced, through the mouth of a sly Santa Slaus :

I'm ready for Christmas. Are you?
Have you opened a bank account?

The greetings, as it were, tumbled from heaven, spread the full length of the advertising panels.

Shell wishes you
health,
prosperity,
happiness.

Peace in Heaven and on earth to men of good will, recalled a metropolitan bakery. The letters were enormous, as was the loaf of bread.

Tires, gasoline, and lubricating oil alike wished men happiness.

Yet this astounding century perhaps excelled especially at drawing the public attention to the unfortunate: Won't you give something to the orphans? Must thousands of the poor go without Christmas dinner? Could you let one single person be alone and sad tonight?

The snow was falling.

A snow-blower was already at work. It sucked up the snow and poured it into trucks which then hurried off toward the dumps. On almost all the streets you could hear the slightly plaintive and powerful grinding of the machine which now, in this city, better than the thin tinkling of sleigh bells, represents Christmas in the depth of winter. In the background sparkled the dazzling show-windows of the stores; in all departments the cash registers must be ringing fast and furious; these were the year's most profitable days. The banks also remained open at this hour; behind their glass walls stood the tellers, pale, impatient in their movements; in front of them long lines of people waited, wedged together. At Christmas—such is the fact —large sums went into the bank and little ones came out.

Yet was it not during this silly time, this spendthrift time, that men were perhaps at their best?

"The Dorval radio predicts a heavy storm," said the chauffeur.

Deep in the back of the car, their eyes as wide as two children's, Eugénie and Alexandre held each other by the hand.

CHAPTER XIX

Silence
Hospital Zone

THE CAR was approaching the sign . . . in French and English, as always, and as must needs be, for you are in a city which thinks and suffers in two languages.

Alexandre's eyes sought the driver's face in the little rectangle of the rear-view mirror; he seemed to be begging him not to go so fast; it was dangerous to go so fast; and, after all, was it necessary? But now the compassionate request to think of others was behind them. And basically there was no more silence here than anywhere else. Used to watching the meter closely, Alexandre had slipped a glance at the little box with its upsetting clicking noises. They were pulling up to the hospital. As he got out, Eugénie helping him, Alexandre put his hand in his pocket.

"I'll pay; don't bother," said Eugénie.

Not at all; he wasn't ready yet to let her, with all the world watching, take over the man's business of getting out the money and paying. His dignity, his man's self-respect would this once more remain inviolate. After this she could handle the purse strings. And she'd have to be mighty careful about it, since, as he had tried to make her get it into her head when they were leaving, "from now on money would go out much more easily than it came in." On their way he had passed a few hints on this subject, whispering them on account of the chauffeur—and also because of the Christmas spirit, a spirit which made his words seem a bit mean and stingy—"No nonsense, Eugénie; it's bad enough to be sick. Do try to understand that I can't be sick in the hospital and at the same time going to the bank and earning my salary. . . . Do try to get that through you head. . . ." She had said she would try.

And now he himself, having paid the amount on the meter, hesitated over giving a few cents more. It was not the first time that the problem of a tip had confronted Alexandre. It could even be said that that problem had spoiled the few rides he had ever taken in cabs. For the softness of the seat, the shelter against the rain or the snow, the comfort, the speed—pleasures so unaccustomed that they inclined him to think that for them he was in the driver's debt—had all led him to feel that he should give a little more than asked. But, as he had so clearly repeated to Eugénie, Christmas or no Christmas, they had to make up their minds not to spend an extra penny. Moreover, would not a tip be out of place when given by a sick man to a gay, hearty fellow with chubby cheeks?

This must have been the chauffeur's view of the matter. He was in such a hurry to cut short his customer's hesitation that Alexandre would not even have had time to figure out the ten per cent. Before going on his way, the man was also considerate enough to smile broadly, giving clear proof that he hadn't a shade of disappointment.

"Try to get well soon," he called out. "We'll be back to get you in a few days."

"A fine, likeable chap," remarked Alexandre. "You don't run into them too often these days," he added, "drivers as obliging as he is."

At the top of the wide entrance steps, Alexandre and Eugénie fought for a moment over the suitcase. In the end Eugénie won the day.

"Come on, how do you think it would look! People would take me for a woman without a heart in her body. . . . Give it to me," she ordered.

And Alexandre pouted.

The rattle of typewriters greeted them. In the distance a telephone was ringing, which no one seemed in a hurry to answer. People were flitting back and forth along the corridors. When you first arrived, the hospital was not too unlike a business office: a counter, notices, an information desk, and even what looked very much like a wicket. Alexandre felt himself a trifle comforted. A tumour . . . well, it might possibly be nothing more than a tumour.

He was confronted with paper and ink. Here, as everywhere else, the first thing you had to do was fill out forms. Alexandre adjusted his spectacles. "No thanks; I prefer my own fountain pen—I'm used to it." Family name, given name, age. Occupation? Why on earth did Alexandre hesitate once again to inscribe "teller"? Was he thinking of claiming another occupation? Of writing on the dotted line, "explorer, bee farmer, world traveller"? Then he had to state his nationality, his religion, and whether he expected to pay himself, or if not, "give details." The prices varied according to the number of beds in the room. For form's sake, he weighed the matter. His health insurance guaranteed him up to a certain maximum. It also provided an end date for payments—not months and months;

Alexandre was suddenly appalled at the possibility of an abnormal illness, that would last too long, the expense of which would fall back on him.

Meanwhile, terribly annoying, Eugénie kept suggesting that Alexandre, who had never allowed himself the tiniest little luxury, might well at last pamper himself a bit, since the insurance covered him, and he was foolish not to take advantage of it.

"No! And I mean NO," said Alexandre, really put out.

It was because of people's acting in just that way that taxes kept going up all the time, and that they spoiled a good thing like social security.

At last everything was settled, and Alexandre had become merely another sick man following a nurse along a corridor, now to the right . . . now to the left. . . . "This way, please . . . watch out for the step . . ." The elevator hoisted them at a snail's pace, participating in all these unexpected attentions by an exasperating lack of speed. Why did hospital elevators move so slowly, the only ones in our day and age to drag so? It made Alexandre scowl. Then he glanced in discomfiture at Eugénie, because he knew they would have to part.

Her features contracted in emotion; suddenly she turned red in the effort she was making to restrain her tears. Poor woman! He had been short-tempered with her, even today, just a moment before, in the hospital office. And now, had he been able to be alone with her, Alexandre would have taken advantage of it to make his honourable amends. But there were always people around! He half suspected that from now on perhaps there would never be a time when there were not people around him. Oh! You went to the hospital to be quiet . . . how wrong he had been!

"Well, then, get going! Go on back home," he urged her, on tenterhooks to be over with it.

Would he ever get to the point of knowing what he wanted!

Now he was in bed, with no more work to do, free of any worry except over the seriousness of his condition; but the bed was too high, and they had rigged him out in what he considered a most inconvenient and not altogether decent nightgown. Then, too, he had no desire to be in bed so early; never did Alexandre retire at such an hour; it made him nervous when he got to bed too early, and when this happened, he slept less than ever. Someone came to do what was necessary for him. In his sillier moments he had thought that this also should be pleasant; yet how hateful and unseemly was this solicitude, or rather this seizure of his person! He had to submit to humiliating procedures, and be scolded into the bargain because he tried to cover himself with a sheet.

And now, tucked in, enclosed in the sheets as though in a bag—could they be fastened down, those sheets, to give him so little freedom of movement?—he could have been at his ease had there been real quiet. But on this point too he had been cheated; in fact there was much less silence here than at the bank. Nuns were praying somewhere in the distance, and they continued for a long while, their voices whining and monotonous. Why do people pray with that tiresome intonation which tears the heart with anxiety? It made them seem to be addressing themselves to a very harsh person, and without much hope of being heard. When they stopped, Alexandre noticed all sorts of vague, stifled sounds—no real outcries, but moans, perhaps uttered in sound sleep. In this very room someone was groaning behind the folding screens which surrounded his bed. Words, little tag ends of sentences, probably muttered in unconsciousness. That poor unfortunate, in his cabin of screens, seemed to sleep yet still to suffer. He must not be truly aware that he was sighing.

Abruptly Alexandre felt it unbearable that he should thus be handed over to sickness, perhaps to death. Were not one's defences against death a thousand times better outside this place? There work and the needs of each day made death keep its distance.

He got up, taking care not to let the bedsprings creak. Anyone who had seen him so cautiously placing one foot in front of the other might well have concluded that he was up to no good.

They had, however, removed his clothes, as he might have suspected. Alexandre missed, as though they had been a joy, his discomforts of years gone by, and even the quite acute pain of the last few months. Never should he have complained about them. Had he kept them to himself, he might have managed without an operation. He would have accustomed himself to his troubles; he might even by himself alone have thwarted them.

He drew on his bathrobe and pushed his feet into his slippers.

He looked like a man who had been walled in and who still was searching on every side for some avenue of escape.

All that remained was the window; he went over to it and looked out.

The weather bureau had been right: a storm was raging through the city.

Such precision on the part of mere men reassured Alexandre

a little. They didn't make so many mistakes nowadays in fore-telling the weather.

To Alexandre's eyes, however, it seemed somewhat doubtful that there still was any city. The sidewalks and streets had disappeared. And the wind lashed out at what was left of them, wave after wave, like the sea pounding an unhappy coast line. Even as high as the hospital's third floor, with its defending storm windows, and right up to this overheated room, came the onslaught and rebelling of the gale.

For a moment Alexandre's soul was delighted at what he saw, as though the whirlwind might have unleashed itself for his express benefit. For if he derived pleaure from accurate fore-casts, this little man loved even more the raging of the elements.

This evening, his face glued to the glass, he would have liked once more to inhale this violence of his native land : the winter which on occasion had made him—sickly, sunk deep in a rut, inactive as he was—feel greatness.

So then he began searching back through his life, as though it might offer him the thrilling surprise of an action he did not know he had performed, such as having gone to the South Pole with Scott or Amundsen; Scott had been only a small man, scarcely more sturdy than he himself; or, less ambitiously, hav-ing been good. . . . He would have liked to appropriate to him-self the lives of noble people. Yet in the midst of this passage from existence into death, had he any business priding himself upon the undertakings of others?

Down below the snow crests rolled along; without obstacle and free, they rolled as though through abandoned spaces. The wind made dunes of them, pale channelled stretches, craters. A street light, most likely very close at hand, blinked like a distant, undecipherable star.

Civilization seemed a trifling thing, this evening, sickly, terribly vulnerable, in great peril, constantly on the road to ex-tinction.

And Alexandre reflected that all in all this must be a bad time to have to report one's presence to eternity.

He cupped his hands on either side of his eyes to cut off the light in the room and let him see better out-of-doors. A man was moving along, all alone. At every step he sank deep in the snow; around him swirled white, screeching shapes; his head sunk between his shoulders, the sides of his coat flapping behind him, he was heading painfully into the wind.

And Alexandre envied this happy one of the earth, who was still going about his business in the snow.

Beyond this pedestrian, further even than the blinking street light, another glow sought to pierce the night; probably the headlights of a car caught in the storm; but its meagre brilliance served merely to call to Alexandre's mind the illumination produced by his gooseneck lamp when, on grey mornings, he had to light it to be able to make out what he was doing.

His customers, gathered in a loyal little group in front of window number two, must have been waiting for him for hours. What on earth was Monsieur Chenevert doing? Never before had he been late. It was suggested that they move to the neighbouring wicket. No indeed; they preferred the second teller, with whom they had always done business. Violette Leduc, the widow Honorine Blanche Mathieu, Monsieur Dubois, Honoré Laplante . . . there was quite a queue of them, comforting in its length. The more people there were today clamouring for him, the stronger he would feel his defences.

In his mind's eye he dusted the small plate which bore his name and bore witness in his behalf. So close to the end of the month and during the days when they were the busiest, how would the others do without him? He was clever at unearthing minor mistakes in the figures. . . . And where in the world is there a greater human solidarity than in a bank? One employee's error worries all the others; all lend a hand to try to bring it to light.

A long sigh slipped through Alexandre's lips.

More even than to be happy, more than greatness, he wanted to be back in his cage.

The door into the room opened. Someone was coming. His heart thumping, Alexandre jumped back into his bed and dove between the covers while trying to free himself of his wrapper.

A priest was approaching him. He leaned over Alexandre. "Would you like to make your confession? It might be more prudent. . . . I'm quite certain," he hastened to add, "that you're going to get well. . . . Are you in for an operation? . . ."

He showed that he was pretty well posted, that he had already been informed of what was on the carpet, and he was trying to convey encouragement.

"A man's disease, eh? . . . The prostate?"

He pointed out that it was a common ailment . . . often curable. . . . He had known hundreds of men who had suffered from it. . . . Generally it worked out well. . . . Still, it was better not to wait to set oneself straight with our Judge.

And he quickly asked, as though to humanize the situation, to bring it within bounds, to pull it from the plural into the singular, "What parish do you belong to, Monsieur Chenevert?"

Alexandre left the unexplored regions through which he had been journeying and out of politeness attended to this detail : "The parish of Saint-Honoré-du-Sacré-Coeur."

"Oh! Yes. I see . . . I see . . ." the chaplain affably remarked. "That's the big stone church, very modern, which stands on the corner. . . ."

He was trying to enlist Alexandre's attention, which was somewhat bewildered and beyond belief surprised that the subject of streets and addresses should again have arisen . . . in connection with eternity. And why was it that eternity suddenly seemed to him to be like another savings bank, situated upon the world's topmost pinnacle?

The sense of his final destination tore open his heart. Rather than meeting God he would almost have preferred continuing to suffer with the rest of mankind on earth. But the time for human preferences was certainly past.

Alexandre moved his dry lips. "Oh, yes!" said he. ". . . I want to settle my accounts . . . get my columns to balance . . ."

And the priest sat down beside Alexandre, both of them in the shelter of the white cotton screen. He spread out his cassock; he seemed at his ease here, quite in his element.

CHAPTER XX

HIS PRINCIPAL bulwark against pain was not to ignore it completely—his eyes had seen too much suffering for that—but to take it down a few notches: as a businesslike fellow with a practical turn of mind, to strip it of the exaggerated importance which, in his opinion, men attached to it. First of all, suffering was pretty monotonous; nothing more closely resembled the death of one man than the death of another. Then too, whatever people said, it was short-lived; sick persons got well, or else they were freed of their troubles quickly enough when you stopped to think of it. As for generalized suffering through epidemics, wars, and cataclysms, he said it was exaggerated by the newspapers; either it didn't amount to anything, or else it was sent in chastisement. Convinced, moreover, that pain is the coin of all bliss, how could Father Marchand not have found it basically rather inexpensive?

He had drawn up a chair quite informally, with signs of fatigue, and was striving to take on the appearance of a friendly neighbour.

He was a strong man of reasonable stature, with thick wrists and ankles, scoffing at the subtleties and reserves of timid souls, a man of good will, with no great sensitiveness, and a man who perhaps imagined that a familiar tone toward the very sick lightens the burden of their loneliness. He chatted a few moments, speaking of the storm which would perhaps have the happy effect of keeping people from crowding into the night clubs, as was their sad habit during this Christmas season. He indicted the silly expenditures common in such places, men's need for comfort, their false standards of life, apparently seeing therein the essential reason for their unhappiness rather than a miserable compensation. Then he cast toward Alexandre a penetrating glance.

In that drama which is the life between men and God, he naturally upheld God; to men he attributed all wrong; his blind loyalty, his entire adherence were bestowed upon the winning side. So for him, the only thing that could matter at the end of the human story was to reconcile man with the inevitable, by virtue of what he called resignation.

To obtain this, and as the circumstances dictated, he had set up a method of attack by several stages which did not greatly vary from one case to another, death—according to him—being the great democrat which levels all situations and the whims of individuality. First he talked about "one thing or another." Secondly, if it was indicated, he "shook the soul a little," through the spectacle of God obliged by His perfect justice to take account of every sin. Then, when he had succeeded in getting the admission of trespasses, Father Marchand let himself go in praising at length, and with less anxiety all the same, the forbearance of God.

At heart he was a lonely person who, like a goodly number of priests, felt no real attachment for human beings. There are priests who have come to God through a burning compassion for man; there are others to whom men are endurable only because of God. To sensitive souls, this subtle difference is ever perceptible.

Fearfully Alexandre watched the priest whom destiny had set aside for him at the most solemn hour of his life. The man displeased him. There close beside him—how could he fail to notice—was a ruddy face with heavy features and thick hair. He averted his eyes, unaware, poor Alexandre, that his bad breath was for the priest a sort of minor torture, which he was most careful not to allow the least gesture of repulsion to betray. Love of God aroused in this man of the Church penances rigorous enough, continual acts of charity, but never—how could such a thing have been possible in him?—a surge of tender preference on his penitent's behalf. His protective glance, unbeknownst to him, let slip an aura of superiority over the suffering soul.

Two or three times Alexandre's worried face twitched on the pillow as though in a gesture of refusal. So often, by now, had he been offended by those priests who set themselves up as God's policemen rather than men's allies, who seemed less to be on the side of God than to have God on their side.

He would have needed a wholly different help in this extremity.

A friend, partial to him if need be, and who would not have said, "Alexandre Chenevert, here is your Judge . . ." but who would have made the introduction in another fashion, saying rather: "Lord, here is a man I warmly recommend to you, for whom we stand guarantee, a man whom we send you provided with the best references; we call him Alexandre Chenevert, and do not forget, Lord, that what you do for him will affect each one of us. . . ."

Probably only his own silly imagination was capable of conceiving any such fine talk. Alexandre, however, remembered a curate in his parish, a man who had been ill all his life and who sometimes spoke in an odd way, never saying, "You will give an account of yourselves; you will be judged . . ." but "We are all in the same boat." Or this, even more reassuring: "In union there is strength; only the organized workers are strong. . . . Even before God, in union there should be strength. . . ." A curate who concerned himself specially with social questions.

As an intermediary between him and God, Alexandre wished for this man, who had gained much experience and knowledge of how to handle people in the negotiations between workers and employers. Yet he had not the courage to resist Father Marchand, nor did he have the intention of raising any fuss, either. It occurred to him that it was perhaps precisely the terrible will of God that he had to confide in a man the least able to understand him, God, as Father Marchand depicted Him, having more than one trick in His bag.

And Alexandre, for whom confession was in itself already a torture, began whispering the avowal of his sins. This whispering went against the natural movement of his soul, against the taste for frankness and openness which endured within him.

The presence of other sick persons in the room likewise disturbed Alexandre. And to cap it all, he felt unbelievably embarrassed to confess his sins lying down. He could not help acknowledging to himself that in this position he was more vulnerable, more guilty.

". . . often impatient, angry over little things, sharp-tongued," Alexandre was saying.

"Yes, yes, yes," interjected the chaplain, himself almost impatient to harvest more serious matters, indulgent enough toward peccadilloes of this sort.

It was not the lack of charity in this world which most seriously aroused Father Marchand's indignation. For offences against charity, he found justifications in man's nature and also in the organization of society. How could you be gentle, wholly just, and honest? He was especially on the lookout for sins attributable to the flesh.

"I have sinned also . . ." began Alexandre.

But in reality he was accusing another than himself, and how far away he was, that other Alexandre, from the little worn-out man who was speaking: that younger, active, alert fellow, who had known demands of the flesh now become incomprehensible.

To be accurate about it, what he had really wanted in those days was to be unburdened and made free of that desire. It had been like an obsession, then, this sad physical need, a kind of constraint much more than the healthy, beautiful thing you now read about in certain books. In one way it had been to avoid having to think of it all the time that he used to have recourse to Eugénie. Still this motive, of which his wife was not unaware, could scarcely please her, as Alexandre would now have admitted. But then he held it against Eugénie. She, the poor woman—how clearly he could see it, now, and indeed had always seen it, save that his needs made him less compassionate at that time—she had been in some way offended against love, because of the lack of joy in him, and of spontaneity as well. Oh! how sad everything had been between them, when they resorted to a kind of hypocritical trickery one toward the other; he would get around her with little gifts, gestures of tenderness that humiliated him, for he thought he saw she realized their selfish intent; and she, when she was too weary to resist him, or else wanted to get it over with, or, again, to avoid having to mention certain things in the confessional, she —poor Eugénie—"resigned" herself. How unlovely is love in the confessional! There only the vulgar facts emerge! Alexandre took pity on Eugénie, to whom her confessor had assuredly preached submission. Perhaps it was a great sin he was going to commit, but he almost felt a desire to have sinned more gravely, as though he could thereby take upon himself Eugénie's wrongs. To her, how frightful must have been the act of love, which had given birth to two children who could not live! Afterward, the pitiless need still pressing on him, he had, at least to avoid the consequences, to spare Eugénie . . . how could he put it . . .

"You sinned against nature?" the chaplain prompted him.

Yes, exactly that. Alexandre acquiesced; he remained a long moment without stirring, his eyeballs dry, as though this sin of his life, the only one that had injured nobody, this poor, wretched sin was precisely what had removed from him the right to understanding and to love.

"Is that all?" asked the priest.

"All! . . ." repeated Alexandre not in reply, but saddling the word with a question.

"And now you are set free," insisted the chaplain.

He thought that the hardest part of it was over, and he was keen to get going with the wholly joyous final part of his mediation.

"God has forgiven you. You have nothing more to worry over, to question yourself about," he said roundly.

But this vast affirmation had the effect of alarming Alexandre even more.

Astonished at the anxious countenance, the chaplain hesitated a little and inquired with dread—he felt a kind of fear and fascination for such headstrong people.

"Surely you have no doubts about God? Of His existence?"

"Oh, good Lord! no!" As though someone had asked him whether he had doubts about his own torment.

"Well, then?" the priest rejoined.

His wrist was seized by the sick man's fingers, who drew him close so that he might unburden himself in secret.

"He does not love me . . . Father . . ." whispered Alexandre.

And he made a tiny sign as though to urge discretion and silence on this matter. A terrible sorrow spread over his countenance, so black a sorrow that the priest recoiled from it. Then he pulled himself together.

"How dare you say such a thing! Poor friend, there's not the least doubt about it: God loves you. Can you conceive of a God creating us and casting us onto this earth out of sheer curiosity?"

It was very difficult indeed to imagine such a thing, and Alexandre seemed appalled at it.

"Has He not sent His Son to suffer and die for us?" continued the priest. "Think of the sufferings of Jesus Christ. Reflect on this consoling mystery: God making Himself man to effect our salvation. . . ."

Alas! precisely because He was God, Christ's passion had not completely stirred Alexandre. Had there not been thousands of men who had suffered as much if not more than Christ, and for laughable reasons—frontiers, quarrels over oil, selfish interests; because they were Jews, because they were Japanese? And how many men, had they had the opportunity like Jesus to save others by their death, would have hesitated for long? To die without its profiting anyone—there was the true passion. But this was a thought that must be hidden from all, even from the chaplain, for fear of giving scandal. Alexandre was lost in fear at the idea that God would punish him for such freedom of thought concerning Him. Then he changed his accusation, reversing it completely.

"I am afraid of not loving Him . . . sincerely. . . ."

The chaplain stopped him short.

"We must love God; that is the first commandment. Come now, stop tormenting yourself. It is only necessary to think, to say, 'My God, I love you. . . .'"

But Alexandre was still unconvinced, his forehead drawn, his heart pounding.

Was it enough to say a thing, or should it not well from the heart? He tried to picture God to himself. Was He like a king, a majesty seated upon a throne, a president? In that case, like the poor Great Ones of the earth, He also should content himself with our official attitudes. Yet was it not possible that, as aspiring as a poor man, He would rather wish for our absolute and total frankness?

What a danger, all the same, to let Him see that perhaps he did not love Him, in the last analysis. And yet if this feeling dwelt in a heart, God had already seen it. He knew from then on what to expect from Alexandre Chenevert, and what good would it do, what earthly good, to try to put Him on the wrong scent!

"What does He want?" asked Alexandre. "Do you know, Father?"

"Love. God wants love," said the chaplain.

Alexandre watched him from the corner of his eye, shaken, but still so distrustful of words. For if this were true, God must then run the risk that the feeling would not have Him as its object.

"He created us free," said the priest, "to love Him . . . or not to love Him . . . I grant you that," he was induced to concede. "But if we do not love Him, we risk being deprived of Him."

Alexandre meditated on this absurdity, this terrifying position: love God or lose Him, or rather, love Him because He is to be feared. Even a man would not be satisfied with such a love. Even Alexandre had had on this earth a desire for a freely given love, a love wholly free. Did God, with His Heaven, think, then, that He could buy men's affections?

And he gathered the notion that God must indeed be very little loved for Himself, but almost always out of interest, since He held eternity in His gift. And thus it was that the other world made men the slaves of God. Abjuring it seemed the only proof of disinterested love. Alexandre was tempted by an everlasting despair.

But God would hold it against him all the same. He would perhaps hold it even more against him than if he lied a little bit. He wanted no slaves, but He wanted to be loved.

After all, God wanted too much.

The feeling of God's unimaginable solitude began to penetrate Alexandre's heart. So exacting, without a peer, how could He not be eternally alone!

The chaplain was insistent: "Say it with me: 'I love you with all my soul. . . .' "

Meanwhile all that Alexandre could say to himself, he who so carefully watched his own motives, was rather: How can one love at the point of a bayonet! . . .

But out of fright he yielded. Was it surprising that the world had so great a horror of candour, candour that left the soul open to so much mystery! He thought that with God as with men, one could keep something for oneself, for oneself alone, act on the authority, too, of a doubt in one's favour. . . .

In terror of perhaps offending against the truth, he agreed to what the chaplain wanted.

"I love," said Alexandre in an apprehensive voice.

When he was alone, however, he corrected himself, and asked God's pardon for it.

"I don't know! How can you know you love! In what can you recognize it! Do I love You?" he asked God.

But he was disturbed in his thoughts by the voice of the man fresh from the operating table who, behind the other screen, was groaning, "What have I done to You, God?"

Alexandre got up. He went toward this loneliness. Leaning over the sick man he asked, so upset that his mouth trembled as he spoke, "Are you suffering? Are you suffering that much?"

Feverish eyes, besotted by narcotics, fastened on him, wavered without seeming to have recognized a human presence. Yet the intonation changed. The thick voice, almost unintelligible, at once asked, as though of an ally:

"What ever have I done to God?"

Alexandre took the sick man's hand. He clasped it awkwardly and gave his name.

"This is Chenevert, your bed neighbour," said he. "Are you thirsty? I'll stay right here beside you," he promised him.

And suddenly he knew that he was less alone before God.

"My name is Chenevert," he resumed. "I'm a bank teller, in the Savings Bank."

His own misery had never seemed to him very meritorious.

But at that moment he clothed himself in that of another, inexplicable, as though it were his sole refuge.

CHAPTER XXI

CALM, THE two long folds of his mouth at rest, accepting death—such was Alexandre's present state, and Dr Hudon was, as it were, provoked at it. For Father Marchand, a submissive man was a success. But he, a doctor, needed a human being to want to live with all his strength.

He was standing still near the bed.

With his stethoscope slipped into one of his pockets, wearing a white coat, sure of his right to heal, he was a more imposing figure than when seated behind his desk, trying to ferret out the cause of suffering. A cruel curiosity got the best of Alexandre.

"What I have, doctor . . . is it? . . ."

And the doctor spoke in the same elliptical fashion. "Why no, we are not in any position to be sure." Yet he had very few doubts in his own mind, and not much hope either. "And even if it were! You know that nowadays we get excellent results."

"Yes, I know that it's not the way it was years ago," said Alexandre. "So, it's an operation?"

"Yes, and you have a good chance to recover nicely."

"What kind of operation is it, exactly?"

"Well," said the doctor, "since a cystoscopy is wholly out of the question, we'll have to take more radical means and try a cystotomy."

"A cysto . . .?" said Alexandre, embarrassed at not understanding.

When he did understand, his eyes filled with indignation. He cried out, as though cured forever of any hope in life: "Oh! in that case I'm all for death!"

"It's still not as terrible as you think it is," said the doctor. "I'll have the operation done by one of our best urologists, let's say Lebrun."

Alexandre shook his head violently.

He refused to accede; to live you at least had to have your body whole. A life sustained and continued with the help of external objects aroused in him too great a pity.

"The operation could be done in two stages," Dr Hudon explained to him. "If all goes well with the first surgical intervention, we might easily, after a certain passage of time, remove the tube and sew everything up again."

"A second operation after the first?"

"A mere nothing."

"But all that would take time, and what would I do in the interval? Could I even earn my living?"

"Why not?" the doctor asked. "I had very good results with a patient in just about your situation. It's now three years ago that I had him operated on; there's been no change in his condition. My chap is working; he goes to his office every day."

"Is it possible!" Alexandre exclaimed in sorrow for the man. "Poor fellow! You say he's working? Did they keep him?"

"Certainly. The thing is much more commonplace than you think."

At this juncture Dr Hudon offered his strongest argument in favour of life.

"And he's still of great use to others."

"Oh! . . . yes . . . useful!" muttered Alexandre.

Would this be the road of penance which would wipe away the ill temper, the lack of joy in a life that had been relatively good? But he saw himself at the Savings Bank, hemmed in by shocked whispering: "Notice that little man?" people would say, giving a tiny shove of the elbow. "Take a good look at him . . . but not now; he knows we're talking about him. . . .

The poor man lives with one of those gadgets stuck in his side. . . . He must be awfully anxious to keep on living!" people would say.

No, he thought; since you have to die sooner or later, it was better to die now than little by little. Moreover, it would be to Eugénie's advantage that he die before the operation and convalescence swallowed up all their savings.

"Anyway," he sighed, "it's far from a sure thing that I'd recover!"

"Come, now; it's pretty close to sure!"

A great dignity overspread Alexandre's tormented features.

"I thank you for having spoken to me frankly," said he. "But weighing everything, allowing for everything, it would be better that I go my way as soon as possible, without its having cost me too much. I have insurance to protect my wife. And what's more, someone will take my place at the bank; were I to go back there, I'd be putting that person into the street. . . ."

At last he saw the whole puzzle falling approximately into place: his wife would have enough to live; his successor at wicket number two would have no worries about his job.

But Dr Hudon, if at times he had to tell his patients a few white lies, at times also owed them the devastating truth.

"If you refuse operative treatment, you'll not necessarily die right away and easily."

"It might drag on?"

"That's not unlikely," said the doctor.

He was astounded at this man's courageous taste for truth, even though he had seen him so scandalized by the falsehoods of the day.

"Months?" asked Alexandre. "A whole year?"

"Perhaps. What's more, you have a certain amount of retention and a little uremia. The pain might become . . . "

At last Alexandre understood; it was true—death could hold him at arm's length, turn him away, and that for a long time—could be as difficult as life. The decision confronting him was turning into something far more overwhelming than he had thought.

"But I haven't the means to drag on," said he, reflecting that it would be really too sad to use up absolutely all his meagre resources.

"One of the advantages of the operation," urged the doctor, "is that it almost always eliminates suffering. And you insist on seeing things in their worst light. If all goes well at the first operation . . ."

"Yes . . ." Alexandre interjected reflectively.

He finally could see the advantages that still remained to him. He could return to his cage, stick at work for a year or perhaps two; with a great deal of care and strict cleanliness, he could succeed in not making himself too odious to others; he might even pull the wool over their eyes, succeed in preventing anyone near him from knowing how much he clung to life.

And he, who had sometimes invoked death when a cold had added its complication to his queasy stomach, now asked, "Rigged up that way, at least I could work?"

"Certainly."

"For a good while?"

"Of course. Five . . . ten . . . years."

Alexandre seized on the higher figure. For the moment it was the very prolonged prospective of the ordeal which made it acceptable to him.

"For six months it wouldn't be worthwhile," said he. "But if it were for a few years!"

He did some more mental arithmetic. Ten years would carry him to the retirement age. In the meantime he would have been able to lay aside a bit more money for Eugénie, Irène, and the little boy. To leave a thousand dollars to Irène had been one of his ambitions. Irène was like him; it infuriated her to owe anything to others, to be a cause of worry; she was extremely independent. But once he was dead, she would no longer resent his help. At last they would know each other, both of them, too much alike ever to have agreed in life. Money to be earned— that was still his best incentive.

He was telling the doctor, "I had almost made up my mind to tell the world good-bye, you know. I even offered my 'resignation' to the chaplain," he added, trying to smile. "But I think I'll go back to your way of seeing things. . . ."

Then he pleaded, with his eyes, "But don't turn me over to someone I never even heard of, that Dr Lebrun. . . ."

"Even though you never heard of him, he's very far from being unknown," Dr Hudon corrected him.

"Oh, I know . . . but you . . ."

"Don't be afraid," Dr Hudon promised him. "I'll be right there on tap. We'll do everything we possibly can."

Alexandre looked searchingly at the fraternal smile bestowed upon him. And he said, "Well, the die is cast, Doctor. I put myself in your hands."

The doctor grasped both of Alexandre's in his own—small, slender, already whitened hands that quivered between his fingers.

Certainly more than any other person in the world, he was

resolved to save Alexandre Chenevert. Yet what did he expect by this but to preserve this man a little longer for human pity!

Who would ever have recognized Alexandre Chenevert, he who arrived at his bank every morning, his stiff hat tipped slightly over his forehead, a little man who looked irascible in an iron-grey suit? He could have gone without buying that last suit; he'd perhaps never succeed in wearing it out, even though it was the most expensive he had ever bought. That purchase was still troubling him as they rolled Alexandre toward the operating room.

He caught a glimpse of another aspect of "his doctor," more impressive than ever, recognizable only by the eyes peering out above the mask. Alexandre greeted him, "Good day, Doctor . . ." as though happy and a bit astonished still to run into an acquaintance at so dire a moment. But already he felt sleepy and little concerned about his own fate. It was the pentothal which provided him with this well-being. His eyelids were slipping shut.

As soon as he went under, the table was turned end for end; Alexandre's head now lay where had been his feet. Tubes linked it to a sort of complex control panel. Gauges there indicated the consumption in litres per minute of the gases contained in the cylinders flanking the anaesthetizing apparatus, protoxide of nitrogen, CO_2, oxygen, cyclopropane, ethylene. In his most outrageous dreams, Alexandre had not glimpsed half the importance he was to acquire. The apparatus recorded his blood pressure; his nostrils, his mouth, almost the whole of his leaden face was tucked into a very tight-fitting mask; into the vein at the bend of his elbow flowed the plasma which helps to hold down operative shock; at his head, sitting on a stool, the anaesthetist watched the general tone and pulse, pressing his finger against Alexandre's forehead.

But already the only haste the surgeon felt was to close and sew up the incision, to replace the covering of flesh upon the palpable mass of growths. Till this moment he likewise had been passionately interested in Alexandre Chenevert; and he liked him still, though he could expect from him not a single happy result. Confronted with such an invasion of mischief, what could he even try to do?

They were talking about it around Alexandre, in succinct sentences deadened by their masks: . . . absolutely useless to do anything at all . . . all the same, from the sick man's point of view, the operation held certain advantages: ease retention

. . . avoid infection . . . lessen uremia . . . the respite might be three months . . . perhaps six . . .

Alexandre did not yet know that that ugly, vulgar moaning, very far off, came from himself. He was back in his bed. Two screens ensured him a little privacy. Anaesthetics were now so gentle that the patient awoke without nausea, the mind only slightly confused. Almost at once he would be back in reality.

Thus Alexandre saw Eugénie, who was asking, "Do you see me—at least hear me?" Already he was indicating by a wrinkle on his forehead that the question did not need asking. "Do you recognize me?"

He was even aware that henceforward he would have no control over his natural functions, that a tube and some sort of receptacle seemed to be joined to his body. And he no longer wanted to live under such circumstances. If he had agreed to it, it had been through ignorance. He would gently turn his back on the ignominy that had been done him; he would go away, without any fuss; death seemed to him as good as sleep, attracting him in spite of himself.

Thus did morphine help him. He slept with the feeling, at times distinct and clear, that he should not, that he was too unhappy to sleep.

For two or three days they struggled thus, one against the other, Alexandre trying in turn indignation, sharp-wittedness, and truth against the drug, and the drug exerting over him its solvent power.

Are not narcotics, apart from pain, the most puzzling gift made by God to men?

Although they had to manage without them for a long while!

He thought that he had nothing left to do in this world.

And yet . . . and yet . . .

A few days later he succeeded, by himself, in lifting a glass to his lips, in eating a mouthful or two. Things had been arranged to yield this fine result, Alexandre having been nourished through his veins with glucose and strong stimulants. Medicine spared itself no pains on behalf of that brief span of life it sought to make sure for him. To keep alive for a few more months this tiny spectre of a man, the doctor, the male nurses, the nuns used heroic measures.

The face was as pinched as that of a child, but of a very aged child, with skin yellowed and sere, whose eyes seemed to be glued to life by dint of disillusionments.

"You're only fifty-four?" asked one of his roommates. "Really? I'd have given you several years more than that."

Out of embarrassment he did not specify how many years, but his astonishment spoke volumes.

Propped up on a number of pillows, Alexandre could look around him. His nurse took away the screens. The room's one window, facing toward the winter sky, became an object of endless observation. Alexandre would study the designs in the hoar frost; he saw forests there, mysterious lakes surrounded with the stumps of trees, such as he had seen in Le Gardeur's clearings. He thought he saw a field of rye growing in the window. "It's quite extraordinary how well he's coming along!" Dr Hudon sought to make certain of all Alexandre's strength of will. He told him he could live for quite a time. He spoke of a man who had lasted for years in Monsieur Chenevert's condition. He omitted explaining that this man had had his operation for a tumour that was not malignant.

And here is what Alexandre then began to think: that he was not the first man, nor certainly the only one, to wear this kind of contraption. That others—many others—must have reconciled themselves to it.

And furthermore: Roosevelt had worn iron braces on his legs the greater part of his life; Harry Hopkins had had a silver stomach. At least Alexandre believed he had read something of the sort. . . . After careful consideration, he preferred his own case to a silver stomach.

He began formulating minor plans and small projects.

At the bank they'd certainly have to take him back for the quite sufficient reason that nowhere else would they want any part of him.

He learned a game of solitaire from the fellow who had been operated on and who was now getting well enough to show the others card tricks.

Alexandre realized that he had been too serious throughout his life; no mistake about it: the simple little diversions were the ones made to man's measure.

Meanwhile he spoke of going home, of going back to work, of putting a stop to so expensive an interlude.

Occasionally he would anticipate "one year, two years, three years" of life, with the cunning natural to man who thinks it suitable to ask a bit more than he really hopes to get.

More often he employed a wholly different tactic. He would think *six months*, convinced that by asking so little he would put life in a better frame of mind toward him.

In spite of everything, he knew happiness each day when

Eugénie entered the room and there arrived with her the pressing cares, the feeling that he should quickly get back to work, the regret over nasty things said and anger that had served no purpose. Such indeed was the untouched wealth of an elderly couple, a couple like himself and Eugénie: their lost youth together.

But now that Alexandre had so many good intentions, his body would not listen to further talk about life.

As for his soul, it was aware that never could anyone wrest from him beauty and a certain share in joy. Just the snow against the pane now sufficed to bring a smile to this small face that had smiled so little.

And therefore joy in the human soul could not be killed.

The initial stages of pneumonia set in. Dr Hudon got the best of it with massive doses of penicillin. To complicate matters, the kidneys became infected. "That was just what we needed," growled Dr Hudon. He got the best of that with other medication. But these medicines did the liver no good. His blood count tumbled.

Alexandre was lost.

But before dying he was to have time to glimpse a little of Heaven on this earth.

CHAPTER XXII

PEOPLE COME to see him from the opposite end of town—such as, for instance, Mademoiselle Violette Leduc, who had journeyed by streetcar over a route involving two or three rather complicated transfer points—people come from afar had the ill fortune to arrive while he was dozing. They looked at his closed eyes, his hollow cheeks, his open mouth, and—since he seemed to suffer a trifle less when he was asleep—rather than deprive him of one single brief moment of rest, they went back home with their kindly words still locked in their hearts, and that is a distressing thing to have to do.

Sometimes Alexandre learned what had happened, and it offended him. Above all did he regret Violette Leduc's visit. In his gratefulness he began to make calculations: "An hour and a half's trip, at the least!"

In view of the amount of time still left to him, they might at least have waked him up.

But the hour had come when they would have walked on their heads rather than steal from Monsieur Chenevert one minute of very sparse sleep, a sleep, too, which gave him little rest and which, as of old, had the great disadvantage of coming at inopportune moments.

"Wake me up when people come," he begged his kindly neighbour.

He had two of them; one, on his left, no more remarkable than the run of human beings; but the other, to his right, in Alexandre's eyes made amends for the whole species.

His nurse wanted to protect him against prolonged visits. They had squabbled at first, because he had had no intention of letting her wash him, and she had then said, "Listen, Monsieur Chenevert; ten more like you, and I'd go out of my head; you've got to be more co-operative; it's time you learned to be co-operative. . . ." And he had given in. Now that he no longer liked to be left alone she drove away his visitors.

"You're getting tired, Monsieur Chenevert; that's enough for today."

Alexandre would be angry to see "his people" thus shown the door.

He was overwhelmed by the importance he had acquired, though through no fresh merit of his own; quite the contrary, it seemed to him that he had less and less, now that he no longer was earning any pay; what was more, these courtesies reminded him too vividly of how often he had wished to be rid of his clients. Within reach of his hand were lovely fruits—expensive during this frosty season—a generous choice of apples, oranges, and California grapes; this had been a gift from the bank. His neighbour to the left, who was not the most sensitive fellow in the world, wondered, "what did such a basket of fruit set them back? Anyway, it certainly was plenty. They must think pretty highly of you, Monsieur Chenevert," he remarked with a kind of sly envy. And he it was—the only occupant of the room with an unrestricted diet—who in the end fell heir to the largesse of the Savings Bank of the City and Island of Montreal. Alexandre deplored this; happily he had made Eugénie take home the best of the fruit. On "Little Christmas"—the Feast of the Epiphany —despite the stormy weather, he had flowers on his section of the dresser. They were sent by the employees of the bank, who had levied an assessment against themselves to get something for Alexandre and had also sent him a card wishing him, in printed letters, "a prompt recovery." And he, who had often been put out of humour by these conventional gestures, was this time annoyed only at the waste of money involved. He longed to know who could have started the ball rolling; the initiative, he learned, had come principally from the little red-head, Alice. She it was who had kept after all the others, insisting that each make his small contribution. "We certainly owe that much to Monsieur Chevevert." In former days he had thus shared with the rest of them the stipend for a Mass and even, when one of the group was getting married, the cost of a sensible wedding present. All of which had been quite normal. But that he himself should be the beneficiary of a collection!

The two "little girls" at the bank came, moreover, in person, a little after the arrival of the flowers. He reproached himself for having thought them silly kids. They were sweet, these children, and how lovely was youth—naïve, smiling, unknowing youth!

"Off with you! . . . Off with you!" he sent them packing after five minutes, well aware that they were eager to be gone.

People were too kind to him. He still had the strength to become angry at so much thoughtfulness which was not his due. How ever could he return so many courtesies? He was piling up obligations. He'd never be able to repay them. He protested against the gifts.

"I don't need that," he would growl.

But no one paid any more attention to what he said now than they had in the past. Friends brought him candies and things to read, but light books; "nothing serious," they had decided.

From then on there was nothing serious around Alexandre.

Even Father Marchand treated him like a child. He now spoke to him only of God's loving kindness.

This change did not escape Alexandre.

In all his life he had never been one to indulge in bantering—perhaps that had been the thing he lacked the most—but the morphine muddled his thinking, and in the need to straighten out his ideas, he asked questions which seemed insinuating.

"You speak to me only of His gentleness," he remarked a trifle severely. "You used to talk about expiating one's punishment, purging one's sentence. Are you referring to the same God now as before?"

"Of course," granted the chaplain, with a shade of stiffness in his tone. "God is justice; He must punish evil; but He is also infinite love, boundless mercy. Now don't be so mistrustful."

And he tried to describe the joys awaiting Alexandre. "In Heaven, the angels, each in his proper station, cherubim, seraphim, archangels, will sing the praises of the Lord. The elect will contemplate Him, as though He were a dazzling star."

Alexandre found Heaven sad . . . after earth. What! No more flowers, no more birds with cries as gentle as the rain, no trees! He began to ruminate: How many kinds of trees might there be? Larches, pines, birches—perhaps the prettiest of the trees—then oaks and maples that changed colour in autumn; and one mustn't forget the willows, alders, poplars . . . all those other trees which so loved moist places. Then he thought of lakes, of ponds, of tiny streamlets of cool water invisible in the thick grass. How very comfortable was man amid the birds, the fawns, the forests, the rivers! And why had God created the earth so lovely, only to remove man from its loveliness!

Alexandre asked the chaplain to explain it. This good man smiled at such simple tastes. "It will be much better in Heaven. The earth has never been and never will be really adequate to the human heart."

Alexandre would have preferred a man more aware of the world's joys as recipient of his last intimacies; but even if he had his limitations, the priest still was one of the best friends he had ever had in his life, the most intelligent, the best educated . . . the most exacting, too, and that was as it should be.

All the same, rather than go to Heaven, Alexandre would have preferred returning to Lac Vert. It is true that, free to go to Paradise, he had no choice as to the nature of the reward; he had to take it or leave it. He had not been consulted.

For long moments he thought that if he could only put in his two cents, Heaven would be perfect. He saw just about how it could be worked out: a vast series—but well protected and hidden from each other by the greenery—of small cabins like his at Lac Vert. What better could a man ask?

And the streets would be nothing more than footpaths.

Meanwhile the chaplain was trying to induce him to desire something else, a more worthy recompense, above all glory, to which Alexandre had never been very much inclined; he told him of mansions, some more splendid than others, of precedences, of the right hand and the left. How was it that man, having imagined such specific punishments in picturing hell to himself, should have been unable, for his ultimate happiness, to devise anything besides a sort of pompous boredom!

Alexandre closed his eyelids. As Heaven, he could see

nothing better than earth, now that men had become good neighbours.

"Don't you feel that mankind has made some progress?" he asked, hopefully.

No, the priest had no such feeling; or, if it had made progress, it was merely in wickedness, or in speed or even in material comfort.

"And yet . . ." Alexandre was saying with a hope as obstinate as his life.

"Morally, no," the chaplain undertook to demonstrate to him. "The great thinkers of antiquity," said he, "were as advanced as we are. Since the Greeks, philosophy has not made a particle of progress."

"Ah!" sighed Alexandre, disappointed.

But did the priest really not believe that men would come to love one another? Couldn't one see signs of this happening? Might not Heaven, after all, little by little, come to be on earth?

"No." The chaplain was categorical; such a notion was a positive error. Men would never be ripe for heaven upon earth.

Alexandre let his breath out slowly.

Perhaps you had to reconcile yourself to so sad a fact, when all was said and done. . . . However, it seemed to him that to live without this enticing dream was not good either. . . .

The chaplain smiled at these heresies, innocuous under the circumstances. He spoke of the resurrection of lame, suffering, leprous bodies, become supple, young, and beautiful . . . of the entire reconstitution of the species.

Alexandre always kept coming back to his own small idea of happiness.

"But then, if God could do so difficult a thing as that, why should He not grant men what they desired even more than the resurrection of the body—namely, to agree among themselves and get along together, just as they were? . . ."

"Would you, yourself, my good friend," asked Father Marchand, "be ready to forswear eternal happiness for what you call your better world?"

"Yes," asserted Alexandre.

But he had no sooner said it than he was far from being so sure, and he was deeply troubled to realize that he was more selfish than he had believed. Fundamentally it was true : he still preferred his personal security to the advancement of mankind.

Worn out by the argument, vexed at having given himself away, he pulled at the sheets and began shifting around in the bed.

The chaplain noticed it, and he changed the subject.

Human beings were now no longer arguing with Alexandre; they pretended to grant that he was right.

"In all you say," remarked the priest, "there is perhaps some bit of truth."

The eyes clouded over from narcotics, from his quite human confusion, suddenly shone brightly.

"You see, I've thought a lot about all that," said Alexandre.

Men, during those days, often granted him the joy of believing that he had convinced them, that their armour had been pierced; and thus he no longer knew the sensation of having thought on their behalf to no effect. They were better than you would have believed while you were living among them.

Likewise, when Alexandre began to feel too much pain, when he might have groaned, disturbing the other sick people and making a most painful impression on visitors—whenever that scandal seemed imminent—then, and quickly, he was given an injection.

At first he was uneasy about the well-being which ensued, asking himself, "What can that stuff be? It must be dangerous to do one so much good?" The soul shared in this relief, and soon it wanted to shut its eyes to what was bothersome and agonizing.

He had noticed this.

Now dying was too important for a man to approach it in an impaired state.

In the world organized as it was, dying perhaps remained for him the unique opportunity to perform an act of absolute sincerity.

In short, it was so difficult a business that he would have had to die with all his strength intact, all his powers of reasoning—there lay the crux—in good health.

It had really been Alexandre's intention not to let his reflective faculties be dimmed just at the moment when they were more than ever necessary to him.

Alas! the sharp pangs, the sudden starts of pain—they, too, prevented him from calm reflection.

So he had given his consent to injections, then he had come to look forward to them, a little ashamed of himself deep down in his heart, and regretful of having so little courage.

But he had not quite reached the point of asking for them; he was still too much afraid of dying without being aware of it, stupefied.

All the same, when he had had an injection, he became reassured on this point, through the effects of the drug.

Moreover, human beings were never so kindly in their

ministrations to Alexandre as they were during the time when the drug exerted its full influence. And then, that love which was at last vouchsafed him he transferred to his entire life, so that his life glowed with it.

One day, as his eyes blinked open, Alexandre became aware of a human form standing near him. He no longer always knew, when he awakened, exactly where he was, or, even less, the identity of all these people who seemed to be smiling at him.

"My glasses? Who on earth has taken my glasses again? They take all my things away from me," he complained as he felt among the small bottles which crowded his bedside table.

Then a hand proffered him the offending glasses, and he adjusted them carefully, with that solemnity you see in a man who is about to read an official document. Thereupon, the glasses having already slid down his thin nose, he recognized Godias. Gravely he shook hands with him.

"Oh! Good! You've come at last!" he said.

He seemed bewildered, as though at a surprising encounter.

"I was wondering whether I'd ever see you again. During all the time I've spent at the hospital, you might at least have dropped by. . . ."

And Godias, who had come to see his friend several times, whom his friend had readily recognized just the day before, Godias Doucet—instead of saying something which might lead Alexandre to perceive that he was losing his memory—took the undeserved reproof in his stride, accepting the blame with a slightly awkward smile.

"We're pretty well snowed under with work at the bank. . . ."

"How have you managed things . . . without me?" Alexandre asked.

His memory was coming back to him, little by little; but after intervals when it had been dulled, the facts it presented him were indistinguishable from dreams; the torment he felt at foreseeing that soon, perhaps, he could in no way rely on his recollections made him distrustful.

"You have been here before, though; yes indeed, yes indeed," said he, as though in reproach.

"Yes . . ." said Godias, embarrassed.

"You thought you would trip me up," Alexandre said accusingly. "I've not yet lost as much ground as you think. My memory!" he exclaimed, with the intolerable grief of seeing himself stripped of a belonging which was more than personal since, apart from him, it would no longer even exist.

"Your memory's still good. . . . You've got more left than I ever had to begin with," said Godias to console him.

He tried to jolly him a bit. "As far as memory goes, no one has a better one than you. They were talking about it only the other day at the bank : Alex's memory! . . ."

"They were talking about me?" asked Alexandre, eagerly.

"Yes," answered Godias. "I don't remember who it was who brought up the subject, but he said, 'Talking about memory, there never was another one like Chenevert's in this bank. You could just let him glance at twenty-five figures on a bit of paper; half an hour later he could recite them to you from memory without hesitating a moment. Chenevert was one of our outstanding personalities.' . . . And do you know who is terribly upset by your illness?" he inquired.

"Who? Who is so upset?" demanded Alexandre.

"Robert L'Heureux."

"L'Heureux? Oh! I never would have believed it," Alexandre remarked with pleasure. "Oh! So he's upset!"

"That's the way it is," concluded Godias. "We never know who will miss us the most! L'Heureux, for instance; he says that you were a straight-shooter. Remarkably so. 'Alex,' he said to me only yesterday, 'was certainly quick-tempered, but he remained a small man with big principles. . . .'"

He could not help himself. To recount all these little items without stiltedness, Godias had to make use of the past tense. He needed that gentle, nostalgic form of expression we bestow upon those who are absent, upon visitors who have not abused our hospitality, and especially upon the dead, those who have acquired all the virtues.

But Alexandre was far from noticing any of this.

"I promise you that you're regretted," Godias continued. "It happens all the time; people keep forgetting that you're gone, and they'll say, 'Show that to Alex and see what he thinks about it. . . .' They've given Ferland your job, and the rumour is that Ferland will be replaced by a girl. . . ."

"I've seen that coming for a long while," said Alexandre. "Think of the poor women holding down our jobs." This was said, though, in pity more than resentment. "So it's Ferland who is second teller!"

"But your customers keep asking for you," insisted his friend; "people ask after you . . . almost everyone. . . . Is Monsieur Chenevert coming back to his job? . . . When will we see Monsieur Chenevert again?"

The avid eyes in the yellowed, waxen face of the sick man

inspired Godias, showed him clearly what road to follow if he would fill this soul's cup to the brim with happiness.

Moreover it was the ease of the undertaking which made it so poignant. Was it a matter of lying a bit? Not even that—at the worst selecting one aspect of things rather than another.

"What's his name . . . I mean Eusèbe, thinks highly of you. . . ."

Godias twisted his hat a bit in his hands and admitted: "I hope you won't hold it against me. I had him read your letter. Your beautiful letter you sent me from Lac Vert. And don't you tell me it wasn't a beautiful letter!"

To him, who never wrote to anyone whatever, and received substantially no mail except commercial communications and circulars, this letter of Alexandre's had taken on the stature of an event.

"I showed it to him and I had him read it," said he, "because it would be a shame to keep it hidden under a bushel. . . ."

"Ah! Do you really think so!" protested Alexandre.

He was now more exhausted by the intensity of his satisfaction than he ever had been by the bitterness of constantly being misunderstood. Still people mustn't go to the opposite extreme on his behalf and overwhelm him with praises hopelessly beyond his deserts.

Yet after a short silence, he asked, a trifle hypocritically, "Exactly what did I say in it? As I remember, it wasn't very well put."

"Oh, no!" Godias exclaimed, as though he had to defend an achievement become his own through the admiration it inspired in him.

Truth to tell, however, he did not remember "the exact words," but the letter had given him food for thought—most certainly that.

"You," he said, now really launched upon the subject, "had you had the opportunity, had you been able to finish college, you could have gone far. . . . It's unbelievable the things that have busied that head of yours! . . ."

"Now, now, now!" rejoined Alexandre.

In the midst of so many present ills, he had no intention of reopening the ancient debate, from henceforth so futile. What he could have been! Certainly here was the most entrancing of all subjects of speculation—surely the most captivating dream to which a man can yield, but he no longer had the time to indulge it. From now on he would have to rest content with what he was.

Yet when Godias had left him, Alexandre was for several

long moments at peace with the world, almost in a state of bliss. With a contentment beyond surpassing, he thought: "Godias . . . there's a fellow who will miss me, all the same!"

Eugénie was sitting near him, that day. She must have come in on tiptoe, while he dozed. And not noticing that he had awakened, she thought she was unobserved and she was weeping.

Alexandre's fine qualities, indeed, were the cause of her grief. Eugénie had begun to discover them with amazement from the first day of their separation, the thankless qualities which did not necessarily make life easy—quite the contrary. Prudence, economy, honesty, and, above all, that fearful frankness.

And then, the evening before, while she was ironing the old brown suit, she had found Alexandre's letter, which began with the words: "My dear Eugénie, you're going to find a big change in me . . ." That adjective *dear* at the very outset opened her heart; never had Alexandre given her to think that he thought of her as dear. And in the letter there were lovely bits . . . "the sharp words I have spoken to you were not really in my heart. . . ." He spoke of the raspberries he had wanted to gather so that she could make preserves out of them, but he wondered if they were not already too ripe. Struggling against his sad desire to economize, he explained that if you added it all up, the cost of the sugar and of the necessary jars, it would perhaps be just as cheap to buy jam; and he added that "it would be less work for her who should now, as much as possible, try to look out for her health. . . ."

And this was the finishing touch for Eugénie. As though it was not enough to lose Alexandre as she believed she had known him, she now must lose still another, far more mysterious being, almost a stranger; in some fashion a man who might have been. How hateful it was to have to suffer such a blow! She scarcely knew what she was about, what with all this complication of her sorrow and with wondering which caused her to grieve the most: her loneliness after he was gone, or her regret at not having known him in time; and since these two occasions of her grief mingled together, the one adding to the intensity of the other, Eugénie was quite beside herself. She let her arms slip limply to her sides as she sat in the easy chair, her attitude one of utter exhaustion, and she was about to start crying once more, from weariness as much as from anything else, worn out by her visits to the hospital, her bad nights, her anxiety. Alexandre stopped her, his voice humbled.

He could not bear seeing her cry, he who had judged her on the insensitive side. His punishment was too much for him.

"You're breaking my heart. Stop!" he begged.

And then they looked at each other, almost unhappy to discover, at this moment, so late, that they loved each other. That pain, they seemed almost to be saying to themselves, might have been spared us.

"You've wasted away beyond belief. You're just melting away," Eugénie reproached him. "Do try to stop losing weight."

He turned up his eyes, taking Heaven to witness that this time it was no longer his fault if he still caused sorrow.

"You're still young," Eugénie pointed out to him.

"Listen," said he in a low tone of voice, beckoning her toward him.

The time seemed to have come for him to inform her of a little secret he had kept for a number of years. So he began to tell her: apart from the life insurance policy of which she was well aware, he had taken out another, for a smaller sum, "only fifteen hundred dollars." He had kept it to himself because she found fault with almost everything he did and because she started from a false premise, claiming, "We should live while we are still alive rather than skimp on money for a time when we are dead and past enjoying it." In any case, it seemed to him that he had not acted foolishly: he was the first to go, and that justified his foresight. Thus she would have enough to live on while she waited, as he put it, "to draw your old-age pension." Most likely she would have it from the age of sixty-five; social security would probably get better and better all the time.

He took advantage of the grief he saw she felt to try to win a small concession from her.

So, with the money she would have, if she could see her way clear to help poor Irène a little, not to spend it all too quickly, thoughtlessly, he would be pleased.

If there was one thing that could bring him satisfaction in the hereafter, he gave her to understand, it would surely be to know that she would not spend imprudently the small savings he had had such a hard time laying aside.

He was not too dissatisfied with himself.

He had not put too much trust in God. According to the chaplain, this was the greatest of his failings. "Consider the lilies of the field and the birds . . ." All very well, but neither the birds, which fed on insects, nor the lilies, which quenched their thirst with rain water, had to provide for their own burial, or leave enough to live on to a woman who was none too practical in business, liked to spend money, and was too old to earn her living. It seemed to him that he had not done too badly in steering his way between the temporal and, as the priest put it, "the surprises of the eternal." He had not succeeded in being carefree, untroublesome, joyous, and at the same time meeting his insurance premiums. Those who could manage all that were cleverer than he. In any case, and at the present juncture, he felt more consoled at having pinched his pennies, at having been misunderstood, than if he had relied too wholly on the parables.

The lines of tension, of pain around his mouth and on his forehead diminished. He fell asleep with the feeling that there must remain one last measure of precaution he should take before trusting himself wholly to Providence. But what could it be?

He had rid himself willingly enough of those of his responsibilities which, as the priest put it, did not at all concern him: Palestine, overpopulated and undernourished India, the chances of another war. It was even remarkable to what an extent all that had ceased to fret him. He had left all the balance up to society: Eugénie's old age, the unforeseen things she and Irène might encounter; were his small savings not to suffice for this, he knew he could rely upon his country. Still it had not been without remorse and regrets that he had relinquished to it certain of his duties; one of the very curious longings of this bank teller's soul had been to want to dispense with the help of others as much as possible. But the chaplain insisted upon his banishing all this from his mind: no money worries, no scruples about burdens left behind him; in brief, he too was in favour of social security, although he called it by another name— Divine Providence.

And hence Alexandre had only one preoccupation left; it regarded his funeral. If he was not departing as well provided for as he might have desired, at least he intended that everything should be done according to his means. For after all, Alexandre had achieved that good old ambition of another age —to have the wherewithal to die.

He wanted no quilted casket, nor one of those grey, fashionable coffins, which must cost more than the ordinary caskets, "quite good enough" for him.

As to where his body should be exposed, he realized that their apartment did not lend itself to this purpose, being perched up too high off the street, and not large enough. From now on he must take into account the self-respect of others, try to put himself in their place, at last try to put up with a little human falsifying. So he agreed that he would be entrusted to a funeral parlour, but not to one whose proprietor had fancy ideas about fees. He thought he had heard that a chap named Benoît, with a place on Saint Denis Street, did not take too great advantage of the occasion. But Eugénie would do well to secure prices in advance. In business the best policy was always to ask the price before committing oneself.

Having settled this much, Alexandre went on to consider the place he would continue to occupy on earth.

He was not absolutely against a very small headstone, but the inscription should be brief, and the whole business the cheapest possible. After all he was only a teller, and Eugénie would do well to remember that. Nothing was more idiotic, in his opinion, than to seek to exalt a dead person by the money spent upon him.

". . . something fifteen by eighteen . . . just one single stone . . ." to that much he agreed, but only if Eugénie absolutely insisted upon it.

Deep within him his heart was distressed to think that, even after he was dead, it still would be necessary to take money which had been so hard to earn, harder still to save . . . and to no one's advantage. The world's great crime more and more seemed to him to be waste; and often there appeared within his soul the painful concept that, better employed, money might perhaps have succeeded in making men almost happy. But what good did it do to express his deep desire merely to be laid away in the ground! He dimly foresaw that money-consuming conventions would triumph over him the moment he could no longer stand in their way.

And it was in making known his last wishes, as people put it, that Alexandre saw the good sense, the perfect dignity of death. Thereafter it was life here below which he pitied, poor earthly life, so mindful of the proprieties! With intense compassion he thought of the others, who had to continue to run after their streetcars, get to their offices on time, live in apartments too warm in summer and not sufficiently heated in winter, buy frigidaires, take short holidays, each man in his turn, and, when it was all over, end in a mortuary parlour, a "funeral home," as the ads sometimes put it, and there be made as pretty as possible by the "director's" art in order that people might say, "He looks so lifelike. . . . He must be at rest. . . ."

Where, then, and how had life ever begun to be so amazingly deformed? Now, error having been heaped upon error, it had gone so ridiculously astray that it seemed impossible to catch a glimpse of the prime cause of what was wrong. When he got up there, Alexandre proposed immediately to request an explanation, to set his heart at ease upon this matter.

But he would be unable to explain anything to the others. As always, his experience would profit them nothing.

Yet how Alexandre would have loved to convey to the others what he himself would at last have understood!

Meanwhile, with his affairs in order, he found himself singularly relieved—free, unfettered as he had never been before.

And thus the poor fellow regained his appetite for life.

Eugénie, still distracted by these burial arrangements made in advance, had the dreadful grief of seeing him become animated, regain hope, of hearing this man of skin and bone abruptly ask, "If . . . I recover . . . would you . . . come live with me at Lac Vert?"

They could cut their wood, make their preserves against the winter, he pointed out to her. She would gather the fruit . . . he would take care of the garden . . . they would buy a goat . . . a few hens . . . Barred Plymouth Rocks . . . Edmondine had told him that was a good variety.

Eugénie agreed, seeing no great danger in committing herself if it would give him pleasure.

But, alas! she had not enough imagination to join in his game, speak of the food cupboard they might have filled, think of the bees he was forgetting, remind him that Blacky would probably live with them.

He had all alone to supply the elements of the illusion, and it was so tiring, so exhausting, that after a few hours he wholly changed his mind; as though this, too, could be decided by his will, he declared: "Oh! instead of all that, I'm going to die."

He thought he saw that he would weary the patience of others if he lasted too long, and it was intolerable to him to take advantage of that patience.

Meanwhile this disconcerting kindness all about him no longer required him to be on his guard.

Quite the opposite—this kindliness of others was what finally induced him to imagine God as equally kind.

As he tried, one day, to express it to the chaplain, "If God had as much heart as a man, that would already be a fine thing . . . a very fine thing. . . ."

"To start from a man's wretched heart, from a wretched human intelligence to conceive God is insane!"

Alexandre could no longer recall the chaplain's name. From time to time he called him Béchamp, then Grandchamp; at the moment it was Beauchamp.

Now the chaplain, no more than any other man on earth, did not like to be called by a name other than his own. At first he had corrected Alexandre. Now he allowed himself to be called Beauchamp with a tiny, almost imperceptible flicker of irritation. And he was also indulgent enough toward this new naïveté of Alexandre's, which led him to attribute human qualities to God.

"A man," Alexandre was saying, "is quite something! You know it yourself . . . good, honest, serviceable . . ."

If God was better than the best man on earth, there was no reason to be so anxious.

"Just think how good a thing is a man, Father! . . ."

That was the way he addressed him now, just *Father*, without any proper name.

"Yes," the chaplain agreed, rather niggardly; "there were the saints: Saint Thomas Aquinas, Saint Augustine . . . and many others . . . the popes . . ."

"No, no, no; I wasn't talking about the saints," said Alexandre, annoyed.

For indeed his heart marvelled only at men, ordinary men.

It is true that at the time he was taking a powerful drug. In his case they had replaced morphine, which produces nausea, with heroin, which also has disadvantages, but which at the outset induces dreams more satisfactory than any lucid brain has ever dreamed.

His were in colour.

"Nothing strange about that," explained Dr Hudon, ever inclined to indulge that penchant for scientific things which Alexandre still retained. "Heroin acts on the optic nerve. It augments visual perception. It gives the illusion of amplified colours, more intense than in reality."

"But everything is so green!" said Alexandre.

It was hard for him to believe that one single injection could have succeeded in making grow before his eyes a nature so fresh, luxuriant, and wondrously beautiful. His deduction therefrom was that instead of being at Lac Vert, he must at last have set foot upon his Pacific island.

"Do try to eat a little, Monsieur Chenevert," Sister Alice of the Redemption would say to him. "You have to keep up your strength."

"The Lord awaits you," the priest would promise.

"How goes it this evening, Alex old fellow? You seem to me to look a bit better," would remark poor Godias.

Monsieur Fontaine also put in an appearance, between a heavy day and a meeting of our managing directors . . . just for five minutes . . . to tell Monsieur Chenevert in what high esteem he held him . . . for his absence . . . far too long—it was hoped that it would not continue much longer—this absence had made them all reflect, and they had come to realize this: that Monsieur Chenevert represented that breed of old-time employee, of whom, alas! few remained in these days when everyone was engrossed in demands inspired by the labour unions; Alexandre Chenevert had been much more than a teller; rather, in a fashion, a pivot of organized society, of the whole system, as important—Monsieur Fontaine modestly concluded—as a bank manager, and perhaps even more so.

And then Mademoiselle Violette Leduc again made that long trip from the other end of town.

She excused herself the moment she arrived for not having returned sooner. Alexandre was at once disturbed at how slight she looked; he asked her for his glasses, and scrutinizing the old spinster with attention, he realized that she had become much thinner and had grown woefully pale.

He scolded her about it: "You look very badly. Something has been the matter with you. . . ."

She had to admit that her health had not been of the best and, pressed to say more, that "she had had a little touch of pleurisy . . . nothing much. . . ."

She had had to wait for a day that was not too cold before she could go out.

But today, as it happened, was indeed extremely cold. The windows were frosted over; when they had arrived from outdoors, visitors had complained of a glacial wind.

Very concerned, Alexandre looked closely at poor Mademoiselle Leduc. He fretted about what her age might be, about the condition of her little business, and wondered to himself if there was one single person in all the world to take care of her if things came to the worst. The only person she had ever mentioned to him had been her bedridden mother, who was dependent on her. The sad thing about small independent lives like Violette Leduc's was that they were not protected by retirement funds. What would become of her?

"You should not have come so soon—not today, anyhow," Alexandre spoke severely. "After pleurisy, you have to be careful for a long time. . . ."

She blushed a little, and—at last—he comprehended that she had not dared delay any longer, that she had been afraid of coming too late.

Through the glances they exchanged, they reproached themselves for an instant that each should cause the other so much pain, and this quite beyond their power to avoid; and the old lady's eyes told Alexandre that he afforded her more grief than she could possibly give him. Then he raised his hand to his own eyes to hide the tears he felt were on their way.

He had reached the limit of his ability to endure kindness.

Having reached a stage of anguished oversensitiveness, he saw that everyone else had been kind to him; but he did not see that he himself had ever deserved anything of others.

Kindness was accusing him.

He recalled that one day, when his harassed mother had said something silly, he had told her she was an old fool.

Sobs choked him. At that time his mother already had a bad heart. By saying such a thing to his mother, he had helped her heart to die. In a way he had killed his poor mother.

He was crying and could not stop crying.

The chaplain tried to console him.

"We kill others—all the people we know—a little bit," Alexandre was saying. "Here on earth that's what we do; we kill the hearts of others. . . ."

The tears streamed down his cheeks.

"Come! Come!" said the priest.

He would point out that "it was no great crime, in a moment of impatience, to have let slip an unfortunate word. God would not hold it against you."

The priest saw God as a little like himself, concerned about serious sins, sensitive only within reason, gifted with sound good sense. A God exasperated by suffering, half crazed—no, that he could not see.

They put a stop to the heroin, which might be the cause of this new torment of Alexandre's. It produces serious hallucinations in persons already given to excesses of the imagination. They went back to morphine.

Yet if this drug calmed Alexandre's mind, it no longer held complete sway over this body being eaten alive.

The disease had now attacked the bone, a development which Dr Hudon had above all hoped to avoid. Emigrated to the narrowest portions of the bone hollows, lodged in the very heart of the spinal marrow, the miscreant cells in their growth must be straining those bones to the bursting point. The mouth stayed half-open, as though ready to utter a cry, and Alexandre's eyes remained fixed, attentive, entirely absorbed by the awareness of pain.

Yet at last he had a friend.

It was the postoperative patient whom he had comforted during his own first days at the hospital, to whom he had proffered water when the nurse was slow in coming—this was the very one who now got out of his own bed and shuffled toward Alexandre in his worn slippers the moment he began to stir between his covers.

The friend would watch the tortured features, and when they twisted spasmodically, he would tighten his lips. He would grasp the shrunken wrist and say, "Oh! Oh!" as though to arrest the pain, or at least inject himself between it and Alexandre. Then, sitting beside Monsieur Chenevert, he would talk of some altogether different matter. This Oswald Pichette was a curious man. He had been head cook in lumber camps, a logger, even a prospector. His jobs had merely been pretexts to acquire experience now in one thing, now in another, and satisfy his curiosity by constantly keeping him on the move.

He had, as he put it, "roamed the whole country." "Yes, sir, I've roamed through Abitibi carrying my own packsack, through Lake Saint John, the Gaspé, I've roamed on every side and in every direction, as far as the Great Slave Lake country. Monsieur, there are things to be seen in the world; it's beyond belief how much there is to see! And then the North Shore, the Témiscamingue . . ."

Occasionally a word would capture Alexandre's attention.

"The Témiscamingue! What's it like there? . . . I'd have liked . . . to see . . . to know . . ."

He knew the joy of beholding a man who had been an adventurer in his stead.

There were still moments when Alexandre did not suffer too much. He folded his small hands, so pleased to be able to relax that it made him smile. Then he thanked God, Whom he thought very kind—so charitable, so generous.

At last Irène arrived from Sherbrooke, having come specially to see her father. Her employer would allow her only three or four days off, and, after having put their heads together by letter, Eugénie and Irène, in the interests of economy, had thought it best to locate those few days as close as possible to the end.

But the pain of their meeting made Irène and Alexandre forget other painful but less lovely things in their lives.

Close to her father, her face pinched and aged, Irène began that long and true knowledge of others which comes to us only through grief.

For the rest of her days, during all her own trials, she would be forgiving her father for the anguish he had transmitted to her.

"Poor little girl!" He pitied her, knowing that he would suffer in her, just as his own mother had continued in him to endure the woes of life. "Poor little Paul!" he added, seeing no end to this chain of transmitted anguish; and then feebly, as a distant hope, he seemed to glimpse what might be God's intention; how beings would never be truly severed, one from the other. . . .

One day there even appeared at his bedside a young man with a husky voice who told him : "Horace Desnoyers . . . the name means nothing to you? . . . I've had dealings with you fairly often, but it's quite possible, of course, that you wouldn't remember me. You've taken care of so many people through the years. But when I learned, last week, that . . . that you were . . . when I saw that you weren't at your window, I thought I'd look into it . . . seeing that I was always so well satisfied with the way you served me. . . . A stranger indeed to you . . . Monsieur Chenevert . . . but I thought it would not displease you if a stranger should come to thank you."

Then, for the last time, Alexandre put on his glasses. He stared deep into the face of a young man with a tiny stiff moustache; and abruptly the glint of memory burst over this almost extinguished face and lent it beauty.

"I recognise you," sputtered Alexandre. "You work for Choquette-Grand'Maison, the sacramental wine house . . . church . . . goods. . . . Used to come to the bank . . . Fridays . . . because you people closed . . . all day Saturday . . ."

"That's it, that's exactly it," said the young man, overjoyed.

Before his departure he produced a small box of chocolates.

Who ever would have thought that Alexandre had so many friends !

He grew a bit boastful about it to the chaplain during his last lucid moments.

"People have come to see me," said he, "from every side and every direction. . . ."

It seemed to him that God would take into account this quite extraordinary consideration with which he had been surrounded.

And yet, at the height of one of his crises, this confidence was torn from him. No, God was not touched by the love of men and their pity. He was not human.

Father Marchand was still trying to persuade Alexandre that God sends no man more suffering than he can endure.

But the fury of the pain led Alexandre to an altogether different conclusion. If God could handle him so roughly, it was because He could continue indefinitely to do so. Why would He ever stop? To what reason would He ever yield, He who knew nothing of the reasons of this earth?

An instant of unutterable cruelty ravaged him. Then he recaptured some small capacity of speech and moaned, beyond further astonishment and distress, "It's frightful, Father, when it is He Who is master; when medicines do no more good, when the doctor gives up . . ."

"Patience!" begged the chaplain, himself at last worn to the point where his nerves were on edge. "Your liberation is at hand."

But suppose they were still deceiving him? That was clearly what Alexandre feared. Suppose the living had an interest in wanting to see him go quietly? So that they might continue to live!

"No, no! I know it! I'm sure of it!" asserted the priest, this time committing himself so deeply and so positively that his features suddenly paled.

And Alexandre then began to whisper, as to an earthly witness who must even so be warned in time.

"God goes deeper than we. He it was Who invented making people suffer. . . . He knows far more about it than we. . . . No one has yet gone as far as He. . . . It's strange! Strange! . . . Even the Nazis . . ."

And then at last the priest admitted, "I don't know what it means . . . but you—you will know very soon. . . . Have trust . . . You it is who will know the answer."

"But I'll not be able to tell you what it is," moaned Alexandre.

"Perhaps you've already made me understand it," said the priest, bowing his head.

Alexandre's agony had stripped his faith of all proud pretension.

It was not his assent to God's own good reasons that was shaken, nor even his certainty that man up to a certain point deserves suffering. But he thought he realized that he was not perhaps intended for his role with those who were dying.

Never had he been very ill.

He slept well, he ate well; up until now he had never suffered anything worse than twinges of rheumatism.

Obviously the exercise of a ministry like his required steady nerves. An impressionable man would not have lasted long. In their wisdom, did not the church authorities consider as likely to exert a good influence on the sick and as, after all, the only kind of person able to persevere in the task, a man naturally healthy and somewhat on the simple, jovial side?

But he was a man who had been extraordinarily spared.

He had not even ever had to earn his living.

To earn his living, thought he; that means to give his time, his energy, the greater part of his life to the sole care of obtaining bread and a few sticks of furniture! He became aware of the lot of the greater part of men, which is to remain chained to life's insignificance: selling shoes for thirty years, being a tax collector . . .

He though also of the slavery which their earthly affections must impose on men: the need of providing for a wife, for children. How much he did not know, in short, about the life of an ordinary man! And then, in place of a feeling of superior freedom, acquired through the choice of his vocation, the chaplain felt a sensation of unworthiness.

Short of suffering as much as, if not more, than all others, by what right could he serve as interpreter between God and a human being!

The poor priest bent his shoulders. He who until now had rather given thanks for his good health, for his freedom from too human bonds, today was tempted to count them as a grievance against God.

"I am not a man whom others have succeeded in making suffer much. . . ." said he to himself.

Suffering alone began to seem to him worthy of suffering.

He went to the chapel. On his knees in a low voice he earnestly asked for Alexandre's death.

And that, moreover, was what everyone now hoped for Alexandre. The love people had for him had taken this direction. The very persons who had prayed the most for his recovery, now that he was dreadful to behold longed for his death as a benefaction. Perhaps they also longed for the removal from their sight of this worrisome witness of God.

So simple-minded was he, in spite of everything, that the chaplain came back to Monsieur Chenevert's bedside to see whether his prayer had not been answered.

Alexandre was still living, but just enough to be able himself also to ask for death. He had reached the point of no longer expecting help from anyone save from the One alone who tortured him. He had changed his desires at almost every season of his life; hundreds of desires had worked at cross purposes, jostling each other in his heart; and, now that he believed himself free of them, without the strength to harbour a single one of them, he was himself nothing but one unbearable desire:

"My death . . ." he implored, with a humility which pierced the soul, "please . . . today . . ."

Meanwhile human solicitude did not let him go completely; they placed a little ice on his tongue; they arranged his pillows;

Sister Alice of the Redemption came to whisper to him that she had had from God Himself an assurance that tomorrow, at the latest, he would be in Heaven; but at the same time she wanted to make him swallow a little spoonful of broth.

Alexandre half opened his eyelids. He made out Dr Hudon in evening clothes. For one last time he grumbled,. ". . . you shouldn't have . . . taken the trouble . . . others in greater need than I . . ."

To him the full dress could mean only one thing, and he said ". . . to the Opera . . . of course . . .?"

When he began to choke, there was nothing they could do except give him oxygen. So invigorating an air, like that in the mountains, must have brought back to life a few thoughts in his brain; perhaps he saw that he had exceeded all the bounds of health insurance, of patience, of human love, for he tried to tear himself from the hands that were caring for him. He made gestures as though to push them away, but he did not even succeed in preventing the others from continuing to give him repulsive care.

Fingers were trying to get his now almost imperceptible pulse. An instrument placed against Alexandre's heart sent its last tremors to a human ear.

It was an intern, stethoscope in hand, who was keeping watch.

To the very end, now one person, now another defended this poor life as though it had been precious, unique, and in some sort beyond replacing.

During the last moments, so great a gentleness had touched his face that those who saw it might have persuaded themselves, with this dying man, that the only assurance on earth comes from that tenderness for human beings which goes furthest beyond the bounds of reason.

Even after his death, men did not yet abandon Alexandre Chenevert to God.

There were Masses requested in his behalf by people who had known him, some in one connection, some in another . . . and even one from a donor who preferred to remain anonymous.

What, indeed, is the limit of men's tactfulness!

Eugénie was a little put out, for she could not concede that, having paid for a Mass, a person might not wish to reap from it esteem for himself, for the deceased, and also for those whom he has left behind.

And yet, elsewhere than in churches, it happens still today, after these several years, that name is uttered—and is it not a thing tender and mysterious that to this name there should attach a bond? . . . It happens that here or there in the city someone says:

"... Alexandre Chenevert .."

THE AUTHOR

GABRIELLE ROY was born in St Boniface, Manitoba, in 1909, of a French-Canadian family of pioneer stock. She first taught in rural Manitoba schools, but becoming interested in the theatre, she went to Europe in 1937 to study drama. She began writing at the age of twelve, some of her early stories being published in St Boniface. While she was in Europe, some of her articles about Canadian life were published in a Paris weekly. Returning to Canada in 1939, she lived in Montreal, supporting herself by writing for various journals. Her first novel was *Bonheur d'Occasion* (published in English as *The Tin Flute*), which appeared in 1945 and was a Literary Guild selection and won the Prix Fémina in France in 1947. *La Petite Poule d'Eau*, published in English as *Where Nests the Water Hen*, appeared in 1950. *The Cashier* (*Alexandre Chenevert, Caissier*) was her third novel. *Rue Deschambault*, first published in 1955, was a semi-autobiographical work, and was translated in 1957 as *Street of Riches*. The latter and *The Tin Flute* both won Governor General's awards. Miss Roy is particularly noted for her sympathetic but realistic portrayal of working-class city dwellers. She was married in 1947 to Dr Marcel Carbotte.

THE NEW CANADIAN LIBRARY